RUIN BEACH

KATE RHODES

**SIMON &
SCHUSTER**

London · New York · Sydney · Toronto · New Delhi

A CBS COMPANY

First published in Great Britain by Simon & Schuster UK Ltd, 2018
A CBS COMPANY

1 3 5 7 9 10 8 6 4 2

Simon & Schuster UK Ltd
1st Floor
222 Gray's Inn Road
London WC1X 8HB

www.simonandschuster.co.uk

Simon & Schuster Australia, Sydney
Simon & Schuster India, New Delhi

A CIP catalogue record for this book
is available from the British Library

Hardback ISBN: 978-1-4711-6543-6
Trade Paperback ISBN: 978-1-4711-6544-3
eBook ISBN: 978-1-4711-6545-0

Typeset in the UK by M Rules
Printed and bound by CPI Group (UK) Ltd, Croydon, CR0 4YY

CUNARD

Library

Out of respect for your fellow guests, please return all books as soon as possible. We would also request that books are not taken off the ship as they can easily be damaged by the sun, sea and sand.

Please ensure that books are returned the day before you disembark, failure to do so will incur a charge to your on board account, the same will happen to any damaged books.

RUIN
BEACH

Kate Rhodes grew up in London, but now lives in Cambridge with her husband, the artist and writer Dave Pescod. Kate began her career as an English lecturer and still works part-time as an educational consultant. Before becoming a crime writer she produced two award-winning poetry collections. In 2015, Kate was awarded the Ruth Rendell Short Story prize.

Also by Kate Rhodes

Hell Bay
Blood Symmetry
River of Souls
The Winter Foundlings
A Killing of Angels
Crossbone's Yard

For the heroic staff and volunteers of the
Royal National Lifeboat Institution

Round
Island

St Helens

St Martin's

Tean

Bryher

Northern Rocks

Tresco

Samson

Eastern
Isles

St Mary's

Bishop Rock

Annet

Gugh

ISLES OF
SCILLY

Western Rocks

St Agnes

Tresco

Kettle Island

Piper's Hole

Tregarthen Hill

Tom's cottage

Merchant's Point

Mike and Diane's House

Cromwell's Castle

Ivar Larsson's cottage

The Dive Shop

Dolphin Town

Ruin Beach Cafe

Frenchman's Point

Denny's house

Braiden
Steps

Post
Office

Church

Cradle Point

Vicarage

Smuggler's
Cottage

New
Grimsby
Quay

New Inn
Hotel

Vane Hill

Lizard Point

Jamie's house

Saffron
Cove

Great Pool

Sophie's cottage

Abbey Gardens

Tresco Abbey

David Polrew's
house

Pentle Bay

Appletree Bay

Valhalla Museum

Oliver's Battery

PART ONE

'How that personage haunted my dreams,
I need scarcely tell you. On stormy nights,
when the wind shook the four corners of
the house, and the surf roared along the
cove and up the cliffs, I would see him in
a thousand forms, and with a thousand
diabolical expressions.'

TREASURE ISLAND,
Robert Louis Stevenson, 1883

It's midnight when the woman begins her steep descent down Tregarthen Hill. Excitement washes through her system as she follows the rocky path, with the breeze warm against her skin, a kitbag slung across her shoulders. She pauses halfway to catch her breath, staring up at the granite cairn that lowers over the bay like a giant's silhouette. When she drops down to the beach, she can feel someone's eyes travel across her skin, but the sensation must be imaginary; if she had been followed, she would have heard footsteps pursuing her through the dark. The woman takes a calming breath, remembering why she must take this risk, as moonlight glances off the Atlantic's surface. Her family need her help, there's no other choice, and the tide is drawing closer. If she works fast there will be time to complete her task before the returning surge floods the cave.

She presses sideways through a chink in the granite, the temperature dropping with each step. A sense of awe overtakes her as the cave expands. Her torch traces a line of brightness over sea-scoured walls that soar like a cathedral's nave. The smell of the place intoxicates her, reeking of

3

seaweed, brine and ancient secrets. When she catches sight of the black water at her feet, the cave's history fills her mind. Pirates were slaughtered here for stealing smugglers' cargo, their ghosts hiding in the shadows. She has to suppress a shiver before retrieving the wetsuit and mask she hooked to the wall of the cave days ago, to prevent the tide from carrying them away. The woman checks the oxygen gauge on her aqualung, before clamping the regulator between her teeth. She takes the package from her kitbag, then lets herself fall backwards into the water. After diving alone hundreds of times, she knows how to avoid unnecessary risks. Nothing can disturb her now, except the measured rasp of her own breathing and her lamplight distorting the velvety blackness. She lets herself float for a minute, enjoying the solitude. Few other divers have experienced the beauty of this hidden fracture in the earth's surface, extending far below sea level.

The woman understands that losing focus would be dangerous. She stops to check her pressure gauge at twenty metres, the beam from her headlamp catching grains of mica in the granite, glittering like stardust. She locates the familiar opening in the rock, then places the package in the crevice where it will be easy to find, her fingers gliding through clear water. She's about to swim back to the surface when a light shines beneath her, then disappears again. It must have been a reflection; the depths seem to extend forever, the water a dense, unyielding black.

She kicks to the surface fast, relief powering each forceful stroke. It will be days before she must dive here again, and tonight she can rest easily, knowing she's done the right thing.

The woman is about to clamber back onto the rocks when something hits her so forcefully there's no time for panic. The regulator is yanked from her mouth, a hand ripping away her mask. Her headlamp falls into the water, piercing the dark as it plunges. She lashes out, but someone has gripped her shoulders, her arms flailing as she's pushed under again. A face looms closer, its familiarity too shocking to register. She fights hard, but the breathing control techniques she has practised for years are useless while her lungs are empty. The woman's fists break the surface again, before something cold is rammed between her lips. Terror is replaced by a rush of memories. She pictures her daughter's face, until a last flare of pain stuns her senses, and her body floats motionless on the water's surface.

1

My day off begins with a canine wake-up call. Something rough scrapes my cheek at 6 a.m., and when my eyes blink open, Shadow is sprawled across my pillow, his paw heavy on my chest.

'Get off me, you hellhound.'

I jerk upright to escape his slobber, wondering how he managed to break into my room again. Shadow skulks away to avoid my temper, a sleek grey wolfhound with glacial blue eyes. A stream of curses slips from my mouth as I emerge from bed, my lie-in ruined by an unwelcome pet inherited from my old work partner. Loyalty would never allow me to abandon him at a dogs' home but it crosses my mind occasionally, depending on how many rules he breaks. When I open the front door, it's impossible to stay angry. The dog bowls across the dunes, the cottage filling with the cleanest air on the planet.

Bryher is at its best in early May, before the beaches are invaded by day trippers keen to photograph every bird, flower and stone. This morning there's not a soul around. Sabine gulls spiral overhead, the Atlantic a calm azure, no sign of the storms that thrashed the western coastline all winter long. This is the view that summoned me home from my job as a murder investigator in London. I took the quality of light for granted as a kid; it's only now that I appreciate the way it makes the landscape shine. There are no houses to spoil the scenery, except the square outline of the hotel on the far side of Hell Bay, ten minutes' walk away. My own home is much humbler; a one-storey granite box built by my grandfather, with extra rooms added to the sides as his children arrived. The slate roof needs repairs since last month's gales played havoc with the tiles, but my DIY plans will have to wait. I owe my uncle Ray a day's labour in return for hours of dog-sitting, and an early start will give me time for a swim afterwards.

I glance at the letter that lies unopened on my kitchen table before I leave. My name and title are printed in block capitals on the envelope – Detective Inspector Benesek Kitto – and I already know what it contains. It's a summons from headquarters in Penzance, telling me to report for a review meeting, to decide whether I can continue as Deputy Commander of the Isles of Scilly Police, now that my probation period is ending. I've spent three months fulfilling every obligation, but the judgement is out of my hands.

Shadow traipses behind when I take the quickest route through the centre of the island, my walk leading me eastwards over Shipman Head Down. The land is a wild expanse of ferns and heather, the fields ringed by drystone walls, with flowers rioting among the grass. If my mother was alive, she could have named each one, but I only remember those that are good to eat – wild garlic, parsley and samphire. No one's stirring when I cut through the village, passing the Community Centre with its ugly yellow walls, stone cottages clustered together like old women gossiping. When I reach the eastern shore, I admire the repainted sign above my uncle's boatyard. Ray Kitto's name stands out in no-nonsense black letters, as clear and uncompromising as the man himself. I can hear him at work already, hammer blows ringing through the walls. The smell of the place turns the clock back to my childhood when I dreamed of becoming a shipwright, the air loaded with white spirit, tar and linseed oil.

'Reporting for duty, Ray,' I call out.

My uncle emerges from the upturned frame of a racing gig, dressed in paint-stained overalls. It's like seeing myself three decades from now, when I hit my sixties. Ray almost matches my six feet four, his hard-boned face the same shape as mine, thick hair faded from black to silver. He looks less austere than normal, as if he might break the habit of a lifetime and let himself grin.

'You're early, Ben. Prepared to get your hands dirty for once?'

'If I must. What happened to the boat?' Its prow looks battered, elm timbers splintering, but its narrow helm is still a thing of beauty, just wide enough for two rowers to sit side by side. Gig racing has been a tradition in the Scillies for centuries, the vessels unchanged since the Vikings invaded.

'It needs repairs and varnish before the racing season starts.' He gives me a considering look. 'Ready to start work?'

'I'd rather have a full English.'

'You can eat later. Bring the delivery in, can you?'

A shipment of materials has been dumped on the quay that runs straight from the boatyard's back door to the sea. Three crates stand side by side, waiting to be carried into Ray's stockroom. It takes muscle as well as patience to heft tubs of paint and liquid silicone onto a trolley, then shelve them in the storeroom, but the physical labour clears my mind. I stopped clock-watching weeks ago, no longer measuring hours by London time. Days pass at a different pace here, each activity taking as long as it takes, the sun warming my skin as I collect another load. My stomach's grumbling with hunger, but the view is a fine distraction. Fishing boats are returning from their dawn outings, holds loaded with crab pots and lobster creels. Many were built by Ray years ago, when he used to employ shipwrights to help him construct vessels with heavy oak frames and larch planking, strong enough to withstand the toughest gales. I shield my eyes to watch them battling the currents that race through New Grimsby Sound, and an odd feeling travels up my spine.

One of the fleet is approaching the quay at full speed, black smoke spewing from its engine, while the rest head for St Mary's to sell their catch. The boat is a traditional fishing smack called the *Tresco Lass*, with red paint peeling from its sides, skippered by Denny Cardew. The islands' permanent population is so small I can name almost every inhabitant, despite my decade on the mainland. I don't know Cardew well, but the fisherman's son was a classmate of mine twenty years ago. I remember Denny as a quiet man, watching football at the New Inn, where his wife Sylvia worked as a barmaid, but his composure is missing today. He's signalling frantically from a hundred metres as his boat approaches. As it draws nearer I can see that the decking is in need of varnish, and there's a crack in the wheelhouse's side window.

When I jog down the quay to help him moor, Cardew stumbles onto the jetty. He's in his fifties with a heavy build, light brown hair touching his collar, skin leathered by a lifetime of ocean breezes. I can't tell whether the man is breathless from excitement or because of the extra weight he's carrying, banded round his waist like a lifebelt. Words gush from his mouth in a rapid mumble.

'There's something in the water, north of here. I

saw it when I was collecting my lobster pots.' His mud brown eyes are wide with panic. 'A body, by Piper's Hole.'

'You're sure?'

'Positive. I went so close, I almost hit the rocks.'

His tone is urgent, but I'm not convinced. Last week a woman on St Agnes reported seeing a corpse on an offshore rock. It turned out to be a grey seal, happily sunning himself, but the tension on Denny's face proves that he's convinced. The coastguard would take an hour to get here, so my day off is already a thing of the past.

'Come on then,' I reply. 'You'd better show me.'

Ray is standing on the jetty as I climb over bait boxes strewn across the deck. The dog tries to jump on board, but I leave him on the quay, whimpering at Ray's feet. My uncle watches the boat chug away, his expression resigned. He's grown used to our time together being cancelled at short notice, even though I'd like to repay him for his support since I came home.

Denny Cardew's skin is pale beneath his year-round tan as he focuses on completing the return journey, the fisherman's silence giving me time to watch the scenery from the wheelhouse as we sail through the narrow passage between Bryher and Tresco. Cromwell's Castle hangs above us as the boat chases Tresco's western shoreline, its circular stone walls still intact after four centuries. The bigger island has a hard-edged beauty; its fields are full of ripening wheat running down to its shores, but the coastline is roughened by outcrops of granite, Braiden Steps plunging into the sea like a staircase built for giants.

Cardew steers between pillars of rock at the island's northernmost point, waves pummelling the boat as we reach open water, nothing sheltering us now from the Atlantic breeze. A few hundred yards away, Kettle Island rears from the sea. It earned its name from the furious currents that boil around it. I can see a host of gannets and razorbills launching themselves into the sky, then winging back to settle on its rocky surface.

'Over there,' Cardew says, as we approach Piper's Hole. 'I'll get as close as I can.'

The fishing smack edges towards the cliff, with the shadow of Tregarthen Hill blocking out the light. From this distance, the entrance to Piper's Hole is just a fold in the rock. No one would guess that the cave existed without local knowledge; it's only accessible at low tide, when you can scramble down the hillside, or land a boat on the shore. Right now, the cavernous space will be flooded to the ceiling, my thoughts shifting back to a local woman who died there last year, stranded by a freak tide.

I peer at the cliff face again, but all I can see are waves breaking over boulders, a row of gulls lined up on a promontory. Several minutes pass before I spot a black shape rolling with each wave at the foot of the cliff, making my gut tighten.

'Can you land me on the rocks, Denny?'

Cardew gives me a wary glance. 'You'll have to jump. I'll run aground if I go too close.'

'Lucky I've got long legs.'

My heart's pumping as the boat swings towards the cliff. If my timing's wrong, I'll be crushed against the rocks as the boat rides the next high wave. I wait for a deep swell then take my chances, landing heavily on an outcrop, fingers clasping its wet surface. When I climb across the granite, the soles of my trainers slip on a patina of seaweed. I give Cardew a hasty thumbs up, then turn to the wall of rock that lies ahead, marked by cracks and fissures. Below it a body is twisting on the water's surface, dressed in diving gear, too far away to reach. I can't tell if it's a man or woman, but the reason why the ocean has failed to drag it under is obvious. The oxygen tank attached to the corpse's back is snagged on the rocks, anchoring it to the mouth of Piper's Hole.

I dig my phone from my pocket and call Eddie Nickell. The young constable listens in silence as I instruct him to bring a police launch from St Mary's; it will have to anchor nearby until the tide ebbs and the body can be carried aboard. The breakers cresting the rocks are taller than before, but the *Tresco Lass* is still bobbing on the high water, ten metres away. I make a shooing motion with my hands to send Cardew away before his boat is damaged, but he gives a fierce headshake, and I can't help grinning. The fisherman is a typical islander, unwilling to leave a man stranded, despite risking his livelihood. I turn my back to the pounding spray, knowing the wait will be uncomfortable. It could take an hour for the tide to recede far enough to let me reach the body. When I lift my head again, the corpse is rolling with each wave, helpless as a piece of driftwood.

2

Tom Heligan reaches Ruin Beach earlier than planned. He looks more like a schoolboy than a young man on his way to work, an overgrown fringe shielding his eyes, his legs spindly. He pauses on Long Point to catch his breath, images from the sea cave making panic build inside his chest. From here he can see the black outlines of Northwethel, Crow Island, and the Eastern Isles scattered across the sea. On an ordinary day he could stand for hours, picturing shipwrecks trapped below the ocean's surface. Spanish galleons lie beside square riggers and tea clippers. He could draw a map of the wooden carcasses that litter the seabed with his eyes shut, but even his favourite obsession fails to calm him today. Tresco's rocky shores have destroyed hundreds of boats, their precious cargo stolen by the waves, ever since Phoenicians sailed here to trade jewellery for tin. Now his own life is foundering. He drags in another breath, weak as a castaway stumbling ashore.

The boy crosses the beach towards the café at his slowest pace. How will he be able to work after what he saw? He should never have followed Jude Trellon from the pub last night; it was a pathetic thing to do, especially after spending the day in her company, but he hates letting her out of his sight. Tom comes to a halt, eyes screwed shut, trying to erase the memory. The shame of his cowardice will last forever. He saw a figure emerge from behind a rock in Piper's Hole, but was too afraid to act: he hid in the darkness until the terrible cries and splashing ended, then ran for his life. Fields passed in a blur as he sprinted home to Merchant's Point. Last night he convinced himself that everything he saw was a waking dream, but now he's less certain. Surely the woman he's obsessed with is strong enough to defend herself from any threat? There might be nothing to fear after all.

3

Cardew's boat is still bobbing in the distance. The life-belt he has thrown towards me floats close to the rocks; at least I'll be able to grab it if the next breaker drags me into the sea. I cling to wet granite for another twenty minutes with waves lashing around me, until the tide recedes, then scramble across to the diver's body, still trapped by the cave's entrance. Curses slip from my mouth when I see that it's Jude Trellon, a local woman in her late twenties, employed at her father's diving school. I remember her as an attractive dark-haired girl who attended my school with her older brother. When we were in our teens she was full of restless energy, but the sea has erased her beauty; the skin on her face and hands is blanched with cold, her cheek marked by a ragged tear. I know immediately that she's been mur-dered. Someone has wedged her oxygen tank between two boulders, a rope bound tight around her thigh, tethering her body to the cliff.

When I lie the victim on her side, brine gushes

from her mouth. I remember hearing that people can sometimes survive long periods of immersion, the cold slowing their metabolism. My first-aid training rushes through my head as I pull her tank free, then lift her body from the water. Something hard is lodged in her throat when I try to clear her airway, too deeply embedded to remove. CPR would be pointless while her throat is blocked. It's clear that she drowned hours ago, face misshapen from being pounded against the rocks. She looks nothing like the woman I saw enjoying herself last summer in my godmother's pub, surrounded by friends. All that remains is to work out how she met such a painful death. The mouthpiece from her aqualung is dangling at her side, but when I check her oxygen monitor, the tank is almost full. Such an experienced diver should never have drowned while she had access to a good air supply. It's only when I straighten up again that I notice something else. A blue plastic bottle has been tied to her ankle with a piece of wire, but the object seems irrelevant, compared to the bigger questions. What made her risk diving alone, and who hated her enough to leave her body tied to a cliff face, to be tormented by the waves?

I scramble back over the rocks to peer through the narrow entrance to Piper's Hole, but there's no point in trying to go inside. The cave is still half full of water, thrashing against its walls. If Jude Trellon met her death there, any evidence will already have been claimed by the tide. I'm still muttering questions to myself when the islands' biggest police launch arrives. It's a powerful rescue vessel built from glass-reinforced plastic, with yellow and blue flashing marking its sides. The boat is capable of travelling at thirty-two knots, but it's moving at a snail's pace today. Constable Eddie Nickell is preparing to jump ashore, while my boss, DCI Alan Madron, steers the boat onto a newly exposed strip of sand. The men make an odd contrast. Eddie is pink-cheeked and excitable as a choirboy, face framed by blond curls; the DCI nearing retirement age, frowning with disapproval. They have taken an hour to cover the short distance from St Mary's, but at least the ebb tide will make it easier to transport the body.

Denny Cardew finally swings his boat around, prepared to return to the harbour now my safety is guaranteed. I make a mental note to thank him, once the grim task of informing the relatives is over.

'You took your time,' I call out, as Eddie scrambles across the rocks.

'Sorry, boss. The DCI said it was too dangerous to go round the headland at high tide.'

'Great,' I reply. It's typical of Madron to observe health and safety protocols while I cling to the rocks like a drowned barnacle.

Eddie's eyes turn glassy when he sees the body, and it hits me that he must know the Trellon family well, having grown up on the island. The woman's parents are prominent members of the community – Jude

Trellon's father owns the local diving school and her mother manages Ruin Beach café.

'How did it happen?' Eddie mutters. 'She's got a four-year-old kid.'

'Sit down for a minute, catch your breath.'

Nickell squats on the rock beside me, thin shoulders hunched, his face pale. His reaction proves that we're chalk and cheese. A decade with the Murder Squad in London, witnessing many fatal stabbings, beatings and gun crimes, has dulled my sense of horror. Eddie is ten years younger than me; a smart, fresh-faced twenty-four-year-old. His fiancée is expecting their first baby in July, yet it's deceptively easy to view him as a child. I'd like to give him more recovery time, but the DCI is beckoning urgently from the boat's wheelhouse. I remove the plastic bottle from its length of wire and stow it in the pocket of my hooded top. Once Eddie has stumbled to his feet we carry the victim's slim body over the rocks, the slick material of her wetsuit slipping from our hands. Madron is fuming when we clamber on board.

'We haven't got all day,' he snaps. 'The islanders mustn't get wind of this before the relatives. How the hell did it happen, Kitto?'

'She was attacked, then someone tied her body to the rocks. I think she died hours ago.'

'You're certain it wasn't a straightforward drowning?'

'Positive, sir. I took photos, showing how she was left.'

21

'I'll check them later.'

Madron's face is pinched with fury, as if I had swum across to Tresco and killed the woman myself. Even at sea he looks immaculate, shielded from the cold by his smart black coat, grey hair cropped short, boots glittering with polish. He has managed the local force for eleven years with ruthless efficiency, but always reacts badly to crises, as if the population's welfare was his sole responsibility.

'She can't have been gone long,' he insists. 'Someone would have reported her missing.'

I keep my mouth shut to avoid a row. I have only worked under Madron for a few months, but already understand that neither of us likes being contradicted. The ocean breeze sets my teeth chattering, penetrating my wet jeans, the sensation making me wonder what kind of hell the victim experienced before she died. I go below decks to grab a towel from the hold and rub brine from my hair, blotting the worst of it from my clothes.

'You should change before you see the relatives,' Madron says, when I return to the wheelhouse.

'There's no time, sir. Cardew will have told people about the body already. You'd better drop me at Ruin Beach.'

The DCI gives a curt nod of agreement, then heads the boat into Old Grimsby Sound. On an ordinary day it would be a scenic trip down Tresco's eastern coast, passing unspoiled bays, covered in glittering sand. The sea here is studded with outcrops that make night-time sailing treacherous, even with state-of-the-art GPS, it's hard to avoid the spikes of basalt marking the entrance to Ruin Beach. The harbour is a low expanse of shingle, guarded from storms by the long arm of its quay. The café resembles four large beach huts with picture windows overlooking the beach, and steps leading down to the shore. A handful of white dinghies and motorboats are moored to the jetty beside the diving school fifty metres away. Half a dozen houses lie further inland, on the far side of the track.

'The ambulance will take the body to the mortuary when I get back to St Mary's,' the DCI says. 'You can see Jude's family together, but don't tell them she was attacked until we've had the pathologist's assessment. Scaremongering won't help anyone.'

Madron's reaction makes my temper rise. He always errs on the side of caution, even when victims deserve the truth, but I keep my irritation quiet. Eddie observes me closely as we walk up the beach. He seems to believe that the skills of first-class detection can be learned by tracking my every move, but I'm not looking forward to giving the Trellons the worst news imaginable, then repeating the performance for Jude's boyfriend.

My breathing grows shallow as we approach the diving school, but judging by the sleek speedboats waiting to be hired, the place has prospered since I took my first diving lesson there as a teenager. An ocean-going cruiser with state-of-the-art satellite antennae bobs on the tide, with the name *Fair Diane* stencilled on its prow. The diving school is a modest two-storey brick building, its front room operating as a shop. When we step inside, wetsuits are hanging from the walls, shelves are filled with halcyon flares and wrist-bound computers, and a box of underwater cameras is waiting to be unpacked. Mike Trellon emerges from the stockroom as we arrive. He's around sixty, medium height, with chiselled features. Mike hasn't changed much since he taught me to dive two decades ago; he still carries himself with the authority of a Hollywood film star. It must be life experience that has given him such natural confidence. He's been diving here since he was a child, and no one knows more about the local waters. The lines bracketing his mouth may be deeper, his hair a lighter shade of grey, but his voice is the same baritone grumble when he claps his hand on my arm.

'You're soaked, Ben. Did you fall off the quay?'

'There's been an accident.' I keep my gaze steady when he meets my eye. 'Is Shane with you?'

Mike shakes his head. 'He's taken a party out seal watching, they'll be gone all morning. What on earth's happened?'

'We need to talk to you and Diane together.'

I consider advising him to lock the door, to protect thousands of pounds' worth of stock, but security here is rarely an issue. Mike Trellon marches away from his shop without a backward glance.

Ruin Beach café is only a minute's walk south along

the shore. Its tall windows reveal a scrubbed wooden floor, and waitresses bustling between tables positioned to enjoy the immaculate view of the Eastern Isles strewn across the sea. Diane Trellon is serving breakfast to some early holidaymakers, her wavy chestnut hair tied back with a green scarf, her top the same rich emerald. She must be fifty-five, but looks years younger, famous for her warm welcome. Diane's grin widens when she catches sight of us, then quickly vanishes. Two police officers arriving on your doorstep rarely means good news, even when you've known them all their lives.

'Can we have a word, Diane?' I ask.

I stand beside Eddie in her tiny office. The room should feel comforting, with its wood-lined walls and the soft hiss of waves landing on the beach outside, but it's a tight squeeze for the four of us. The couple sit on hard plastic chairs, while Eddie and I stand by the door, like a pair of reluctant sentries. On the other side of the wall, strangers are laughing while they enjoy their breakfasts, the air salty with fried bacon, yet my appetite has deserted me. The couple watch me fumble for the right words, but there's no good way to explain that their daughter has drowned. Mike collapses first, his face dropping forwards into his hands.

Diane's green eyes are glassy with disbelief. 'That can't be right. Jude dropped in last night, on her way to the pub.'

'What time was that?'

'Eightish, the place was packed; we had a big party over from St Mary's for dinner.' Hope still burns in her eyes, like she's praying for a miracle.

'It happened later. Jude's body needs to be identified, but I'm afraid we're certain it's her. She was in her diving gear, by Piper's Hole.'

'It's my fault.' Mike's head rears back suddenly. 'I should have stopped her night diving, the bloody idiot. I knew it would kill her in the end. She always has to do everything bigger and better than her brother.'

The statement strikes me as odd; there's no clear reason why Mike Trellon should blame himself for his daughter's death.

'Shut up, for Christ's sake,' Diane snaps. 'It's too late for talk like that.'

'Jude always has to break every rule.' His fist smacks down on the table, sending a cup and saucer smashing to the floor.

His wife ignores the sound and turns to me. 'Does Ivar know?'

'We're seeing him next. Will he be at home?'

'He's looking after Frida. I should be there when he hears.'

'We'll call you afterwards, or bring them to your house.'

I want to ask more questions about whether Jude had worked the previous day, and how her brother Shane spent the evening, but the couple are in no fit state. When we get up to leave, Mike Trellon's fury has already turned to grief. He's weeping into his cupped hands, Diane's arm circling his shoulders, our visit shattering their peace with the force of a grenade. Eddie is quiet as we leave the café, his chatter silenced by the couple's misery.

We walk towards the centre of the island at a steady pace. Tresco is dominated by the Abbey and its famous gardens, which attract thousands of tourists every year, yet the place has kept its tranquillity. There are no cars here, but the lane is wide enough to accommodate local traffic, which consists of horse-drawn carts, bicycles and golf buggies for the elderly. Dolphin Town sits in a valley lined with grassy fields, where goats and sheep are grazing. The village would only qualify as a town on an island two miles long, with a permanent population of less than 200. It consists of a row of photogenic cottages, the old vicarage beside St Nicholas's church, and a one-room primary school. Jude Trellon's property is a small whitewashed house at the end of the village. I come to a halt fifty metres away, to plan my speech to her boyfriend.

'When did Anna Dawlish drown at Piper's Hole, Eddie?' The landlady of the New Inn died sometime last winter, while I was still living in London, but I remember hearing about her funeral.

'Last November, she wasn't much older than Jude. The tide caught her when she was taking an evening stroll.'

'We'll have to check the details.' I study the victim's

cottage again, where a child's red tricycle stands beside the front door. 'We'd better break the bad news.'

'Do you want me to do it, boss?' Eddie asks. 'At least I'm a familiar face.'

'It's my job. The senior officer always draws the short straw.'

I rattle the door knocker, but there's no answer, so we approach the back entrance, and Ivar Larsson steps out to greet us. The dead woman's boyfriend has a slim, tennis player's build, his blond hair slicked back to reveal pale blue eyes and high Scandinavian cheekbones. His features are so flawless they look computer-designed. When I lived in London, I forgot about the lack of diversity here until I came home; most of Tresco's permanent residents have been rooted in island soil for generations. But the reason why a Swedish academic would choose to live on a piece of granite barely two miles long is obvious. I fancied Jude Trellon too, back in the day, the woman's good looks and high spirits making her hard to resist. I remember hearing that Larsson came here to do scientific research, but know little more about him. He's dressed in faded jeans and a black T-shirt today, clutching some papers in his hand. The expression on his face is so resolute, I can't imagine him taking orders from anyone.

'If you're looking for Jude, she'll be at work by now.' His voice has a strong Scandinavian inflection, its tone cool.

'Can we come in, please, Mr Larsson?'

His daughter is kneeling on the kitchen floor, so focused on completing a wooden jigsaw puzzle she barely registers our presence. Frida must be around four years old, a wave of dark hair obscuring her face, and I feel a pulse of sympathy. Losing my father at fourteen was bad enough, but she's far too young to make sense of her mother's death. Ivar must have been working while the girl plays: a nautical map is spread across the table, the metre-wide sheet marked with dotted lines and small red crosses. He turns the paper over, concealing his documents. I'd like to know what he's researching, but it's the wrong time for curiosity.

'I'm in the middle of something. Is this important?' Ivar's gaze shifts between Eddie's face and mine.

'I'm afraid so. Is it okay to leave your daughter here for a minute?'

'If we keep the door open.'

When Larsson leads us to his living room, framed photos of his homeland stand on the mantelpiece: pine-clad mountains are outlined against clear skies, brightly painted cabins studding the foothills. Jude's face beams out from a set of pictures taken on a local beach, her golden-brown eyes giving the camera a forthright stare. She is sitting with her daughter by an elaborate sandcastle. Larsson's arm circles his girlfriend's waist, while her dark hair billows in the breeze. Jude looks gorgeous and carefree, but even on a day out with his family, Larsson's smile is reserved. When I look at the man again, his posture is rigid with tension.

'There's no easy way to say this, Mr Larsson. I'm afraid your girlfriend's body was found a few hours ago, in the sea.'

His eyelids flutter rapidly. 'You're telling me she drowned?'

'That's right, I'm sorry.'

'Is there someone we can call for you?' Eddie murmurs. 'Jude's parents, maybe?'

He gives a fierce headshake. 'I don't need anyone. Just tell me what happened.'

'We think Jude was diving, then ran into difficulties.'

'At Piper's Hole?'

'You knew she was going there?'

His gaze slips from mine. 'She was planning to stay at Shane's overnight. We ate dinner together, before she went out.'

'How did you spend the evening?'

'Someone had to look after Frida, and Jude likes seeing her brother alone now and then.' Ivar's hands twist in his lap. 'Someone killed her, didn't they? We've dived together dozens of times, she knew her limits.'

'We can't be sure what happened yet. Did you leave the house at all last night, Mr Larsson?'

'Of course not, I was looking after Frida.' He rises to his feet suddenly, then stands there swaying, his veneer of toughness slipping away. 'Leave us now, please. I want to be alone with my daughter.'

'I'll send someone round to help you later today.'

Shock is seeping through his composure as he

retreats into the kitchen. Larsson stands with his back to the window, eyes glazed, clearly willing us to go. When I turn round, his daughter has appeared in the doorway, clutching a battered doll. She scurries past me to her father's side, hiding her face against his hip, the man's hand settling on her shoulder.

'Finish your puzzle, Frida,' he says quietly. 'You don't need to worry.'

Eddie and I step into the living room, to give him time on his own. The DCI calls my deputy a few minutes later, already requesting an update, his hectoring tone leaking from the handset. I put through a call to my friend Zoe Morrow, asking her to catch the ferry to Tresco immediately. Any of the islanders would keep Ivar company, the community drawing close during crises, but I have a feeling that Zoe's presence will be easier for him to handle. He seems unwilling to face Jude's parents' distress, or questions from well-meaning friends. Zoe is around the same age, with a warm, no-nonsense manner. She seems like the right person to penetrate his frozen exterior and coax out details to reveal whether his girlfriend had enemies.

I take a quick look around the ground floor of the cottage on our way out. Books on shelves in the hallway provide the only evidence of the victim's passion for diving. There are dozens of trade magazines featuring the latest breathing apparatus, glass-bottomed boats, and submersibles, beside marine surveys of the Great Barrier Reef. But her possessions can't explain why she took the night dive that led to her death, or her boy-friend's knowledge that she had been found at Piper's Hole, before he was told. He could easily have left the house once his daughter was asleep, then walked to the sea cave to kill his girlfriend, after a bitter row.

4

Offers of help flood in once the islanders hear of the fatality. The most useful one comes from Will Dawlish, manager of the New Inn Hotel. He's in his mid-forties, with an unassuming manner, his shirt stretched tight over his paunch, bald head shiny in the overhead light. He looks more like an avuncular geography teacher than the landlord of a thriving inn. Dawlish's voice is quiet as he offers us the hotel's attic as our temporary headquarters. I ask to see it immediately, because public space on Tresco is hard to find, and the New Inn stands at the centre of the island, only five minutes from Dolphin Town. The place has expanded in recent years from a modest hostelry to a boutique spa with a swimming pool, yet the manager looks embarrassed as he presses the key into my hand.

'We're renovating this room next year. Sorry it's such a mess, but it's yours for the taking.'

'Thanks, Will. If we use it, the room has to be secure. No one can enter without our permission.'

'You'll be left alone, I promise. I'll get a table and chairs brought up.'

Dawlish's manner is flustered as he hurries away, and I can understand why. Hearing about another death in the same place as his wife's drowning must have triggered bad memories. Instinct tells me that two fatalities in the same location can't be a coincidence, but I'll need to find out more before drawing conclusions.

The room he's offered us appears to be falling apart, but it's better than nothing. Bare plaster is shredding from the walls, the floorboards are grimed with dust, and cobwebs shroud every corner, but the bird's-eye view is a fine compensation. Through the smeared glass, I can see the sloping hills of Bryher, hazed by purple heather, and the Atlantic glittering for miles.

When I take off my hooded top, the blue plastic bottle from the crime scene falls to the floor. It was attached to Jude's ankle by a length of green plasticised twine, of the kind people use to secure plants to frames in their gardens. I pick it up without worrying about leaving fingerprints; DNA evidence will have been scoured from the bottle's exterior by seawater long ago. It's a far cry from the romantic notion of messages in bottles, cast into the brine by lovesick mariners. This one would have held half a litre of drinking water originally, but now the plastic is scuffed, its label soaked away. When I hold it up for closer inspection, the slip of white paper inside is neatly folded. I unscrew the cap and shake it out onto an evidence bag. Eddie passes me some sterile gloves before we both peer down at the message, which is handwritten in square block capitals, as if the killer went to great lengths to disguise his writing style.

> THE SEA GIVES, AND THE SEA TAKES,
> NEVER MIND THE DANGER,
> NEVER MIND THE CARE.
> THE SEA GIVES AND THE SEA TAKES
> YET TREASURES AWAIT FOR THOSE
> THAT DARE.

Eddie gives a low whistle between his teeth, but makes no comment. The message is as simple and repetitive as a lullaby, and it interests me that the killer has chosen such a practical method of communication. A glass bottle would have been smashed on the rocks by the first tall wave, but he has insured that his odd statement reaches us intact. I have no idea where the phrases come from, but the message seems to blame Jude Trellon's death on the sea itself, with its elemental ability to give and take life. A quick internet search reveals that the words come from an eighteenth-century sea shanty. Sailors would have bawled the song at the top of their voices while they battled with the elements, the wind lashing their ship, aware that the ocean could wipe out their lives in an instant. But why did the killer attach an ancient rhyme to his victim's ankle in a used water bottle, of the type that litters our beaches by the thousand every year? There's no time to discuss the message with Eddie before our next distraction arrives.

A group of locals have appeared to enquire about Jude Trellon's death, even though no formal announcement has been made. The people of Tresco have the same outlook as those on Bryher, where I grew up, always prepared to abandon petty conflicts in a crisis. Lives here are so tightly connected that weddings and funerals often last for days, the community celebrating and mourning together. The first person to approach me is Justin Bellamy, the vicar of St Nicholas's church. He's only lived on Tresco for a year, relocating from Birmingham, but he's adapted well to island life. Apart from his dog collar, he looks like any other man in his late thirties; his lanky figure is dressed in jeans and a short-sleeved shirt, brown hair shorn into an ugly buzz cut that demonstrates his lack of vanity. The priest gives me a concerned look, as if he's longing for opportunities to minister to his flock. His only distinguishing feature is a scar that bisects his cheek, running from his eye socket to his jaw, puckered by a dozen stitch marks. I'd love to know how a man of the cloth received such a savage wound but have never found reason to ask. Bellamy's expression is earnest as he crosses the room.

'I just heard the news, Ben. What can I do to help?' His voice is a soft Midlands drawl.

'The family are in shock, they'll need all your support.'

'I'll pop round today,' he replies. 'It's hard to believe. Jude was a force of nature; she'll be missed by all of us.'

'When's the last time you saw her?'

'Friday morning, she was teaching me to dive – it's always been a fantasy of mine. We went out to St Helen's for a few hours.'

'Can we talk about that, when things settle down?'

'Anytime, you know where I am.' Justin peers deeper into my eyes, as if he's checking the condition of my soul. 'I hear it was you that found her. Are you all right?'

'Fine, thanks. I'm trained to deal with it.'

He taps my arm. 'But no amount of practice prepares us for the reality, does it? Call me, if you feel like talking.'

The vicar hurries away once we've said goodbye, leaving me envious of his ability to comfort people. My years undercover with the Murder Squad taught me to keep my emotions under wraps as effectively as Ivar Larsson, blunting my ability to show compassion. Eddie fulfils that part of the policing role much more easily. I can see him on the other side of the room, busy comforting Elinor Jago from the post office. She has been Tresco's postmistress since I was a child, striding round the island delivering letters, cheerful even in winter's storm-force gales. Her appearance is uncompromising, a big woman with grey hair cut into a mannish crop, her sturdy walking boots and jeans designed for practicality, but she's one of the kindest people on the island. Her blunt manner disguises the fact that she's always the first to help when someone is sick or in need. Jude

Trellon's death seems to have destroyed her unflappable calmness. She barely acknowledges me when I say goodbye, her face blank with shock as she listens to the few details Eddie can offer.

A child is skulking in the porch when I step outside. I recognise the boy's face, but his name escapes me. He's thin as a wraith, eyes half hidden by curtains of chocolate brown hair, dressed in a grey T-shirt and designer jeans. When his gaze connects with mine, I realise that he's older than he seems, probably late teens. The look in his eyes is much too serious for a child.

'Can I help you?' I ask.

'It's nothing,' he stammers. 'I was just passing.'

'Did you want to talk about Jude Trellon?'

The lad shakes his head. Before I can say another word, he's hurrying away, hidden already by elder trees that line the track to Ruin Beach.

'Nice to meet you too,' I say under my breath.

The boy soon slips from my mind as I take the five-minute walk to New Grimsby Harbour. Warm air has glued my salt-encrusted clothes to my skin as I wait for the ferry. My uncle's boatyard stands on the quay on the other side of the channel. I wish that I could strip to my boxers and swim home to Bryher, like my brother and I often did in high summer, pitting our strength against the currents, but the boat is already chugging across the water. Arthur Penwithick is steering the *Bryher Maid* towards the jetty. The ferryman has changed little in the twenty years since he carried me to school on the mainland, a navy cap is still glued to his frizz of brown hair, buck teeth protruding as he offers a smile of greeting. Penwithick is too shy to volunteer questions, even though he's sure to know about the fatality, island gossip spreading like wildfire. Instead he focuses on collecting half a dozen passengers from the quay, before transporting us to St Mary's at top speed. My fellow passengers are a party of French tourists, their faces pale as the small craft judders over choppy waves.

I hurry along the quayside once we reach Hugh Town Quay. St Mary's is going about its business as usual, fishing boats beached on the shingle like rows of colourful fish, while gaggles of visitors loiter outside gift shops, with ice creams in hand. Cars are proceeding down Quay Road at a respectful pace, as if the drivers know how lucky they are to live on the only Scilly island where driving is permitted. When I check my phone, DCI Madron has left three voice messages, advising me how to do my job, but his nagging can wait until the day's worst duty is over.

St Mary's Hospital is one of the smallest in the UK. It doubles as a doctor's surgery, with a basic operating theatre for emergencies and a handful of treatment rooms for patients too sick to be flown to the mainland. The room at the back of the building serves as a mortuary, a refrigeration unit built into the wall to accommodate the dead. Dr Keillor is drumming his fingers when I arrive. The pathologist is a portly figure, grey hair combed over his bald patch, dressed in a navy linen suit and Oxford brogues. The man's black-rimmed spectacles magnify his eyes, making his stare inescapable. Keillor retired here after working for the Home Office, but still provides his services as a consultant whenever there's an unexplained death. He gives me a brisk nod before pulling on his white coat.

'Thanks for waiting,' I say. 'Sorry I'm late.'

'Not a problem, but let's begin, shall we? I'm missing a round of golf for this. The post-mortem can't happen until the relatives have identified her, but I'll try to establish cause of death.'

The pathologist's words are addressed to me, but he already seems more interested in the dead than the living. He pulls on surgical gloves, then draws back the white sheet. Someone has removed Jude Trellon's wetsuit already; apart from the superficial wounds on her face and bruising around her throat, the woman appears to have been in athletic shape when she died, no spare fat on her muscular frame. It feels invasive to stare at a woman's naked body, but it's the only way to find out how she died. The thing that strikes me immediately when the pathologist rolls her body gently onto her front is that her back is almost covered in tattoos. Even in an age when body art is the norm, so much of her skin is covered with illustrations, she must have spent days in a tattooist's chair.

'Let's find out what happened to you, young lady,' Keillor mutters to the corpse.

He takes his time examining the victim, checking the condition of her palms and fingertips, then shifting her gently onto her side. Her tattoos all have a nautical theme. A sea snake curls across her shoulder in blue-black twists, a detailed picture of a galleon riding out a storm inked across her shoulder blade. It's only when I study the words that scroll down her arm that I realise they're the names of ships: *Destiny*, *Esmeralda*, *Good Fortune*. Every dive the woman made seems to have been recorded on her body. I'm still staring at her illustrated skin when Keillor makes a startled sound. He pulls a piece of seaweed from Trellon's mouth, then inserts surgical tweezers to draw something else from her throat. The pathologist mutters an exclamation before rinsing it under the tap, then showing me the item on the flat of his palm.

'Here's your cause of death, Inspector. I've cleared plenty of blocked airways in my time, but never seen anything like this. Don't touch, it needs to be analysed.'

The object is made of metal, six inches long, about an inch wide, covered in verdigris. It's a figurine of a mermaid, her features glossy with water. If I'd spotted it in a gift shop window, I'd have said it was beautiful, with minute hexagonal scales carved across its tail. I stare at it in silence until my brain starts working again.

'How did it get there?'

'Someone shoved it down her throat. There are cuts in her oesophagus, enough swelling to seal her windpipe. It would have been a vicious attack.'

'Could it have been put there after she died?'

'She's ingested very little water. This blockage stopped her breathing, not the sea. Someone rammed it into her mouth with considerable force.' He turns away, attention drifting back to the corpse. 'You'll get my report tomorrow. We'll keep her body in the fridge until the relatives have said their goodbyes.'

'Did you carry out the autopsy on Anna Dawlish too, Dr Keillor?'

He nods but doesn't look up. 'That was a different case entirely; she fell on a Tresco beach and drowned from a simple head injury. There was nothing unusual about the circumstances.'

The pathologist's certainty that Will Dawlish's wife met her death accidentally is a relief, because it allows me to focus on the reasons for Jude Trellon's death. Witnessing her autopsy has revealed the violence of her attack and made me more determined to find her killer.

I'm still processing Keillor's words as I return to Hugh Town. The police station is an unprepossessing grey building one road back from the quay, its front door permanently open. Sergeant Lawrence Deane sits behind the reception desk. He's a stout, red-haired man of around fifty, inclined to long bouts of sulking. Deane still hasn't accepted my appointment as Madron's deputy. Until I arrived he was the longest-serving officer on the island force; the man must have believed the job was his by right.

'Up to your usual heroics, Ben? I bet the girls are

swooning.' There's no trace of humour in his voice.

'I doubt it. Pulling a corpse from the sea isn't exactly glamorous.'

'The DCI's waiting for you. He's not in the best mood.'

Deane's attention flicks back to his computer screen. The other officers on the team claim that Lawrie has a sense of humour, but at this rate it could take years to make him crack a smile.

Madron listens in silence when I pass on Keillor's view that Trellon was murdered by asphyxiation. The only sign that the DCI is displeased by the news is his rigid posture, backbone stiffer than before, his chest puffed out like a sergeant major.

'Have you put a stop on people leaving the island, Kitto?'

'We've told everyone on Tresco that all journeys have to be authorised.'

He gives a rapid nod. 'Nothing like this has happened there before. The islanders might panic; I don't want the family upset.'

'I'll handle them with care.'

'Remember you're still on probation. Your final evaluation is next month; my report will decide the outcome.'

'The review meeting's in my diary, sir.'

'You can be too plain-spoken, and I want you to smarten up. An SIO should wear full uniform.'

'I've worked in plain clothes for ten years. Everyone here knows who I am.'

'It's a matter of showing respect. I could get a detective from the mainland to lead the investigation.'

'The islanders will clam up if outsiders interfere.'

The DCI looks exasperated. 'I'll keep the press at bay, but they're bound to leap to conclusions and assume it was the boyfriend. What's your impression of him?'

'His distress seemed genuine when he heard about Jude. He's a cool customer, but I don't want to prejudge him. I'll wait for more evidence. Right now, all I have is the murder weapon and the written message left at the scene; they'll be sent to the lab for analysis.'

'Don't take any risks. One sign of drama will make me change my mind.'

'Thank you, sir. I'll want Eddie on Tresco for the investigation. If we need more officers, I'll let you know.'

I back out of the door before he can change his mind. I'm the only member of Madron's team with experience of murder investigation and a glowing reference from the Met, but after so long in charge, the DCI hates ceding control. He's dangled the threat of my last evaluation over me for months. I'm not sure why the desire to find Jude Trellon's killer is building inside my skull, like a headache coming to the boil. There's something obscene about the way she was choked to death with a trinket designed to adorn someone's mantelpiece. The woman was five years younger than me, but we grew up in parallel, with just half a mile of water separating us. I heard that she was a talented diver, making a living from the sport for years before returning to Tresco. She used to be a wild child, but must have grown up since then, leaving her daughter motherless. The afternoon light is starting to dull as I reach the quay. A few people from Bryher are queuing for the ferry, but I keep my head down, too preoccupied to communicate. My mind is already clicking through pieces of evidence, working on angles to pursue when I get home.

5

It feels like a miracle that Tom has passed the day without breaking down. Shutters still cover the diving shop's windows, but the café has remained open, the boy's movements mechanical as he unloads the dishwasher. Steam damps his face when he leans inside, his mind echoing with questions. What will he do now? The person he cared for most is gone, and only he knows why, but there's no one he can tell. The big cop he saw outside the New Inn stared at him like he deserved to be in jail. Since then his grief has turned to anger. Through the serving hatch, he can see diners gorging themselves. Many of them knew Jude well, yet they're ploughing through fish and chips like nothing has happened. He wants to march over and empty their plates onto their laps, but forces himself to continue polishing wine glasses.

At six o'clock, Tom hangs up his apron and nods goodbye to the manageress. His home is ten minutes away, but he walks at a snail's pace. The sun fades as he crosses the sand, avoiding a handful of beachcombers and joggers, until he reaches the next bay and finds himself alone. When he drops behind a breakwater, sobs spill from his throat with the raw sound of an animal in pain. It has been years since he let himself cry, but now there's no choice; the rush of grief is overwhelming. Once the outburst passes he dries his face with the sleeve of his sweatshirt. His guilt feels too heavy to carry when he thinks of all the days he spent with Jude. She taught him to dive for no payment, always teasing and encouraging him, treating him like a kid brother. He owes it to her to discover the name of her murderer, but speaking to the police would only get him into trouble.

Tom rises slowly, then brushes sand from his jeans. He walks past the high outline of Merchant's Rock to reach his cottage. The boy wishes just for once to find the place empty, but his mother calls out a greeting when he closes the front door. Tom rushes to the bathroom without replying, his reflection confronting him in the mirror; his features are gaunt with misery, skin blotchy from crying. He splashes his face with cold water before returning downstairs.

His mother is in her wheelchair, a novel open on her lap. She looks up at him when he appears, her smile artificially bright.

'You're late tonight, love. Everything okay?'

'Fine, Mum. What do you want for tea?'

'Whatever's in the fridge. Is something wrong? You look pale.'

'It's nothing.'

Tom's gaze lingers on his mother's face, taut with pain, behind a layer of make-up. He loves her, but the time when he could confide in her passed years ago; she has grown weaker since his father left, only her invalidity benefit and his small wage keeping them afloat. Sooner or later he must share the news of Jude's death, but not now. He can't face adding to her sadness, and his voice would give too much away.

'How about pizza and salad?' Tom asks, hovering in the doorway.

'Perfect, love. Do you want a hand?'

'No need. It won't take long.'

'Why not meet Gemma at the pub later? You haven't seen her in ages.'

'Her dad won't let her go out till after her exams.'

'All right, love, it's up to you.'

His mother's attention has already drifted back to her book, as if the people described on its pages matter more than the ones right under her nose.

6

Shadow is sprawled across the doormat when I get home. He gives a bark of disapproval, expressing his opinion of my absence. When I put my hand down to greet him, he bares his teeth.

'Remember who feeds you, buddy,' I tell him as he slinks inside.

His manner warms considerably after he's demolished a bowlful of dog biscuits. He settles in front of the empty hearth, napping while I peel off my clothes. It's a relief to shower away the salt that has clung to my skin all day, but the memory of Jude Trellon's body in the mortuary is harder to remove. I always feel a mixture of excitement and tension at the start of a murder investigation, the thrill of the chase battling with concern about letting a vicious killer walk away. Nine times out of ten, the motives for a murder are easy to identify, but I need to understand the woman's life better before jumping to conclusions. It still bothers me that her boyfriend guessed she had been found near

Piper's Hole, yet refused to explain why. I've always respected the victim's parents. Diane has transformed the Ruin Beach café into a welcoming hub for the local community, and I can still remember Mike teaching me to dive as a teenager, explaining oxygen calculations with infinite patience. It's a year since I last wore my wetsuit, but the first dive of the season used to be a summer ritual. My brother and I would sail Ray's dinghy until Bryher was just a speck on the horizon, then hurl ourselves overboard, plummeting into a field of turquoise.

I sit at the kitchen table, too preoccupied to eat, picturing the island where Jude Trellon met her death. Tresco lies less than half a mile away, yet I know little about the place, apart from local folklore. Augustus Smith leased the island from the Duchy of Cornwall in the mid-nineteenth century, then built his lavish home beside the ruins of an ancient abbey. The man's descendants still control the place, most of the properties rented, but the land was inhabited long before the monarchy got their paws on it. Some of its cairns and hill graves are Neolithic. I drop my pen on the table and rub my hands across my face, aware that I'm drifting off course. The island's past can't explain why a young mother met such a violent death. The message in the bottle proves little, except the killer's interest in history and his desire to taunt us.

The second I rise to my feet, the dog's eyes flick open. 'Coming to see Zoe?'

Shadow jumps up at the mention of her name, the prospect of visiting his favourite islander cancelling his bad mood. He sprints ahead as I follow the shingle path down to the beach. The hotel on the far side of Hell Bay is owned by Zoe's parents, who retired to the mainland five years ago, leaving her in charge. It looks like a row of clean white boxes strewn across the headland; the place is so popular with tourists, the summer season books up months in advance. Shadow chases my heels when I jog up the steps to the hotel's veranda. There's no sign of Zoe through the bar's panoramic window, just a few dozen guests, lingering over nightcaps and enjoying the immaculate sea view, while waiting staff buzz between tables.

I trot up the back stairs but no one answers my knock on the door to Zoe's flat. When I push it open, she's sitting at her dining table, ears covered by headphones while she pores over something that looks like a legal document, with an ornate crest at the top of the page. I've enjoyed looking at Zoe ever since we were kids, so I linger in the doorway. Her short blue dress showcases her curves, long arms and legs tinted gold by the sun. My friend's short hair is the same platinum blonde she's favoured since she hit sixteen and decided brown was boring. She announced her plan to become a world-famous rock star in the same year, but her dream never materialised.

Zoe almost jumps out of her skin when she finally spots me. 'Jesus, you scared the living shit out of me.'

She's on her feet, scrabbling papers back into a yellow plastic wallet.

'What were you reading?'

'Just business stuff. I wasn't expecting you till tomorrow.'

I can tell something's bothering her, but it's the wrong time to ask. Shadow has picked up on the atmosphere too. He's behaving himself for once, his muzzle propped on her thigh while he gazes at her adoringly. Zoe fusses over him before fetching us both a beer. She slams the bottle of Grolsch down in front of me, hard enough to make the table rattle.

'Is that how you serve all your customers?'

'Only ones that piss me off royally.'

I take a long swig of beer. 'What did I do?'

'You wasted my morning, when I could have been looking after guests. I made a hamper for Ivar and Frida, then used the hotel dinghy to get over to Tresco. He's got the place locked up like Fort Knox; he wouldn't even let me inside.'

'Larsson was shell-shocked when I left. I thought he might open up to you.'

'I bet poor Frida hasn't got a clue what's happened.' Zoe's expression softens. 'Ivar looked scared, under all that hostility. Do you think he's afraid of someone?'

'I won't know till he starts talking.'

'How are Diane and Mike taking the news?'

'Not great. It'll be a while before it sinks in.'

'Was it a diving accident?'

'Too early to say.' It would be a mistake to give Zoe information; she's always been lousy at keeping secrets. 'Have you seen Jude and Shane recently?'

She shakes her head. 'Not for a while. Do you remember what they were like, back in the day?'

'Not really, they were a few years below us at school.'

'All the boys fancied Jude, including you, I bet, by the time she hit sixteen. Her brother's less confident, even though he's a year older. She was so charismatic, Shane didn't stand a chance. Jude was one of those people everyone wants to know.'

'Were they close?'

'I think so.' Zoe stares out at the empty beach, streaked with light from the hotel's windows. 'Shane grew up in Jude's shadow, but that didn't seem to bother him.'

'Do you know how she met Ivar?'

'He came over from Gothenburg University to research a book; the guy's so serious, it seemed an odd choice. Some of her friends disliked him from day one.'

'That must have caused ructions. Do you know what he was writing about?'

'Something to do with the sea. Ivar doesn't do small talk.'

'Did they have a close relationship?'

'Jude came here last summer and sat at the bar chatting when I was closing up. She said her dad's business was having problems, but didn't mention anything else.' Zoe's gaze slips from mine. 'It's so awful, Ben.

She was a livewire, always the first to dance at parties, and she was so thrilled to be a mum.'

'Where was Ivar the night she came over?'

'With Frida in Sweden, visiting his folks. He goes back every few months.'

When I study Zoe's face again, her smile is still missing. 'That's enough work for the night. I bet those papers are from a posh dating agency, aren't they?'

'I'm happier single. The last guy to ask me out was the vicar, but I declined. There's something scary about him.'

'Justin Bellamy fancies you?'

'Don't look so shocked. Men still try to seduce me, occasionally.'

'The only reason I've never made a move is because you made me sign an oath of eternal friendship when we were twelve.'

'I was wise before my time,' she says, patting the back of my hand. 'What happened to that girl you fancied on St Mary's anyway?'

'One date; no spark. Don't change the subject, Zoe. Tell me about the folder.'

'None of your business.'

'Sooner or later I'll find out, so why not come clean?'

'You're such a cop, Ben. Everyone's got secrets, even you.' She gives me a curious look. 'There's no way I could do your job, investigating all that evil. What made you choose it?'

'I was too stupid to do something easy, but it was the

right choice. It's not just the victim that gets destroyed in a murder case; whole families fall apart if a killer isn't found.'

She narrows her eyes. 'I thought you'd end up in Ray's boatyard, or journalism. You read all the time when we were kids.'

'I still do. Should I hand in my badge and become a librarian?'

'You'd last five minutes behind a desk.' She lets out a hoot of laughter. 'I've been thinking about my own future lately, that's all.'

Our conversation echoes in my head as I walk back across the beach. My job is the one thing I rarely question, because the emotional pay-off when a killer is found always justifies the graft, and moving home has given me a clean slate. The tide is coming in as my house looms into view and the urge to swim overwhelms me. The hiss of waves against the shore is a direct invitation, so I make a quick decision, abandoning my clothes on the beach. I enter the water in my boxer shorts, the chill sharp enough to make me hold my breath. When I swim against the current, my thoughts clear, as cold air and exercise work their magic, while my dog splashes in the shallows. I left most of my mistakes behind in London, but I'll need to uncover every error Jude Trellon made to find out what caused her death. Talking to Zoe has proved that the victim had more charisma than her older brother;

she won prizes for diving in international competitions, yet someone wanted her dead. Jude's adventurous personality is starting to emerge, but the only fact at my disposal is that her killer chose last night to snuff out her life. I swim a few more hard strokes, then let the tide carry me back to shore.

7

Tuesday 12 May

The ferry from Bryher to Tresco is packed on Tuesday morning, with more than a dozen people heading for work at the Abbey Gardens. Most of them sit on the narrow wooden benches that line the deck, but I stand by the gunwale at the bow, while Arthur Penwithick twists the wheel against currents that are rippling the surface of the sound. The journey to Tresco only takes five minutes, but it gives me time to remember my life in London, when I used to march through streets heaving with pedestrians, the sound of traffic assaulting my senses. There are no disturbances here, except occasional gulls squalling overhead and the drone of the ferry's motor as it battles with the tide. Eddie is waiting for me on New Grimsby Quay, shifting his weight from foot to foot, like a kid before his first day at school. Words bubble from his mouth as Shadow leaps onto the jetty.

'Good news, boss. I've found out how Jude spent Sunday.'

'Slow down, Eddie. Leave it till we're indoors.'

The fact that my deputy would happily blab confidential details in front of passengers leaving the ferry is another reminder that he's inexperienced. At least he doesn't have long to wait before spilling the beans. The bar of the New Inn is empty as we climb the back stairs. Through the open window I can see down to the quay, where Arthur Penwithick is preparing to sail back to Bryher, with miles of mid-blue Atlantic unrolling behind him.

Eddie starts gabbling immediately as the door closes. 'Jude was with a couple from London called Stephen and Lorraine Kinver on Sunday. She was working as a diving guide on their boat.'

'Are they still here?'

He shakes his head. 'People saw them sailing west from Ruin Beach, the afternoon before she died. Jude went home for dinner, then spent the evening in the bar downstairs with her brother until around eleven thirty. Will Dawlish heard them rowing, before Jude stormed out. Shane left around midnight. One of the punters said he was in a foul mood.'

Eddie's triumphant expression suggests that the case is solved, but I feel less certain. Jude's route to Piper's Hole will be impossible to retrace without any witness information. She could have crossed the fields to Tregarthen Hill, or followed any of the winding paths that lead north from the village. There was no evidence on the shore where I found her either, the sea destroying any clues to how she died.

'Have you got much background information on Jude?' I ask.

'Only that she had no record, and was popular with the islanders.'

'Come on, Eddie, you grew up here. There must be gossip; this place thrives on it.'

'It won't help us, boss. People make up crap for the hell of it.'

'Tell me anyway. I need to hear people's opinions.'

'Jude was a big name on the island when I was a kid, winning diving championships and being interviewed on TV. Her confidence came over as aggression sometimes; she wasn't afraid of men, that's for sure. Jude never stepped down from an argument if something pissed her off.'

'Was she on bad terms with anyone?'

'Only her ex-boyfriend, Jamie Petherton, the manager of the Valhalla Museum. He was in the pub early on Sunday night, on his own. Apparently the two of them fell out a few weeks ago. I don't know why.'

'We'll have to follow that up. What do you know about her current partner?'

'Ivar doesn't socialise much, apart from diving trips in the summer. Jude often went out with friends and her brother, but he spends his time at home, even though plenty of people could babysit.'

'Not a great relationship then?'

'Who knows, boss? They say opposites attract. She was the outgoing type, but he prefers his own company.'

'Can you check his record with Europol? We need to know more about his time in Sweden. The guy's reaction to Jude's death was muted, to say the least.'

Eddie's mouth purses shut, as if he's reluctant to criticise the dead. I flip open my notebook and stare at my to-do list. The couple Jude spent her last day with will need to be interviewed, her relatives, then friends and acquaintances, to find out who hated her enough to watch her drown. Jude's parents must be taken to see her body too, but not until I've broken the news that their daughter was murdered. Shane's argument with his sister on the night of her death makes him an obvious suspect, but suppositions are pointless without evidence to back them up.

'Look after the dog, can you, Eddie? I need to see Shane. Where does he live these days?'

'Smuggler's Cottage, on Cradle Point.'

'Start phoning round for more witness information. Contact the couple she dived with on Sunday too; see if you can set up an interview.'

'I'm on it, sir.'

'Stop calling me "sir", for Christ's sake. Ben's fine, unless Madron's here.'

Eddie gives an uneasy nod. My deputy is easily the brightest member of the islands' force, studying law at university until he opted for a more practical career. He prefers rigid protocols to thinking outside the box, but he's always industrious. Before I'm halfway to the door, he's on his phone, scribbling notes at a hectic pace.

My curiosity rises as I approach Shane Trellon's home. I can't forecast how I'd react if my only sibling was killed. Ian is two years older than me, and his endless Skype calls from America can be annoying, but the gap would be hard to fill if they ever stopped. Our childhoods were shaped by the wildness of these islands; the pair of us turned feral every summer, only returning home when hunger overwhelmed us. I'm guessing it was the same for Shane and Jude Trellon, but they were even closer in age, making the experience more intense. The landscape is a child's paradise, with hundreds of bays, caves and hill graves to explore.

When I head south along the coastal path, the sun is obscured by cloud, a freighter on the horizon keeps its distance from the rocks. Lumps of granite that pierce the water's surface are surrounded by hidden outcrops, making the Eastern Isles a ships' graveyard for centuries. Smuggler's Cottage stands alone in a small inlet, above a pebbled beach; it's one of the oldest houses on Tresco, with a commanding view of the Atlantic. Local folklore says that it was a haven for smugglers carrying contraband from Europe, using their navigational skills to escape the excisemen, but now it's too pristine for such lawlessness. The cottage looks like an advert for elite holiday homes, with a herring-bone brick path snaking through a garden full of lavender and jasmine, its six large windows facing the sea.

I rattle the door knocker but no one appears. I'm about to turn away when a pair of bloodshot eyes study me through a window in the door.

'Shane? It's DI Ben Kitto. Can we talk?'

'Not now, come back tomorrow.' His voice is a gruff whisper.

'I'm afraid it can't wait. I need information about your sister today.'

His footsteps drag as he leads me to his kitchen. The place is too well-decorated for a bachelor pad, but an empty whisky bottle stands on the table, beside some crushed beer cans. It doesn't take a stellar IQ to realise that Shane Trellon went on a bender after hearing of his sister's death yesterday. But there's no way of knowing whether his splurge was prompted by guilt or grief. His full mouth and dark hair make him resemble Jude, yet the family's good looks have bypassed him by a few inches. His pitted skin and heavy jaw make him average instead of handsome. Shane lowers himself onto a stool, his frown deeper than before. The man has the same athletic build as his sister, dressed now in jogging pants and a white T-shirt, with the diving school's logo emblazoned across his chest. When I ask how he's doing, his reply is a shallow groan.

'Have you taken some aspirin?' I ask.

'It won't make any difference.'

I hunt for an empty glass in his kitchen cupboards.

'Drink some water at least. It'll flush the crap out of your system.'

Shane swigs down a few mouthfuls, then finally makes eye contact. 'Have you got news about Jude?'

'I need to get some facts straight first.'

'Like what?'

'Why did she go diving so late at night, alone?'

'Fuck knows. Jude had been keeping secrets recently.'

'How do you mean?'

His tone is as sour as lemon juice when he finally replies. 'She was tense about something, but wouldn't say a word. I knew she was troubled.'

'Why are you so touchy, Shane? Did Jude tell you she was going to Piper's Hole?'

'I thought she'd go home.'

'The bar staff at the New Inn say you two had a row.'

'It was nothing.' His gaze drops away. 'My sister could pick a fight with a brick if she was in the mood.'

'What got her started on Sunday?'

'I asked what was wrong, but she told me to back off. Jude trusted me more than anyone. She'd never locked me out before.'

'Your dad says that she often went on night dives. Is that right?'

'She loved it when we were kids. Jude said it was like entering another universe, nothing around you except silence and the dark.' Shane stares at me like I've missed something obvious. 'You know about her background, don't you? My sister was a professional free diver, swimming to a hundred and fifty metres without oxygen, incredible breath control. Diving alone wouldn't have bothered her, but it doesn't make sense that she got into trouble. She'd clocked up thousands of diving hours.'

'We think she may have been attacked. Can you think of anyone she'd clashed with?'

Shane closes his eyes, frowning with pain. 'She wasn't crazy about a couple of clients, but she kept it quiet.'

'The Kinvers?'

'She called them a pair of greedy amateurs. They normally dive with Dad when they visit Tresco; this was the first time she'd dealt with them.' He rubs his hands across his face. 'Jude could be a pain in the arse, but we saw eye to eye on the important stuff.'

'You cared about her, despite the rows?'

'Always.' He sucks in a deep breath. 'She stayed here every few weeks, after the pub, and we'd sit around, talking for hours. She pissed me off sometimes, but I'll never be that close to anyone again. If I find out who killed her, I'll finish him.'

'Don't take matters into your own hands, Shane. Leave it to us. Have you got anyone to support you?'

'Like who?'

'A girlfriend, or a close mate?'

The anger returns to his face. 'I'm not seeing anyone, but the people I care about won't let me down.'

Shane has described his sister's flaws, yet the guy

looks heartbroken; their relationship seems to have thrived on conflict. It's too soon to know whether the chemistry between them spiralled out of control, resulting in Jude's death. He has had plenty of time to scour the place, removing any evidence that he harmed his sister, but there may still be clues about what had been troubling her.

When I get up to leave, Shane looks relieved, until he sees me scanning the sparse contents of his kitchen.

'This place was a holiday cottage once, wasn't it?'

'The museum employs me as caretaker now. Visitors can book appointments each summer to look around. I show them the old well in the garden and the false floor, where the smugglers hid their stash.' His voice tails away, as if his mind has suddenly defaulted back to his sister's death.

'I'll come back another time, for a formal search.'

'Why?' His blurred gaze finally comes into focus.

'You were one of the last people to see Jude alive. She may have left something here, to help us understand why she died.'

A vein bulges in Shane's neck, his face reddening. 'It sounds like you're accusing me of killing my sister.'

'We both want her killer behind bars; I'm just gathering evidence, like I said.'

The conversation remains in my head as I head north to Ruin Beach. Right now, Shane is the most likely culprit, and his temper runs so near the surface it wouldn't take much to ignite the flame. There's no circumstantial proof yet, but he could easily have followed his sister north from the pub, drunk and fuming from the insults they'd exchanged. It doesn't surprise me that he's taken a second job, to supplement his income from the diving school. Islanders must turn their hands to anything to make a living, knowing that pickings are slim during the winter. But it's the look on Shane's face when he spoke about Jude that interests me, anger combined with intense regret. It could just be the rawness of grief, but I need to understand the chemistry of their love/hate relationship.

The tide is out when I walk along the shore, past the old Block House. It hangs over the beach as a reminder of the island's military past, battalions stationed here to ward off invasions since Elizabethan times. Not much remains of it today, except a stone tower and a wall with its square rampart still intact. Once I round the headland it's a quick walk to Ruin Beach, where a notice in the diving shop's window states that boat trips are cancelled until further notice. Fifty metres away, the café is thriving, most of the outdoor tables filled with tourists drinking coffee as the sun intensifies, oblivious to the local tragedy.

Mike and Diane's house lies on the far side of the track. It's a handsome stone building with a large front garden that must consume their spare time. A climbing rose has been trained across the roof of their porch, borders rioting with colourful blooms, but there's no sign of anyone tending the plants today.

Diane looks like a different person from the friendly, exuberant woman I saw yesterday. Her eyes are shadowed, chestnut curls snagged back from her face in a messy ponytail. I catch sight of a photo of her children on her sideboard, taken in their teens; Jude is clowning in the foreground, oozing charisma, while Shane stands in her shadow. It can't have been easy playing second fiddle to his younger sister. Diane's green eyes zero in on my face, as if she's expecting me to announce that her daughter has been found alive after all. I can tell it's the wrong time to announce that Shane is being treated as a suspect.

'Is Mike here, Diane? I'd like to see you together.'

'He's asleep, and I don't want him woken. Neither of us got a wink last night.' Her hands jitter in her lap, unable to keep still. 'I'm worried about Frida. Ivar's kept her locked indoors since we got the news.'

'Why not ask him to bring her round?'

'My granddaughter needs me, but he's not the type to care about anyone else.'

'What makes you say that?'

'He's so aloof, most of the time he hardly gives us the time of day.'

'I'm sure Ivar will make contact soon. It would help to know a bit more about what happened on Sunday night. Did you and Mike have to work late at the café?'

'Mike stayed here, but it was past midnight when the café emptied. I didn't get back till two in the morning.'

'Were any of the dive boats used that evening?'

'I doubt it.' She shakes her head blankly. 'Mike would know, he keeps records of every trip.'

'Do you want me to come back later to see you together? I'm using the top floor of the New Inn until we find out what happened to Jude.'

'What do you mean? It was a diving accident, wasn't it?'

There's no way to shelter her from the pathologist's report. 'We think it's more complex, Diane; she may have been attacked. Something was blocking her airway.'

'Someone killed my daughter?' Diane says the words in a quiet monotone.

The information snaps the thin band of courage that's been holding her together. Jude Trellon's mother ignores my presence while she weeps, sobs racking her body. Watching women cry always makes me uneasy. It reminds me too strongly of my mother's tears after my father drowned; she cried for weeks, impossible to console. I gaze at my scuffed boots, then fish in my pocket for a tissue to offer Diane. All I can do now is wait in silence while her emotions flood out.

8

Tom jogs down the steps to the beach when his morning break starts, hoping not to bump into anyone. Since Jude died, his need to be alone has deepened. The boy skirts around the side of Tregarthen Hill, over a landscape pockmarked with history. The horizontal stones of entrance graves loom above him, funeral cairns, and trenches from ancient tin mines. His father used to tell him stories about the island's past, but after he left only Jude shared his interest in history. She lent him nautical maps of sites where ships foundered, until his fascination with the subject grew overwhelming. He had never realised before that the local waters are full of perfectly preserved wrecks.

The boy's thin arms swing at his sides as he marches north. Why didn't he spend more time with Jude while he had the chance? Now the big diving trip they were planning will never happen. The fact that she had a boyfriend and a kid makes no difference. The space inside his ribs feels empty, eyes blurring when he considers all he's lost. But he keeps on walking, determined to discover the truth. Jude told him months ago that her life was in danger, but he didn't believe anyone on the island could act so violently. He will have to retrace her footsteps to find out why she died.

He drops down to the beach, east of Piper's Hole, with his torch inside his pocket. It takes courage to slip through the narrow entrance again. He has heard stories of pirates being hung here long ago, as punishment for their crimes, angry ghosts still lurking in crevices. The smell of rotting seaweed almost makes him gag, blackness cloying against his skin as he follows the passageway down into the cave. Tom's torch beam skitters over granite walls, droplets of icy water falling from rock formations that hang overhead, like a monster's fangs. The place contains nothing except silence today, the air unnaturally still. He kneels beside the pool, the black water unwilling to yield its secrets. It strikes him suddenly that he might be the only person to know why Jude dived here alone at night. Memories overwhelm him, making him cover his eyes with his hands, until he hears a sound. Someone must have followed him, but when he turns round, nothing is moving among the boulders. The boy drags in a deep breath to calm himself. His imagination must be working overtime because he's so spooked by Jude's death. The sound comes again, even nearer than before. In the stillness he can hear the low rasp of someone's breathing. When he spins round, a figure is coming towards him through the dark.

Tom stumbles to his feet and begins to run. As he gathers speed, the torch slips from his fingers, smashing apart on the rocks. Suddenly the darkness is absolute. He crawls over wet boulders, blind panic forcing him towards a crack of light in the distance. Jude's killer must be metres away, the only illu-mination coming from a torch beam that flickers behind him. Tom has no idea who's chasing him, but the man must have seen his face. He's too terrified to look back, all of his energy focused on reaching the daylight before it's too late.

9

Diane clings to my hand while she digests the news of her daughter's murder. It's a relief when Elinor Jago arrives; the postmistress is dressed in her usual severe clothes, but her voice is gentle when she comforts her friend. By the time I leave she's made a pot of tea, and Diane is weeping on her shoulder.

Eddie is still on the phone when I get back to the New Inn, but I can see he's been busy. The floor of the attic has been swept, cobwebs brushed from the walls. Pages full of notes lie on the trestle table in front of him, but he's so focused on his conversation that he barely raises his head. When I peer at his call log, I see that he's had no luck in tracking the Kinvers down. The couple who employed Jude Trellon as a diving guide aren't answering their phone. Shadow is trying to attract my attention, whining quietly in the corner. It's only a question of time before he starts clawing holes in the walls, making me wish I'd left him at home. He races through the door when I set off to see Ivar

Larsson again, celebrating his freedom with a chorus of loud barks.

'Where's your self-restraint?' I ask, as he sprints away, oblivious to criticism.

The dog only reappears outside Larsson's house. The man's skin is paler than before, muscles taut around his mouth, but his expression brightens when he sees Shadow. His pale eyes examine the dog's face closely as he leans down to stroke him. To his credit, Shadow doesn't flinch, even though strangers normally make him skittish. When Ivar finally returns his attention to me, he seems embarrassed by his display of tenderness.

'I grew up on a farm. My father keeps dogs just like him. He's a husky, right?'

'Czechoslovakian wolfdog, but all dogs are ninety-nine per cent wolf anyway. Is it okay to bring him inside? His name's Shadow.'

'Because he's always with you?'

'He's got no loyalty whatsoever. He'll follow anyone that feeds him.'

The small talk seems to relax Larsson, but only by a fraction; he looks thinner than before, his ash-blond hair uncombed. Soon I'll need to question him about the state of his relationship with Jude, but not today. He's retreated too far inside himself to give reliable answers. His daughter is sitting on a stool at the kitchen table, scrawling lines of colour across a sheet of paper, completely immersed. She seems to be using drawing as her means of escape, just like I took refuge in books after my father died. I keep my voice low to share the news that Jude was murdered, when Ivar follows me into the hallway. His reaction is quieter than Diane's; he rocks back on his feet, remaining silent until his anxiety bubbles to the surface.

'Promise to keep Frida safe, if anything happens to me.'

'Of course, Ivar, but who would harm you?'

His pale gaze meets mine. 'I don't know why Jude was killed. Maybe I'm their next target.'

'I doubt it. She must have fallen out with someone on the island.'

'Only Jamie Petherton. They went out for less than six months, but you'd think I'd stolen his wife.'

'Did she often have rows with people?'

'Jude was a passionate person. There were stand-offs with her family, but they never lasted. She was incredibly close to her father.' His voice falls by half an octave, gaze slipping away. 'When can I see her? I need to say goodbye.'

'Why not go over with Diane and Mike this afternoon?'

Ivar frowns at me. 'I need to see her alone.'

'Can I ask a question first? It would help to know how you and Jude met.'

He glances through the doorway, checking on his daughter. 'Anyone could tell you. The islanders gossiped about us for months.'

'I never heard about it.'

'She was seeing Petherton, like I said. It was nothing serious for her, but he couldn't accept that it was over.'

'That must have been difficult for you.'

'It settled down after a few months. The guy's never forgiven me, but Jude saw him as a friend, until they fell out recently. She never said why.'

'How did your relationship with Jude start?'

'I'm an oceanographer. I came here to study the local waters, five years ago. The Scillies have a unique ecosystem; the diversity of plants and creatures on the seabed needs to be recorded, before it's lost forever.'

'It's that fragile?'

He nods his head. 'The seas register the chemicals we burn, every rise in temperature. Jude took me out diving each day for weeks. So much time in someone's company is a good way to learn about them. I didn't pursue her at first, but the feelings wouldn't go away. By then I'd fallen for the island as well.'

'You were prepared to lose your job because the relationship was so intense?'

'I still work part-time. The university are paying for my research until the survey ends in five years' time. Me and Jude had been talking about getting married; we planned to stay here with Frida permanently.' Suddenly the chill returns to his voice. 'Why are you asking me these questions?'

'Someone hated Jude enough to attack her. I'm sorry

if this is hard for you, but I have to know why. You said yesterday that you thought she'd been murdered. I'm not accusing you of anything, Ivar, but how did you know she'd be at Piper's Hole?'

There's a hint of panic in his eyes. 'The place fascinated her, and Jude could be impulsive. She dreamed of night diving there, but I begged her to forget it.'

'You seem afraid of something. Why not tell me the reason?'

'Let me see Jude, please. That's all I want.'

'Will Mike and Diane look after your daughter till we get back?'

'That's not necessary.' He shakes his head fiercely. 'I want her with me.'

Larsson rises abruptly to his feet, then goes upstairs to fetch his coat, the dog gazing after him, whimpering quietly. Shadow never misses an opportunity to demonstrate that he would prefer a new owner, even when they're hard to interpret. The little girl is humming to herself, still immersed in her drawing. When I walk into the kitchen, her expression is solemn, more like a small-scale adult than a child. Her gold-coloured eyes are so like her mother's the resemblance is unnerving, until she offers me a smile.

'You look like the giant in my story book.'

'I only seem big because you're little.' I drop onto a stool to study her picture more closely. She has drawn three figures, with hands linked like paper dolls. The details are blurry, but it could be a family portrait, a lopsided white house in the distance. 'I like your drawing.'

'Mummy's are better than mine.'

'No way, I bet yours are twice as good.'

Frida bows her head over the paper again, using a crayon to mark a ragged yellow sun above the house. Her expression is so intent I'm left wondering how much she understands about her mother's absence.

Soon Larsson reappears in the doorway, helping his daughter into a jacket before we set off for New Grimsby Harbour, with the dog trailing behind. The outboard motor churns sluggishly as I steer the smallest police launch across the sound. It's a beaten-up old speedboat that can accommodate no more than eight people, with the police crest painted on its prow in flaking paint, and a fibreglass screen failing to protect us from the elements. When I look back, Larsson is sitting at the stern, upright and immovable as a masthead, his hand on Frida's shoulder. His decision to bring the girl to the mortuary seems bizarre, but he must have his reasons. It reminds me that I need to find out why there's no love lost between him and Jude's mother, but there's no point in asking questions until he has identified his girlfriend's body.

The dog protests loudly when I leave him outside St Mary's Hospital, half an hour later. The receptionist agrees to look after Frida while a young nurse leads us to the morgue. Larsson makes no sound as he studies his wife's damaged face. Once the nurse has stepped outside the room, I retreat to the corner to let him say goodbye. Encroaching on his privacy makes me uncomfortable, but there's no denying that women are most likely to be killed by their partners. If he was involved in her death, guilt may show in his gestures. He keeps his feelings hidden as he touches his girlfriend's hand. His behaviour is so over-controlled, I can imagine him falling apart when the burden becomes too much.

Larsson draws the sheet away from his wife's body, letting it drop to the floor. He runs his hands across her form in a way that would be erotic if she was alive, his fingers tracing the tattoos on her shoulders. My own eyes linger on a picture of an ancient longship that I didn't notice when Keillor carried out his examination. The tattooist has drawn the boat across her left bicep in loving detail, a dozen oars protruding from its side, a picture of a modern cruiser outlined faintly behind it. Larsson murmurs a low stream of words as he bends over Jude's body, but the sounds are unfamiliar. His long, one-way conversation is conducted in Swedish. When it finally ends, it's a relief to escape into the sun outside. I'd like to know what secrets he told his dead girlfriend, but it feels intrusive to ask.

Larsson is too exhausted to speak on the ride back to Tresco, eyes closing as the boat toils over open water, his daughter busying herself by throwing pebbles into the sea. After I escort them back to their cottage, I'm still uncertain whether Ivar could have harmed his wife in a fit of rage, but moral niceties don't bother Shadow, who has clearly taken a liking to the pair. Once the father and child disappear inside, he releases a heartfelt howl.

Eddie is hammering away on his laptop when I get back to the New Inn, his expression subdued. 'I'm not getting much response, boss. No one saw Jude walking to Piper's Hole.'

'If she took the coast path there are no houses nearby, but a witness may still come forward. Have you spoken to the Kinvers yet?'

'Their boat must be too far out for mobile signals. Do you want me to contact the coastguard?'

'Straight away, please. I doubt they were involved, because they sailed on immediately after their dive with Jude, but they could tell us about her state of mind. Have you got anything else?'

My deputy glances down at his notes. 'Only that Jude and Shane's row in the pub got pretty heated. One of the barmaids told me she shoved him off his stool, before insults were exchanged.'

'That's interesting. Shane said it was just a few hot words.'

'Maybe it was him that followed her to Piper's Hole.'

'Right now we can't even work out if Jude was in the cave when she died. Did you find out anything else about the relationship she was in before Ivar?'

'She had strange taste in men. Jude was a gorgeous

party girl, and Jamie Petherton's a geek, but he doted on her by all accounts.' Eddie studies his notes again. 'Her best mate was upset when she got together with Ivar five years ago; apparently she couldn't stand him.'

'What's the friend's name?'

'Sophie Browarth. Do you know her? She got married last year to a bloke that works on the oil rigs.'

'The district nurse.' I can picture the pretty, softly-spoken red-haired woman who made home visits to my mother, helping her cope with her MS. 'I'll pay her a call. But right now we need evidence from someone who saw Jude leaving the pub; even better if they clocked whether someone was following her.'

'I'll keep asking around.' Eddie rubs his eyes, as if too much screen time is making his vision blur.

'Let's visit Jamie Petherton first. We can find out if he's still got hard feelings about Jude ending their relationship.'

The walk to the museum takes us over grassland below Vane Hill. I can tell that Eddie could march all over Tresco with his eyes blindfolded, even though he's just moved to St Agnes. It was that bone-deep familiarity that made me flee to London as a teenager, but almost two decades later my attitude has changed. The Atlantic's shifting tides refresh the landscape daily, pristine light showering over valleys farmed for millennia. Our route takes us past the bird hide by the Great Pool, where terns circle over the water's surface. The reservoir is another feature that's constantly changing.

It's mud green today, but in high summer it matches the vapid blue of the sky.

The Valhalla Museum lies inside the Abbey Gardens, Tresco's biggest tourist attraction. I've always taken the place for granted, but now I'd like time to admire the huge sequoia trees by the entrance, plants imported from exotic countries over the last 150 years. Visitors are enjoying the peace and quiet, couples strolling under tree canopies, admiring the lush surroundings. From April onwards, day boats ply back and forth from St Mary's, but at night the place empties, meaning that only an islander or a guest from one of the holiday properties could have harmed Jude Trellon.

Eddie turns to me as we walk through the arboretum. 'I found something on Petherton's file today, but it could be nothing.'

'He's got a record?'

'A caution from four years ago. He did community service and paid a two-hundred-pound fine.'

'For doing what?'

'The guy nicked stuff from people's homes. Trinkets and small items left lying around, nothing valuable. He agreed to get counselling; that's why he escaped a custodial sentence. All the things he stole from friends and neighbours were found in a box in his parents' shed.'

'I didn't know Tresco had its very own kleptomaniac.'

'Petherton's always been weird, boss. The bloke still

lives with his mum and dad, and he's more interested
in the past than the present. He's so obsessed by the
museum, he even goes there on his days off.'

The information slips to the back of my mind as
we approach the Valhalla Museum. It's a one-storey
wooden-framed building, with deep porches sheltering a display of mastheads salvaged from local
shipwrecks. Most of them are human-sized or larger,
ranging from gryphons and unicorns to yellow-haired
sea goddesses with glassy smiles. Figures loom from
the wall, others hang from the low eaves, eyeing me
with unsettling stares. The mastheads are as gaudy
and cheerful as dolls, yet they represent huge loss of
life. Their painted smiles never flinched while the ships
they adorned plummeted to the depths and every crew
member drowned.

Jamie Petherton is nowhere to be seen when we go
inside. The museum is almost empty, warm weather
keeping visitors on the beaches. Its interior is filled
with cabinets and salvaged objects displayed on
plinths, one of the walls covered with ships' clocks,
telescopes and navigational instruments, their brass
casements glittering. My eyes scan the exhibits, looking for anything resembling the mermaid figurine that
ended Jude Trellon's life, but find nothing similar. The
pieces include the smallest details of mariners' lives,
harvested by beachcombers: brass buttons from cap-
tains' uniforms, dice made of ivory and carved pieces
of whalebone.

When I finally catch sight of Jamie, he's poring over a display case, making notes on a clipboard. My greeting makes the museum manager turn round slowly, and it's only at close range that I remember why his appearance is disturbing. One of his eyes is brown, the other sea blue, when he fixes me with a curious stare. We attended the same school on the mainland, but like the Trellons he was several years below me; he used to stand at the edge of the playground, too odd or solitary to join the fray. Petherton still looks vulnerable, with dark curls falling across his thin, expressive face. No one would ever call me sensitive because of my hulking build, but he must attract that description all the time. He's medium height and fine-boned, with a distracted air, as if his mind is fixed on higher things. The man looks like a throwback to a time when Keats and Shelley were writing sonnets. He's dressed simply in a blue shirt and grey trousers, his expression wary when he agrees to talk.

'Now's as good a time as any, I was just closing for lunch.' Petherton's voice is so quiet, it's a struggle to hear his words.

He hangs a closed sign on the door, then offers us seats at the counter, which carries postcards, mugs and key rings bearing the museum's logo. The man's asymmetrical gaze surveys Eddie's face, then mine when I begin to speak.

'We're talking to everyone who was in the pub on Sunday night,' I tell him. 'Were you there long?'

'I had a meal there around eight o'clock. I stayed about an hour.'

'Did you notice Jude Trellon and her brother having a row?'

He shakes his head. 'I was reading a newspaper. I only saw them briefly when I bought my drink.'

'Can you tell us about your relationship with Jude?'

He shuts his eyes. 'I can't get my head around what happened to her. Was it a diving accident?'

'The cause of death is still unconfirmed. How well did you know each other?'

Petherton's voice is hesitant. 'We had a relationship years ago. You could say we were the odd ones out here: misfits, to some extent.'

'I'm not following you.'

'How many heavily tattooed female diving experts do you know on Tresco? And I was bullied at school, for being different. But Jude was probably more interested in my boat than me.'

'Did she teach you to dive?'

'I often wish she hadn't.'

'Why?'

'I had no skill for it; Jude had to drag me to the surface. She thought it was a joke that my family owns a boat but I hate diving. Maybe it's because I see the oceans as sacred territory. Diving felt like entering a country I had no right to visit. It disgusts me when people throw rubbish into the water.' Petherton's eyes linger on my one piece of jewellery – my grandfather's gold wedding ring, on my right hand. His gaze lands on it, then flicks away.

'How did your relationship end?'

'By text. She said she was in love with Ivar, so it was over.'

'That must have been painful.'

'In a place this small it's a bad idea to have enemies. We were on good terms, most of the time.'

'Until you argued a few weeks ago?'

'We were both at a birthday party on St Agnes. She invited me on a diving trip, but I refused. She said I was too cowardly to face my fears. Jude humiliated me in front of my friends.' A flash of fury crosses his features, then disappears. 'Being near her was like flying too close to the sun.'

'Did you see her much after that?'

'Only in passing. I think life on land frustrated her; she had a quick temper, but she wasn't a bad person.'

Eddie gives me a sideways look after we leave the museum, then whispers the word 'freak' under his breath. I can see where he's coming from; the museum manager's intensity is disturbing, but he doesn't strike me as a murderer. I doubt that anyone could stew over being dumped for five years before taking action, or that a single row about a diving trip could drive a man to murder. But Jude's ex gives the impression of being so highly strung, a single word could unravel him, still dwelling on being bullied at school. He seems the kind to nurse grudges, long after they should have been resolved. Petherton has found the right place to work, given his magpie instincts. He must be in his element, surrounded by hundreds of glittering curiosities dredged from the sea.

10

The rest of the afternoon is spent investigating where the islanders were on the night of Jude Trellon's death. It's so early in the season that most of the holiday cottages are empty, just a few rented out to tourists who will need to be interviewed before leaving Tresco, but something about the attack convinces me that Jude was killed by someone familiar. The modus operandi was horrifyingly intimate. To force an object into a woman's mouth, then casually watch her choke, would require rage as well as a murderous instinct. Most victims are killed by family members, or people known to them, but no one I've interviewed so far seems an ideal fit, except Shane, who may have hated his sister for a lifetime of stealing his glory. Mike and Diane had no reason to harm their much-loved daughter, and although Ivar is mysterious, his manner seems too restrained for savagery. Jamie Petherton's an oddball, but that doesn't make him a cold-blooded killer.

It takes effort to write up interview reports for the

case file, to provide Madron with an up-to-date set of documents so he has no reason to remove me from the case. My need to find Jude Trellon's killer has become a personal mission. The image that sticks in my head is of her daughter, hunched over her drawings, trying to swap the adult world for a simpler place, full of colour and sunshine.

It's five o'clock when I leave Eddie behind and head for New Grimsby Harbour, with Shadow at my heels. I stop at the island store to buy a gift for Denny Cardew, and discover that the shop has expanded, to cater for the tastes of rich holidaymakers. Its shelves are loaded with exotic cheeses, olive oil, sourdough bread and packets of locally grown herbs. There are plenty of sugary treats too: an array of biscuits and cakes, as if the hardships of island life could be softened by indulging your sweet tooth. I select a bottle of Rioja, then go on my way.

The quayside looks much as it did in photos from a hundred years ago. A narrow concrete slipway runs down to the sea, and a line of ramshackle wooden huts face the sound, the air still salty with last night's catch. Denny is sitting on a crate outside his hut, mending a lobster creel. The fisherman's powerful build and quiet manner remind me of my father, as well as his shabby clothes, but Dad would have been a decade older if he'd survived the storm that capsized his trawler on the Atlantic Strait. Cardew gestures for me to join him when I arrive.

'Recovered from your dousing, Ben?'

'More or less, I've still got brine in my ears.'

The fisherman looks shocked when I hand him the bottle. 'There's no need for any fuss.'

'You took a risk, sailing so close to the rocks.' He seems determined to ignore my gratitude. 'How's your wife doing these days? I haven't seen her at the inn.' I remember being told that Sylvia Cardew was unwell, but not the nature of her illness.

'She's been poorly since she lost her job there, but she's not one to complain. The news about Jude upset her though. Sylvia's been worse since she heard.'

'Will she be at the meeting later?'

'I doubt it.' A look of concern crosses his face.

'Tell her I'll drop by if she's got any questions.' The fisherman is keeping his hands busy, patching the creel with strands of willow. 'How's the fishing these days?'

'Most days half my crab pots come back empty, but you're not here to talk about my job, are you?'

'Did you know Jude Trellon well, Denny?'

'I'm friendly with her dad. Last year wasn't great for either of us; Mike had to raise the capital to replace his diving boat, and my wife fell ill. We kept each other sane through the worst days. Losing Jude must be terrible for his family.' The fisherman shifts uneasily on his crate.

'You've heard something about them, haven't you?'

'Only that Mike wanted to retire from the diving

business, but his kids argued over who should take charge. Mike was afraid his business would go down the drain.'

'Did that cause tension between Jude and Shane?'

'No more than usual,' Denny replies. 'They often fought when they were small; strong characters, the pair of them. Jude threw her fists around, just like a boy. She was the fearless one. I saw her dive off Pentle Rock once; no one's had the guts to do it since.'

'Just as well, the drop must be fifteen metres. Diving there at low tide could break your neck.'

'That didn't bother her. If something was off limits, she wanted it, whatever the cost.'

'You're talking in riddles, Denny. Was Jude taking some kind of risk?'

He rises to his feet. 'Sophie Browarth would know, those two were thick as thieves. She lives out at Pentle Beach.'

I want to ask more questions, but the fisherman has retreated into the hut to stow away his nets and bait pots, my presence already forgotten.

There's no time to follow Denny's lead because people are gathering outside the New Inn for the 6 p.m. briefing. Madron is waiting for me in our make-shift headquarters, surveying the dirty windows with distaste, dressed in full uniform. I consider telling him that while I'm the SIO, there's no need for him to attend every public meeting, but he likes to believe he's indispensable. The DCI's expression is sombre as I update him on the case. When we go downstairs, he loiters in the background, observing my every move.

More than fifty islanders are grouped around the bar's handmade tables, which are built from driftwood, carefully sanded and polished. I can see familiar faces from the hotel, shop and Abbey Gardens, most of the island families represented. Justin Bellamy is standing with Diane Trellon, the priest shepherding her to a front row seat. She looks frailer than before, but my admiration increases. It takes guts to attend a public meeting so soon after identifying your daughter in a morgue; every instinct must be telling her to hide at home. There's no sign of her husband, but her son trails in her wake, giving me a hostile stare. It's getting easier all the time to imagine Shane's resentment towards Jude turning violent. I shunt my suspicions to the back of my mind when I rise to my feet.

'Thanks for coming everyone. You'll have heard the sad news about Jude Trellon by now.' Faces are sombre as I scan the room; people's existences are so closely entwined here that neighbours become like relatives. 'We know she died between eleven thirty on Sunday night and seven on Monday morning. Jude was found in her diving gear, by Piper's Hole. Evidence suggests that she was murdered near there, or inside the cave.'

A murmur of shock circulates the room. When my eyes skim the crowd, Shane still looks ready to punch someone, aggression evident in the set of his jaw.

'I want you all to look at this photograph, please.' I

use my laptop to flash an image of the mermaid figurine onto the wall, beside the message left at the scene. Despite being made of tarnished green metal, the creature looks exotic with her form magnified, long hair undulating down her naked body, scales shimmering on her curved tail. The faces before me register appreciation, but they don't know that the object ended Trellon's life. I can hear a few voices mumbling about the scrap of verse. 'The words come from a sea shanty that originated in the Scillies two hundred years ago. If you know anything about these items, or what happened to Jude on Sunday night, please tell me or Eddie today. This was probably an isolated event, but you should keep your homes secure. No one can leave the island without my permission for the time being. If you've got any concerns, we're using the inn's attic room as our base.'

There's a murmur of dissent when the islanders realise that their travel plans will continue to be disrupted for days to come, the session unravelling into questions. Most of them concern where Jude was found, and why she was targeted, but I keep my answers neutral. I can't prove that she was night diving alone in Piper's Hole, because the sea cave floods each day, scouring away every shred of evidence, so the killer must believe he'll never be found.

I scan the crowded bar again as the meeting closes. The islanders are supporting the Trellon family well. Elinor Jago is at Diane's side again, her hand on the grieving woman's shoulder. Denny Cardew is talking to Shane, the younger man's gaze fixed on the ground, but there's no sign of the fisherman's wife. Working in murder investigation has taught me that everyone deals with loss differently. Some crave every piece of information, while others prefer to stick their heads in the sand. Most of the crowd look upset, but Jamie Petherton's thin face is unreadable while he watches events unfold from the edge of the crowd, as if he prefers a bird's-eye view.

DCI Madron prevents me from visiting Sophie Browarth at the end of the meeting by insisting on a case review; he takes an hour to sift through our action log, then subjects me to a lengthy inquisition. His superiority makes me grit my teeth. I've always hated being micromanaged, but Madron loves being in control. He gives a slow nod of approval once he's audited every report, but the meeting leaves me frustrated. I could have used the last part of the day to continue looking for Jude Trellon's killer, instead of defending my strategy. When I finally exit the New Inn at seven thirty, the dusk is thickening. Someone is hunched on the drystone wall opposite. It's the thin, dark-haired boy I saw outside the community hall. He's dragging on a cigarette, and this time he stays put instead of rushing away. The lad's presence makes me wonder why he didn't return home with the rest of the crowd. I've got enough to do without worrying about an inquisitive kid, yet his interest in the case concerns me. I drop onto the wall beside him and let silence unfold, before asking my first question.

'Why did you miss the meeting just now?'

'I got here too late. I was needed at home.'

'But you want to know what happened?' The boy gives a single nod. 'Tell me your name first.'

'Tom Heligan.'

'That's why you look familiar. Your mum taught me English; she even stopped me playing truant for a while. I'm DI Ben Kitto, but you probably know that already, don't you?' He inspects me from the corner of his eye, judging my trustworthiness. 'I held the meeting to find out if anyone knew how Jude Trellon died, and whether they could identify this.' I show him a picture of the mermaid figurine on my phone.

'I've never seen anything like it before.' The words stutter from his lips.

'It belongs to someone on the island. I'll have to keep searching till I find out who.' When I turn to the young man again, he looks more like a terrified child than a teenager. I want to ask what's troubling him, but he seems so fragile, the question could do more harm than good.

'I should go home, Mum can't be left alone.'

'Feel free to come back, if you've got questions. Give your mother my regards.'

The boy sets off in a hurry, almost tripping over his feet in his race to get away.

11

There's no escape when Tom gets home. His mother is struggling down the hallway on her sticks. His longing to be alone
is more powerful than ever, and he resents the way her dark
brown eyes seem to peer inside him to read his thoughts.
When he goes to the kitchen to prepare dinner, her sticks tap
slowly across the lino, before she lowers herself onto a chair.

'Why didn't you tell me about Jude?' Her voice is flat with
anger. 'Elinor let me know this afternoon. She was shocked I
hadn't heard.'

'I didn't want to upset you.'

'So you let me be the last person on the island to find out?'

Tom drops his chopping knife on the counter. 'Is that all
you care about? You're not bothered about Jude drowning?'

'I wish you'd shared the news, that's all.' Her tone suddenly
softens. 'I know you two were close. Are you okay, love?'

'Leave it alone, Mum. I don't want to talk about it.' The
words snap from his mouth. 'Dinner's in the oven, I'll come
down when it's ready.'

He sprints upstairs two at a time, but guilt hits him before he reaches the landing. The top floor is his domain, while his mother lives downstairs in her empire of books, the pair of them occupying separate worlds. He should never have shouted at her like that, but the cop's hard stare has put him on edge. Tom's breathing steadies once he reaches his room. The walls are lined with photos from recent dives: a huge seal grazing on kelp near Gimble Point, the rusting snout of a seventeenth-century cannon poking up from the seabed, and a broken plate that has spent two hundred years under fathoms of brine.

He listens to waves scouring the rocks outside. It feels like the sea is his best companion now his dreams have fallen apart. His room is filled with telescopes, sextants and books about celestial navigation. He wishes he knew the local waters as well as the pilots who once guided ships through dangerous channels between the islands, but the ocean's secrets are lost to him now. Jude had promised to take him on another night dive soon, the depths even more beautiful by moonlight, full of luminous creatures rising to the surface like ghosts.

Tom stands on a chair to reach a package from the top of his wardrobe. Two weeks ago, Jude asked him to keep it safe, making him promise not to open it. She wanted her father to have it if anything bad happened, but that will have to wait. The narrow parcel is less than a foot long, wrapped in brown paper. He must deliver it to Mike once life on the island gets back to normal, but until then it needs a better hiding place. He climbs the ladder to the loft to conceal the package in a safer location, his breathing calmer as he climbs back down.

The boy catches sight of a figure from the landing window,

perched on the granite outcrop that runs down to the sea, and when he hurries outside the air is cooler than before. The girl is wearing a thin summer dress, her long blonde hair ruffled by the breeze. He can see how pretty she is, yet it was Jude that caught his attention, even though she was out of reach.

'I thought you had to stay indoors, Gemma.'

She gives a quick smile. 'I was worried about you. I wanted to check you were okay.'

'It's good to see you.' He sinks onto the rock beside her. 'But it's best you stay away for a while; it might not be safe here.'

'What do you mean?'

'Someone's watching me.' He'd like to say more but the words choke him. 'Jude had been going to Piper's Hole, leaving stuff for people to collect. Something bad's going on there; I got chased out of it today.'

'Tell the police, if you're scared.'

'I'd only get into trouble.' He shakes his head, urging her to drop the subject. 'How are things at home?'

'Dad keeps going on about my retakes. I don't even want to do psychology, I'd rather study garden design.' She checks her watch. 'I'd better head home before they notice I've gone.'

'You'll be off to uni like all the rest when your exams finish.'

'Not if I can help it. I love it here, they can't make me leave.' Her head drops onto his shoulder, just for a second. 'Answer my texts, Tom, so I don't have to worry.'

He waits until the girl vanishes across the bay, then his eyes fix on the flickering lights of merchant ships heading for the Atlantic Strait. He would rather cross rough seas than remain here forever, yet leaving his mother isn't an option. He's trapped, but no longer safe. A pulse of fear travels along his spine. Jude's killer was waiting in Piper's Hole; the man must have seen him running away on the night of the murder. He may already be planning how to silence him.

12

My uncle is sitting on the bench outside the boatyard when I walk up the quay, smoking a roll-up. Ray's habits are unchanged since I was a kid. He still allows himself two needle-thin cigarettes each evening, the smell of Old Holborn lingering on his clothes.

'There's food if you want some,' he says.

'I already owe you half a dozen meals.'

'Who's counting? Come and eat, or it'll be wasted.'

Ray's flat above the yard is furnished with items he's built himself. The kitchen table is fashioned from cedar deck boards, stools made from leftover squares of oak, everything stowed away neatly, as if his old naval commander might return to criticise his quarters. He passes me a plate of fried halibut, mayonnaise and a hunk of bread, then sets down a bowl for Shadow. My uncle often receives gifts from the local fishing fleet for services rendered, if they take a good catch.

Ray lets me eat in silence, sitting in his armchair, facing the sound. His flat fascinated me as a boy, the nautical maps on the walls marked by routes he's travelled, picked out in red. Years of designing boats for fishermen have taught Ray everything there is to know about the local waters, but little about communication. We could spend the rest of the evening in companionable silence unless I ask the question that's been bothering me all day.

'Jude Trellon left the pub around eleven thirty on Sunday night, then we found her body tied to the cliff face by Piper's Hole yesterday morning. Do you think the killer approached the cave by land or sea?'

My uncle rises to his feet, to peer at a tide table that's pinned to the wall, then spends a few minutes studying one of his maps. 'The tide would have cut the cave off from the beach by 1 a.m. He couldn't have climbed back up the hill after that. He'd have needed a fast boat, good sailing skills and a strong set of nerves.'

'How do you mean?'

'The tide races in quickly, north of the island, and the eddies round Kettle Point have strong circular currents. It would take a powerful engine to escape them or the boat would be thrown back onto the cliffs.'

I scrub my hands across my face. 'Why would anyone dive in a sea cave at night, for God's sake?'

'To prove they're invincible?'

'Maybe she had a death wish.'

'Piper's Hole is the wrong place to get marooned. The cave's part of an old mine shaft that drops for hundreds of feet. Once the sea traps you, there's no escape.

It's easy enough to climb down from Tregarthen Hill, but people have died trying to claw their way back up the cliff when the tide cuts them off.'

'It sounds like that's what happened to Anna Dawlish.' I look at him again. 'You're certain the killer used a boat?'

His nod is categorical. 'How else would he avoid drowning?'

I thank Ray for the meal, then go on my way, still absorbing the fact that the killer accessed the cave by sea. It's pitch dark by the time I walk back across the island, stars blurred by a skein of cloud. I spend fifteen minutes on the beach in front of my cottage, hurling sticks for Shadow to chase with joyous abandon, as a reward for being cooped up all day. A dog's life may have its limits, but the pleasure he draws from the simple game is enviable. When he lies down to sleep tonight, no nagging questions will keep him awake. On the other side of Hell Bay, breakers lash the shore, the hotel glittering like a string of fairy lights. It's tempting to stroll across the shingle for another nightcap with Zoe, but something stops me in my tracks. An inbuilt safety mechanism tells me not to rely on the pleasure of seeing her every day.

Once inside, I do an internet search on Jude Trellon. A YouTube film shows a younger version of her diving backwards from a speedboat into azure water: she's wearing a wetsuit, flippers and face mask, but no breathing apparatus. Trellon's body cuts a vertical line through the water, movements sinuous as she dives for the seabed. I hold my breath, trying to imagine her lungs aching as the pressure increases. When the water starts to blacken, she performs a rapid spin, swimming hard for the surface. My own breath gags from my mouth long before she emerges. The camera catches her face cresting the water, giving an ecstatic grin. Trellon's free dive lasted seven and a half minutes. I gaze at the screen in disbelief. Holding her breath for so long must have taken immaculate self-control, aware that a miscalculation would be fatal. A perverse part of me would like to try it, but that degree of breath control takes years of practice. The woman must have been in love with danger to court so much risk.

I watch a few more clips of Trellon talking about her passion for the ocean, and the Zen-like calm that comes from free diving, her face alight with enthusiasm, and for the first time I understand what Jamie Petherton meant about her being a misfit. Free diving is a male domain, yet she chose to battle with the ocean, keen to sink deeper below its surface than anyone before. Very few people would enjoy that degree of danger, yet she stopped chasing adrenalin highs when she had her child. Watching the ten-year-old film makes me uneasy. There's something voyeuristic about hearing a ghost describe her greatest passion, even though it's necessary research. Some part of her behaviour inspired an islander to kill her, but the cause remains out of reach. Maybe her thrill-seeking put someone's nose out of joint, or the bravery that made people idolise her, or want to knock her down.

I'm about to hit the off button when the Skype symbol flashes on my computer. My brother Ian's image fills the screen, a tidier version of mine, clean-shaven, his black hair cropped short. He's sitting in his consulting room in upstate New York, still wearing his white coat, fresh from visiting the hospital wards. His fingertips are pressed together, like a shrink, preparing to diagnose me.

'What do you want?' I ask. 'It's midnight, for fuck's sake.'

'To see your ugly mug, of course.'

'How's my niece?'

'Great, if you don't mind tantrums.' He grabs a photo from his desk and holds it in front of the camera. Five-year-old Christy's image beams at me, face haloed by a mass of blonde curls.

'Lucky she's got her mum's looks.'

'Her charm comes from me. What are you up to anyway?'

'Work mainly, a woman was killed, over on Tresco two days ago.'

'How do you stand it? At least most of my patients survive.'

'Normally I'm just telling kids off for painting graffiti on a neighbour's wall. Go home and let me sleep, for God's sake.'

A sly smile crosses his face. 'What happened to that

veterinary nurse you asked out? Samantha, wasn't it?'

'It went nowhere. Her laugh drove me up the wall.'

'One giggle and it was game over?'

'It sounded like a squeaky door, one hell of a passion-killer.'

'Come over for a holiday. Some of Ella's friends are seriously hot.'

'And two thousand miles away.'

'Zoe's close by.' Ian narrows his eyes. 'How is the blonde goddess these days?'

'Out of bounds, so don't go there.'

'Ship a woman over from the mainland then, before you die, friendless and alone.'

I give a mocking laugh. 'You've forgotten the joys of being young, free and single.'

My brother's warning sticks in my mind as I lie down. Behind all his teasing, I know he worries about me, but being solitary is my natural condition, even if the bed sometimes feels uncomfortably wide.

I read a page of *The Sun Also Rises*, but Hemingway's immaculate prose fails to dispel Jude Trellon's drowned face from my mind, her skin ravaged by the sea. Tresco is populated by less than 200 people. Someone must know who tethered her body to a rock face, then sailed away into the night. I switch off the light and watch strands of moonlight seep through the curtains, while the dog whines quietly outside my bedroom door.

13

Wednesday 13 May

An encrypted email from Europol is waiting for me when I reach the incident room the next morning. I had expected Ivar Larsson's record from Sweden to come back clear, but an old court case is outlined in detail. At the age of eighteen, Larsson stood accused of manslaughter. He had been driving friends home from a party in his father's car when he ran down a middle-aged man, who later died of his injuries. Larsson's parents must have employed a clever lawyer to let him walk free with only a suspended sentence and a driving ban. But the event marked a change in Larsson's life, his family leaving their small village and settling in Gothenburg. The event could explain his remoteness; at that age the trauma of killing a man by accident would be hard to forget.

A second email from the forensics lab in Penzance

tells me that the message attached to the victim's ankle was written with a standard black ballpoint pen, on printer paper, and contains no DNA evidence. The killer is smart and organised enough to wear surgical gloves and choose materials that every islander must possess. The garden twine used to attach the bottle to the victim's body is generic too: plasticised green wire available at every garden centre. I push the information aside to focus on my main task of the morning; discovering the location of the Kinvers' boat. The coastguard officer at the end of the line has such a broad Cornish accent, it sounds like he's been gargling with clotted cream when he explains that the couple's cruiser is on the Atlantic Strait, too far out for phone contact. A radio message has been sent, instructing them to return to Tresco immediately, but the journey will take the vessel all day, so I decide to follow up Denny Cardew's suggestion and visit Sophie Browarth.

The walk takes me down to the southern tip of the island, with Shadow bouncing across the dunes. Pentle Beach is a local beauty spot, its golden stretch of sand half a mile wide, only the low outline of Skirt Island marking the horizon. The shore is empty, except for a few kite fliers and a solitary tourist jogging across the sand. I send Shadow on his way, flinging my arms wide to let him know he's free to roam. He bounds towards the tidemark with tongue lolling, clearly eager to perform his usual trick of rolling in fermented seaweed or rotten fish guts, requiring me to hose him down once we get home.

When I reach Pentle Cottage, someone has arrived before me. Shane Trellon is battering his fist on the door, so I conceal myself behind some bushes to watch. He thumps the wood again, giving it a kick for good measure. Expletives spill from his mouth as he finally turns away. It's not clear whether he's desperate to see Sophie Browarth in her capacity as district nurse or for personal reasons. The man's aggressive body language makes me decide to follow my plan to search Smuggler's Cottage today for evidence that could implicate him in his sister's murder.

Something flickers in a top window of the cottage when I look up again. A woman's face appears, pale as a ghost, and there's a glimpse of flame-red hair before she vanishes. I knock lightly on the front door, hoping for a warmer welcome than her last visitor. The state of the place proves that either Sophie Browarth and her husband are living on low wages or they don't care about home maintenance. The stone cottage has gaps in its mortar, the chimney listing at a dangerous angle. I wait five minutes before peering through the letter box. There's little evidence of the woman's presence, except a row of shoes in a rainbow of colours stacked against the wall. I'm still crouching in the porch when the front door finally swings open. The woman peering down at me is petite with delicate features, her vivid copper hair falling to just below her jaw as she watches me scramble to my feet. Her pale skin is littered with freckles, blue eyes observing me closely. She looks different from the nurse who paid regular visits to my mother during her last illness, her manner quiet and sympathetic. Today she seems preoccupied, wearing a cream linen dress that flatters her colouring.

'Are you okay, Sophie? I saw Shane banging on your door just now.'

She nods her head slowly. 'I couldn't face another tough conversation.'

'Has he been bothering you?'

The question makes her flinch. 'He needs to talk about Jude, so he's been coming here since it happened, but I'm a nurse not a counsellor. I can't fix all of his problems.' Her fingers touch the pale skin of her throat. 'Come in, I'll make some coffee.'

Sophie's smile is warm, despite her distracted air. Her hallway is decorated with brightly coloured paintings of seascapes; a reminder that most islanders are passionate about the ocean.

'I like your pictures; you've got enough to open a gallery.'

'My husband, Phil, collects local art.' She turns to face me when we reach the end of her hallway. 'Sorry the place is a mess. It's my day off; I've been doing chores.'

The kitchen smells of detergent and bleach; a pile of fresh linen is stacked in a laundry basket, the surfaces gleaming. Her table is crowded with folders labelled with islanders' names, the nurse's commitment to her job dominating her home. Her work requires her to travel between the islands each day, visiting the sick and elderly, carrying their treatment plans with her. Sophie sits down opposite, assessing me with a level gaze.

'I haven't seen you since you lost your mum, Ben,' she says. 'How have you been?'

'Okay, thanks.' The question wrong-foots me. In my last role, everyone I interviewed was a stranger, but there's no escaping your history here. 'I could use some leisure time; the case is keeping me busy. Can you tell me how you first met Jude?'

A smile illuminates her face, suddenly turning her into a beauty. 'We were friends all our lives. You know how intense friendships can be out here. She was more like a sister.'

'It would help me to hear more about your friendship.'

She raises her eyebrows. 'Will that lead you to her killer?'

'Anything that gives me a better understanding is useful.'

'Jude and I met in nursery school. I was fascinated by her from day one; she always craved new experiences, unlike me. She loved danger and I'm a homebody, but we stayed close.'

'Until she met Ivar.'

'That was a difficult time for both of us.' Her voice

drops by half an octave, distress flattening her cadences. 'She got on fine with my husband, but I thought Ivar would make her unhappy, and she hated me for saying it. She was passionate about life, but he's frozen. I don't know him any better now than I did five years ago. Our friendship recovered, but it was never quite the same.'

'Maybe Ivar's got reason to be guarded.'

'He would never confide in anyone.' Her eyes blink shut. 'It's my job to preserve life, but I couldn't help Jude. It's terrible that she died while Frida's still so young.'

'Did you see her in the pub on Sunday night?'

'I stayed here by myself. I was tired from being on duty all day.'

The statement lacks detail, but she seems unwilling to offer more information. 'Had you seen Jude recently?'

'Just last week. She brought Frida round for the afternoon.'

'How did she seem?

'Preoccupied, but that wasn't unusual.' Her gaze settles on the waves, unrolling outside her window. 'Jude always had big ambitions, maybe her dreams defeated her in the end.'

'I heard she'd been taking risks recently. Do you know what they were?'

'Everything Jude did involved danger. Each time she took clients out on a wreck dive she was gambling with her life.' Her eyes are glossy with tears.

'This must be hard for you, by yourself. Is your husband away long?'

'He'll be back next month.'

Sophie Browarth's regret over Jude's death is more overt than Ivar Larsson's, even though their friend-ship had grown less intimate. The nurse's manner is sympathetic, while Ivar's coolness is impenetrable, but she gives no more details about Jude's troubles. The raw grief in Browarth's voice rings in my mind as I walk away. But, under all that warmth, could she have been so distressed by her friend's withdrawal that she set out to kill her? It seems a ridiculous idea, but her cottage is so remote, no one would have seen her leave it late at night and sail to Piper's Hole. There's no logical explanation why Shane would want to see the nurse so urgently, unless he believes she has information about Jude's death. The dog catches up with me as I head back to the station, tail wagging madly, even though his coat is filthy with green slicks of seaweed.

Eddie's expression is serious when I reach the inci-dent room, his mobile clamped to his ear as he murmurs reassurances. It's several minutes before he returns the phone to the table with a quiet sigh.

'Is the DCI nagging again?'

He shakes his head. 'Mike Trellon thinks we're taking too long to get answers.'

'That's not unusual. Relatives often go on the attack when they feel powerless.' I glance down at his notes, which are written in immaculate schoolboy script. 'It looks like the killer must have made his getaway from

Piper's Hole by boat. He left it too late to escape on foot, without being swept away, so he must be a good sailor. The sea would've been treacherous. Can you check which islanders own a boat, while I visit Mike? I want every vessel searched.'

Eddie gives a rapid nod, then grabs a folder from one of his piles. 'The lab report on the mermaid just came back. Do you want to read it first?'

According to the forensics team on the mainland, the sea has helped the killer to conceal his identity. Salt water has dissolved any fingerprints on the figurine that ended Jude Trellon's life, which carries no DNA except the victim's blood and bile. It's only when I reach the bottom of the page that my interest rises. The six-inch tall mermaid was cast from bronze, hundreds of years ago, the salt water causing little damage to its structure. I drop the report back on the desk, considering its meaning. Who would take an antique figurine and ram it down a woman's throat? The item must hold a symbolic meaning for the murderer, and it could have a high monetary value too, yet no one on the island can identify it.

Shadow is curled up asleep in a corner of the incident room when I head for the door, exhausted from dashing across the sand, yet he shakes himself awake to follow me outside. When I walk through Dolphin Town, the curtains in Ivar Larsson's house are tightly drawn. Food parcels wrapped in tin foil are stacked inside his porch. After my father died, people gave us an endless supply of pies, cakes and casseroles, most of which got thrown away. I need to interview him again, but another visit so soon after the last might make him clam up even further. The man's tendency to shut people out must be making his situation harder to bear. His character seems so over-controlled, it's possible that something flicked a switch, bringing his violence to the surface.

When I reach Ruin Beach, it's clear that the victim's parents are dealing with their sorrow differently. The front door is ajar, windows gazing down like startled eyes. Mike Trellon appears in the porch before I raise my hand to knock. It's the first time we've met one to one since he heard that Jude had died two days ago. Weight has slipped from him since then, accentuating his bone structure, making him look even more like a veteran actor auditioning for a serious role.

'I expected better from you, Ben. We've heard nothing since yesterday morning.'

'Can I come in please?'

He allows me across his threshold, but keeps his back turned in the kitchen as he makes coffee. 'Diane's gone to Ivar's; he's not making it easy for us to see our granddaughter.' He dumps sugar into my cup, then shoves the mug in front of me. The look on his face reveals the origin of his children's hot temper, his unblinking stare searing my face with the force of a laser.

'I stayed away to give you both time to recover, Mike.'

'That won't happen till we know who killed our girl.'

'We're making progress, but I need more information. Have you got records of Jude's boat trips, and the people she taught to dive?'

He nods vigorously. 'The insurers make us keep them for every boat trip, with passengers' names as well as crew. It's all in our logbook.'

'Jude must have upset someone on the island, Mike. There were just over a hundred people here the night she died. Who hated her enough to do this?'

'God knows.' Mike rubs his hand across the back of his neck. 'I can't sleep, trying to figure it out. Jude couldn't hide her feelings like Ivar; she was hot-headed. If something bothered her, she yelled it to the rafters, but most people respected her honesty.'

'I hear you and Jude were very close.'

'Diving brought us together. She was a natural in the water from day one, but now I wish I'd never taught her to swim. Jude always had to push the boundaries.' There's a mixture of shame and admiration on his face.

'When I told you about her death, you said it was your fault, Mike. Can you explain why?'

He fumbles for the right words. 'If I'd never taught her to dive, she'd still be safe, on dry land.'

'She'd have done it without anyone's help, if she was determined. How would you describe her relationship with Shane?'

'They were sparring partners; Jude was a tomboy, not letting him beat her at anything. She adored Frida, but found motherhood tough at first. It meant she had to give up some of her dreams.' He pushes his mug away, his lips setting in a thin line. 'My kids argued a lot, but never hurt each other. Shane adored Jude when they were small. There's no way he'd attack her. You're wasting your time if you go after him.'

'Sophie Browarth says he's been visiting her every day.'

'He must have his reasons.' His gaze slips out of focus. 'Sophie never took to Ivar; he kept Jude all to himself when they got together, which upset her friends.' He looks out of the window, as if he's longing to escape. 'Jude was angry with me when she died, that's what hurts most. She wanted the *Fair Diane* for a private trip, but I refused. Diesel costs a fortune these days. If a boat goes out, it must cover its costs.'

'Has business been hard?'

'The recession's hit us, but we're managing. There's no way I'll let everything I've worked for go to waste.'

'Why did Jude want the boat?'

He pauses before replying, his arms braced across his chest, as if he's holding himself together. 'She never said. Frustration's the hardest part of all this; it feels like there's bugger all I can do to find out who hurt her.'

'I'm on my way to Piper's Hole. The first high tide will have washed away any evidence, but I want to check again, just in case. Would you like to come?'

Mike nods vigorously. The walk should focus his

energies, and have the side benefit of making him talk more openly about his daughter. He remains silent as he collects a torch then follows me outside, the dog appearing again as we cut a diagonal path inland. Mike's silence continues as we pass a wheat field, the crop vivid green and barely a foot high, our conversation slipping back twenty years as Mike describes Jude's childhood. It sounds like she loved to defy people's expectations: swimming before she could walk, a competitive diver by the age of twelve, beating adults for top prizes while she was still a child. It's only when we reach the summit of Tregarthen Hill that his monologue expires. Mike gazes down at the beach, wide-eyed, like it's finally registering that he's about to enter the place where his daughter died.

'Go home, if you prefer, Mike. I can climb down easily enough.'

'I need to see where it happened.'

'Only if you feel ready.'

The shore below is covered in fist-sized pebbles, a wilderness of granite rocks strewn across the beach. Far in the distance the sea is an empty strip of blue, with Kettle Island punctuating the open water; America – the next landmass – 2000 miles away. I wouldn't want to stand here in winter, with no protection from the wind that howls in from the Atlantic. The dog bounds down the steep hillside, far more sure-footed than his human companions, while I take my time descending, with Mike stumbling behind. The path narrows as it winds between boulders, then there's a sheer fifteen-foot drop to the shore. I find a foothold, then help him down, clinging to the rocky surface, until we both land on the beach. It could be foreknowledge that makes the place look desolate; man-sized boulders sprinkled along the tideline, as if giants have been playing marbles on the sand.

The first time I entered Piper's Hole was with a gang of schoolmates, spending a summer afternoon yelling at the top of our voices, laughing at echoes that bounced back from walls dripping with condensation. The entrance seems to have narrowed since then, and for once Shadow refuses to follow. He whimpers loudly as I head through the slit in the rock face, my feet unsteady on slime-covered rocks, the air reeking of salt and decay. I have to walk sideways as the passage thins, Mike's conversation suddenly falling silent. Black air presses in on us with each step, no light except from our torch beams. We follow the path down for twenty metres until the cave splits open, shards of rock jutting from the ceiling like blackened teeth. The place unsettles me, even though I've never suffered from claustrophobia. Anyone superstitious would say that bad spirits lurked here, but it could just be sea mist trapped from the night before. When I look round, my companion is crouching between two boulders, head low over his knees.

'I should never have let her come here,' he murmurs.

'Are you all right, Mike?' His face is ashen in the

light from my torch. 'Keep your head down and take some deep breaths.'

He's soon strong enough to stand, but it was a mistake to let him accompany me. There's a difference between wanting to help an investigation and being robust enough to visit the site where your child was murdered. When I scan the cave again, an expanse of mirror-smooth water is circled by rocks. I walk to the pool's edge, but can't see past my own reflection: a messy-looking giant, black hair in need of a cut, eyes straining for information. When I straighten up again, I climb deeper into the cave. The ceiling drops suddenly, then I see a fissure in the wall ahead, just wide enough to squeeze through. When my torch beam scans the narrow chamber, something is snagged on a piece of rock. It's an old rubber kitbag, with a drawstring top. The item must have been forced into the cave's furthest recess by the tide. One more sweep of the rocks reveals nothing else, so I return to the main cave to help Mike back along the passage.

I'm so busy making sure he doesn't fall, I don't notice a figure blocking my way until he almost topples me. Will Dawlish from the New Inn stands by the entrance to the cave, wearing a shocked look that must mirror my own. It seems bizarre that both of the men who have lost loved ones would arrive here in unison. The hotelier is clutching two white roses wrapped in cellophane.

'I visit this place each month,' he says quietly. 'It's normally empty.'

'Watch out for the tide, Will. It's coming in fast.'

Dawlish gives an absent nod. 'I won't take long. I just want to leave these where I found my wife.'

Mike is leaning against the sheer wall of the cliff, colour still missing from his face. The innkeeper lays a hand on his shoulder, before offering a few words of sympathy, then disappears inside the cave. When I look up at the cliff, the rock face is so sheer and uncompromising, it's easy to see why two islanders lost their lives here. The path we took down the hillside is already cut off by the rising tide. If we stay much longer, our only means of escape will be to swim round the headland, with breakers forcing us onto the jagged rocks.

Mike lets out a sigh as he straightens up. 'Some sick bastard followed my daughter in there. I can't believe it was an islander.' His eyes catch on the bag dangling from my hand. 'That was Jude's, she used it for her diving gear.'

'I'll need it for a few days, then you can have it back. Let's wait for Will, then we can walk round the headland together.'

It takes five minutes for Dawlish to lay his memorial flowers. He seems surprised that we've waited for him, but I want to make sure that both men return home safely. The cave can't be allowed to claim another life. Shadow still seems spooked as we leave, muzzle pressed against my thigh as the three of us turn away. We walk in silence; both men appear drained by visiting Piper's

Hole, scarcely looking each other in the eye. I lead them back to safety at a rapid pace to escape the encroaching tide, with the cave's saline breath still clinging to my clothes.

14

Tom takes a fifteen-minute break mid-morning, to escape the cloying smells of coffee and fried food. Waitresses are talking about Jude's death like it's no more than a piece of gossip. Two of them stand by the hatch, speculating about why she was killed, sharing their stupid theories. He wants to tell them to shut up, but instead he pulls on his sweatshirt and leaves via the fire escape. It's drizzling as the boy makes his getaway. He pulls up his hood, then jogs south across the beach, not caring if the damp penetrates his clothes. He hunkers down to shelter from the breeze. The horizon is a flat grey pencil line today, no ships in sight. He's still studying the water's blank face when footsteps crunch across the shingle. Before he can move, a hand covers his mouth, and he's struggling to breathe, his shoulders thudding against the breakwater.

'You little shit,' Shane's voice hisses. 'I bet you're heartbroken. You can't follow Jude around anymore, like a lovesick puppy.'

'I never did,' Tom replies, jerking his face clear. 'Leave me alone.'

'My sister confided in you, didn't she?' The man's grip on his arm is tight enough to burn.

'I don't understand.'

'Jude gave you the whole story, on those long boat trips. You were her little disciple.' Shane jerks him closer, until their faces are inches are apart. By now Tom is shaking uncontrollably. 'How come she told you her secret, but not me? If you blab details to anyone, I'll fucking kill you.'

Shane releases him, then swings back over the breakwater, leaving Tom shivering. The drizzle is thicker now, rainwater running down his neck, his shoulder blades aching from being pounded against the groyne. He blinks his eyes shut, because tears would be pointless. There's no one to listen to his fears, and telling his mum or Gemma is out of the question. It would only put them in danger too.

15

There's no sign of Eddie when I get back to the incident room at noon. I assume that he's still out, gathering witness statements from islanders who were in the pub on the night of Jude's death. A voice drifts up the stairs soon after I return, the sound bringing a smile to my face. It belongs to my godmother, Maggie Nancarrow, light as birdsong, with a strong Cornish accent. She bounces in without invitation, her small figure clad in jeans and a red T-shirt, face framed by a cloud of grey ringlets. The carrier bag at her side bears the Rock's logo, the pub she's run on Bryher since I was a kid. Her face lights up as she bustles over to kiss my cheek. When she goes back to close the door, I feel certain she's here to pump me for information.

'I've brought you some supplies. Pasta, garlic bread and some really great coffee cake for afters.'

'This place feeds us fine, Maggie. You're just touting for gossip.'

'What a nasty, suspicious mind you have. Why not let me help you?'

'How, exactly?'

'I'm a fountain of local knowledge.'

'Tell me about the history of Piper's Hole, then.'

'The place is cursed, by all accounts.' My godmother's eyes are brimming with excitement. 'There are hundreds of myths about that place from its tin mining days. People say the tunnel runs under the sea, all the way back to St Mary's. When I was a girl, my grandmother said mermaids lured sailors to their deaths there.'

'Old wives' tales can't explain why Jude Trellon drowned.'

Maggie continues, undeterred. 'Smugglers hid contraband from the customs men in the pool; they slaughtered pirates who stole from them there. The place is haunted.'

I roll my eyes. 'Are you still putting your faith in spirits and séances?'

'Cynicism's so unattractive, Ben.' Maggie prods my ribs. 'You can't prove I'm wrong.'

'What about recent history? Has anyone else been hurt there?'

'Only poor Anna Dawlish last November.'

'Keep your voice down, Maggie. This is Will's place, remember? You never know who's lurking in corridors.'

She replies in a dramatic stage whisper. 'Anna's death was one of the worst tragedies we've seen on the islands – two lives lost instead of one.'

'How do you mean?'

'She was pregnant at the time. Poor Will was inconsolable.'

'I didn't know.' My thoughts churn as I gaze down at her. The double loss explains why the innkeeper carried two roses to Piper's Hole this morning, instead of one. 'It's amazing he's kept going.'

'It's lucky he's got a business to run; it must keep his mind occupied.'

'Thanks for the grub, Maggie. I should get back to work.'

'Dismissing me, are you?' She wags her finger at me. 'Come and have dinner soon, before I forget your name.'

'I promise.'

'Famous last words.'

Maggie gives me a wave, then vanishes in a blaze of energy. It still amazes me that so much vigour can be locked inside a sixty-five-year-old woman's bird-like frame. My godmother has planted a seed in my brain that will keep on growing until I find the answer.

I call Eddie's mobile to let him know that lunch has arrived, but there's no reply, so I use my spare time to request Anna Dawlish's post-mortem report from the coroner's office. Six months ago, the pathologist was confident she met her death in a tragic accident, but I need to reassure myself that there's no link between the two deaths at Piper's Hole. Curiosity has spoiled my appetite, so I investigate Jude Trellon's kitbag instead of tucking into lunch. I empty its contents onto a piece of newspaper, but find only a spare diving mask, a snorkel and a handful of sand. When I shake the bag more vigorously, a metal disc drops onto the table, covered in the same dark green verdigris as the mermaid figurine. It looks like a coin, with a pattern scratched on it. I'm just dropping the piece of metal into an evidence bag when my phone buzzes in my pocket. It's Elinor Jago, but the line keeps breaking up. She must be outside, the wind seizing every other word, but the gist of her message is clear. She says Eddie's name, then summons me to Lizard Point, her tone of voice so urgent that I leave in a hurry, chasing the edges of fields at a rapid jog, with the dog running behind. When I break through the stand of pine trees that separates the beach from solid land, Eddie is lying on the sand with waves breaking over his feet. My deputy looks smaller than I remembered, his face raw white, while blood drips from his temple. Elinor Jago is crouching at his side. The contents of the woman's postbag lie scattered across the sand as I drop to my knees, beside a debris of letters and envelopes. I touch Eddie's neck, feeling for a pulse. Relief surges through me when the steady beat drums under my fingertips.

'How did you find him?'

'I had to pull him out. I was on my round when I saw his body in the water.'

'Thank God you were nearby. Have you called the nurse?'

'She's on her way.'

The next few minutes are a flurry of activity. I give Eddie's shoulders a shake, trying to bring him round, and it's a relief to hear him groan. By the time Sophie Browarth runs across the beach, he's blinking at the sunlight, already trying to speak. I stand back to let the nurse examine him, concerned that my deputy still looks far too pale. Sophie shines a light into Eddie's eyes, checking his breathing, then helps him to sit upright. Her manner is so gentle, I feel a pulse of guilt for believing that she could have hurt her best friend, but it's my job to be suspicious.

'You'll need an ice pack on that head wound straight away,' she tells Eddie. 'If you start feeling sick, your fiancée should call emergency services.'

It's only when he finally stands up that I notice the plastic bottle dangling from his wrist, and my heartbeat quickens.

'Do you remember what happened, Eddie?'

His gaze is unfocused when he looks back at me. 'I went to Rowesfield Cottage, to interview the couple renting it. I don't remember much else.'

'You had a lucky escape.'

Eddie's jaw drops open when I point at the bottle hanging from his wrist. I remove the garden twine and stow the thin wire in my pocket.

'What does the message say?' he asks. It's reassuring that his usual excitement comes over in his voice, even though it's weaker than before.

'Don't worry about it now. We need to get you home.'

'I can give him a ride to St Agnes,' Elinor volunteers. 'My boat's just across the bay.'

Eddie leans on me heavily as I help him across 200 metres of sand and shingle to the postmistress's old-fashioned white cabin cruiser, with an outboard motor hanging from the bow at a precarious angle, deep scrapes along its fibreglass side. The small boat reminds me of one my father gave me and my brother to mess around in, with just two portholes admitting light to the galley. Elinor's boat has the same windows just above the waterline, but I'm too busy helping Eddie aboard to look inside. My mouth is still dry with panic as the small craft recedes into the distance. It would have been tough living with myself if my deputy had been killed while his fiancée is heavily pregnant with their first child. I stare down at the bottle the killer attached to his wrist. It's made of clear plastic, revealing phrases written on the paper inside.

WE THEREFORE COMMIT HIS BODY TO THE DEEP, TO BE TURNED INTO CORRUPTION, LOOKING FOR THE RESURRECTION OF THE BODY, WHEN THE SEA SHALL GIVE UP HER DEAD.

The message is scrawled more loosely than before, and this time I don't need the internet to understand its meaning. It's the prayer used for burials at sea, when a corpse is cast into the ocean because the distance to land is too great for a conventional ceremony. The killer may be indulging a private joke about religion, but his attempt to end Eddie's life almost succeeded. If Elinor hadn't spotted his body floating out to sea while doing her postal round, he would have been the second victim in less than a week. Eddie's attacker has established a firm MO; he seems to like a degree of order that conflicts with his violence. Which islander would have enough physical strength to level a man with a single blow, then drag his body across the beach and into the sea? They must be physically fit and strong, unless two people are working together. They would have to be fearless, too. Although this remote beach is often deserted, a passing dog walker could have seen Eddie's body being cast into the sea. The message in the bottle proves that the assault was more than opportunism. He followed the young sergeant during his house calls, waiting for the best moment to launch his attack.

While I'm mulling over possibilities, Shadow appears with a stick clamped between his teeth, expecting a game of catch. I shake my head at him, but the creature ignores my disapproval, laying the stick at my feet like a peace offering. I brush the sand from my jeans, then walk north across the beach as the breeze cools. Changes in the weather are a fact of life here, even as spring edges into summer, the Atlantic delivering constant shifts in temperature. By the time I reach Smuggler's Cottage, the drizzle has turned to rain, and I'm wondering whether Shane Trellon could have ambushed Eddie and left him to float out to sea. His cottage on Cradle Point is only a ten-minute walk from where my deputy was found.

Shane gives a monosyllabic greeting when I arrive to search his place, explaining that I've got a warrant.

'What have you been doing today, Shane?'

'Paperwork.' He delivers the word with a frown, then stomps upstairs.

He vanishes before I can ask another question about how he's entertained himself since his abortive visit to Sophie Browarth's house earlier this morning. When I glance around the living room, my curiosity surfaces. The place could reveal the reason for Jude Trellon's death, the decor almost as basic as it would have been in the smugglers' day, with bare wooden floorboards, oak beams and a stone fireplace. Three paintings on the wall show the sea mounting a vicious attack on Cradle Point during a winter storm.

I pull sterile gloves from my pocket and set to work. Shane seems to lead a spartan lifestyle, with few ornaments clogging his shelves. His DVD collection shows a taste for action movies, with a smattering of travel documentaries about Australia and New Zealand, the man clearly dreaming of bigger landscapes. The cupboards in his kitchen give little insight into his life, apart from proving that he's no bon viveur. There's a limited supply of crockery, a few battered pots and pans and a coffee percolator that's seen better days. His computer monitor is flickering on the kitchen table, an open document appearing when I press the touchpad. Either Shane forgot to lock it or he wanted me to find the financial report. It's an audit of business at the diving school, showing that it's losing money hand over fist, despite the new boat Mike acquired last year. The *Fair Diane* cost £200,000, leaving the company's finances with a sizeable black hole. If Shane killed his sister to become sole heir to the family business, it was hardly worth his time. I do a final scan of the kitchen, looking for used plastic bottles and a roll of garden twine, but find nothing.

Shane appears on the landing when I go upstairs. He snarls something under his breath, then pushes past me, feet thundering on the stairway. The wardrobe in his bedroom contains jeans, T-shirts and one smart suit, the pockets of his jackets empty. It looks like he has taken care to hide any habits that put him in conflict with his sister. I flick through photograph albums, old correspondence and a box full of diving certificates, but there's no clear evidence of Jude's presence. It's only when I discover a book under the bed in the spare room that my interest rises again. Its cover shows a shipwreck lying on the seabed, its wooden structure resembling a whale's skeleton, with sunlight filtering through a wall of turquoise sea. The book's title is *A Diver's Guide to Shipwrecks of the Isles of Scilly*, and the author's name is David Polrew. The man has lived on Tresco with his family for years; he worked as a historian at Plymouth

University, until retiring recently. The volume is dog-eared with use, scribbled notes in the margins. I return downstairs with the book in my hands, to find Shane standing by the kitchen door, glowering at me.

'Is this book yours, Shane?'

He glances at the cover. 'I've never seen it before. Jude must have left it here one night.'

'I need to borrow it for now, and I'll have to take your computer and phone away for analysis.'

'How am I meant to work?' Shane's frown cuts deep horizontal lines across his forehead.

'They'll be returned next week. But before you go, why were you trying to break down Sophie Browarth's door this morning?'

'We've hardly spoken since Jude died. Sophie was her best friend; I'm worried about her, that's all.'

His statement fails to chime with the nurse's claim that he's visited her every day. 'I'm cautioning you to leave her alone for the time being. Have you been out anywhere since you went round there?'

He stares at me, clearly longing to throw a punch. 'I was doing a tax forecast for Dad's business. Now I'm going to work.'

Shane slams out of the house without a backwards glance. The only evidence I have against him is circumstantial, but his tense behaviour is keeping him on my radar. All that's left is to search the false floor in the kitchen, which is cleverly disguised. If he hadn't mentioned it, the elevated boards would have been imperceptible. When I touch a small lever inside the pantry, a trapdoor rises by a few inches, revealing a two-foot-deep crawl space, big enough to conceal a family, or several tons of contraband. But today the space is empty, apart from a legion of spiders and decades' worth of dust.

I flick through Jude Trellon's book again before I leave. The pages have been heavily annotated, lines sketched across maps and pictures, as if she believed they contained valuable secrets. Once I've pulled the door shut behind me, I set off for Polrew's home, with Shane's laptop and phone in an evidence bag.

One of the beauties of living on the islands is that no one is ever out of reach, suspicions can be followed up in minutes. Polrew's home differs from the simple stone cottages scattered across Tresco. It stands close to the abbey, copying the famous building's grand style, three storeys high, with mullioned windows, the front garden so pristine it looks like someone has snipped the grass with nail scissors. I haven't seen Dr Polrew since he addressed my school assembly the year before I left, giving an impassioned speech about local history that prompted sniggers from my year group. A grey-haired woman is watering hanging baskets that trail from her porch when I arrive. She's around fifty years old, straight-backed, with a slim build and narrow, intelligent features. Her smile is tentative when she finally turns round.

'Could I see your husband please, Mrs Polrew?'

An anxious look crosses her face as she takes off her gardening gloves. 'Let me ask him first, please. He hates being disturbed when he's writing.'

The Polrews' hallway is decorated with ornate wooden panels. The house must be 150 years old, but its high ceilings and large rooms resemble an eighteenth-century nobleman's mansion. I'm still admiring the artworks when Mrs Polrew leads me to an oak doorway. She taps on it twice, then ushers me into a dimly lit office which smells of cigar smoke. Dr Polrew sits behind a mahogany desk, squinting at his computer screen.

'Bloody technology,' he mutters. 'I've lost an entire chapter.'

'That's easily done.'

He's around sixty, with broad rugby player shoulders, a thatch of pepper-and-salt hair framing his craggy face. His braying voice carries the assurance that comes from a lifetime of privilege when he rises to his feet to shake my hand.

'Miriam tells me you want to talk about Jude Trellon,' he says. 'There's something dreadful about the old outliving the young.' His words tail away, as if he's just remembered that he has an audience.

'Jude owned a copy of your book, Dr Polrew. I wondered if you knew her?'

'We dived together often over the last two years. My field of expertise is marine archaeology; I needed someone to assist me, but my wife's an art historian, so she was no bloody use. To put it bluntly, that girl had more balls than most men I know. I was happy to employ her.' He slumps in a wing-backed chair, then gestures for me to sit opposite. 'Do you know anything about diving?'

'I'm certified to level two, but that's my limit.'

He looks disappointed, as if I've failed a vital exam. 'The Isles of Scilly rest on the largest underwater graveyard on the planet. No one knows precisely how many ships foundered here in the past five centuries, but it's over a thousand. Only a tiny percentage of the local waters have ever been dived, because the water's deep and currents are treacherous. Until Jude came along, no one was brave or foolish enough to join me.'

'You chartered one of the Trellons' boats?'

'We used mine. I keep it in St Mary's harbour; it's equipped with echolocation and a decent GPS system.' He rubs his hand across the back of his neck. 'I want to map the local seabed before I die. You could say it's my grand obsession.'

'That sounds like a dangerous hobby.'

Polrew's eyes are almost black when he stares back at me. 'If I succeed, the whole community will benefit. No one can say that I wasted my time.'

'Did you ever dive with Shane Trellon?'

He shakes his head. 'Jude had more experience. I needed someone with local expertise; the waters plummet for hundreds of metres between most of the islands. The Scilly Isles used to be a single land mass, until sea levels rose, then only the highest peaks were habitable, and the archipelago was formed. Each island is the summit of a mountain, which explains why they're studded with graves. Ancient civilisations buried their dead close to their sky-dwelling gods.'

'Have you found any undiscovered wrecks?'

He shifts backwards in his chair. 'My interest is purely academic, I'm not hunting for pirates' gold. I want to create a comprehensive record, for future generations, pinpointing the location of every vessel.'

'There was a problem a few years back, wasn't there? Divers were stealing from wrecks, when the items should have been passed on to the Maritime and Coastguard Agency.'

'I know the law, Inspector. Historic shipwrecks are the property of the state,' Polrew replies in a clipped tone. 'I would never harm a wreck site – most of them are reefs, with delicate ecosystems. I take photos, then leave them intact.'

'Jude felt the same?'

'I wouldn't employ anyone who indulged in looting.'

'Thanks for your time, Mr Polrew. If I have questions about your research, can I come back?'

His face softens into a rare smile. 'Feel free to consult me. I hope my book kindles your interest.'

I leave the room with the dog-eared volume tucked under my arm. Polrew's arrogance didn't stop Jude Trellon diving with him frequently, despite the maniacal glint in his eye. The historian's fascination with undiscovered wrecks is easy to interpret, but his touchiness when asked about taking items from the seabed may be more relevant to the case.

16

Tom walks to Dolphin Town once he finishes work. His heart sinks when he approaches Ivar Larsson's cottage, yet he can't turn back. Jude would expect him to pay his respects. No one locks their doors on the island, but he hears the metallic click of a key twisting before Ivar appears in the porch. He has only met him on a few occasions. The man looks fiercer than he remembered, his mouth set too rigidly to smile.

'I wanted to say how sorry I am about Jude,' he mumbles, even though he wishes he'd gone straight home.

'Come in for a minute, Tom.'

Frida is asleep on the sofa in the living room, the girl's features so like Jude's his guts twist into a knot. Once they reach the kitchen, Tom's distress increases; he can picture her sitting on the same seat, enjoying meals with her boyfriend and child. When he looks at Ivar again, the man seems lost in his own world.

'When I wake up, everything feels normal, until I remember she's gone. I have to go through it all over again.'

Ivar's voice resonates with loneliness, making Tom feel

ashamed. His own grief can't compare, yet it keeps threatening to smother him, making it difficult to breathe.

'We're both in danger, aren't we?' Ivar stares at him again.

'How do you mean?''

'We know what Jude did.' The man's pale gaze refuses to release him. 'Someone wants what she found. It's their obsession; they won't rest until they have every piece.'

The desperation on his face makes Tom panic. When Ivar leaves the room to check on Frida, he rushes from the cottage without saying goodbye.

17

I check on Eddie's condition once I get back to the incident room. His fiancée, Michelle, sounds shaken, but informs me that he's showing no signs of serious concussion, which fills me with relief. My previous work partner's death was one of the reasons why I left the Murder Squad; losing another colleague would be difficult to handle.

It's late afternoon by the time I finally speak to Stephen Kinver. His voice has a hard-edged London twang when he explains that his boat is moored a kilometre off the north-east coast of Tresco. We agree that I will use the police launch to visit him and his wife, so I leave Shadow tied up in the yard behind the New Inn.

The black outline of St Helen's expands on the horizon as I steer the speedboat across open water. On any other day, I'd take time to admire the sun dropping behind the furthest islands, but I want to get back to harbour soon. Light is already fading by the time I near the Kinvers' forty-foot yacht, which bears the name

Golden Diver, stencilled in bright yellow paint on its prow. Even from a distance it's obvious that the sleek grey vessel is equipped with plenty of expensive kit, from the lights studding its waterline to the jet ski and speedboat suspended from the bow. The boat is kitted out for sea fishing as well as diving, and must be worth the price of a substantial house in the Home Counties.

The couple are standing on deck as my launch bumps over shallow waves. Stephen Kinver reaches down to tie my rope to the helm rail of his vessel. He looks like an ageing surfer, dressed in baggy shorts, a Hawaiian shirt and mirrored sunglasses, sun-bleached curls skimming his shoulders. His wife is an attractive black woman, with braided hair and a cautious smile. Apart from a few items of expensive jewellery, her casual clothes are almost identical to her husband's. The couple could be anywhere between late-thirties and fifty, empty-nesters enjoying the trip of a lifetime.

'Welcome to our floating gin palace.' Stephen Kinver gives an ironic grin, acknowledging that the cruiser would be dwarfed by a millionaire's yacht.

When Lorraine offers me a drink, her manner is less effusive, dark eyes watchful as I shake her hand. The deck is scattered with diving equipment: wetsuits hanging over the rail, a box full of acetylene flares and a shot line wrapped in a coil. An array of nets, lamps and rods prove that the couple like to fish as well as dive.

'Thanks for coming back to Tresco,' I say. 'It took a while to track you down.'

'It cost us two days' sailing,' Kinver replies. 'We wanted to catch the tide on Sunday night, so we sailed till dawn. We had no idea Jude had died until the coast-guard radioed us.'

'Her poor family must be in pieces.' Lorraine Kinver's voice is less strident than her husband's, her manner more sympathetic.

'I'm trying to trace her last movements. Can you tell me how the three of you spent last Sunday?'

Stephen Kinver gives a rapid nod. 'Jude took us out to the Western Isles; we picked her up from Ruin Beach in the morning, around ten. She brought a young lad with her, to take care of our equipment.'

'What was his name?'

'Tom Heligan; the kid didn't say much, but he was a good diver. We spent the day exploring a few old wrecks, then dropped them back on Tresco in the late afternoon. Jude was good at her job, but I could tell I got on her nerves.' Words spill from Kinver's mouth at high speed, racing to deliver his message.

'Why do you say that?'

'I don't have an off switch, Lorraine says I should learn to edit myself. Jude's dad tolerated me better. We've dived with Mike loads of times, but the guy's heading for retirement, which is a damned shame.'

'Steve's a natural motormouth,' his wife agrees. 'He's like Marmite, people love him or loathe him.'

'I'm the opposite; people tell me I say too little. Where are you both from originally?'

'Essex,' Kinver replies. 'But I've been based in London twenty years, that's where we met.'

'You seem to take your diving seriously.'

'We've been addicted since our first dive. Both of us gave up banking careers to buy this boat. There's a world down there that's more fascinating than ours, with twice as many secrets. I swear I've seen fish that have never been identified.'

'It's the marine life that interests you?'

'Hell, no.' His laughter is as rapid as machine-gun fire. 'I'm looking for Atlantis. Blame my mother for reading me *Treasure Island* at an impressionable age.'

'Are you serious?'

'The lost city may never be found, but I know it exists. You've heard the legend of Lyonesse, haven't you?' Kinver seems more interested in folklore than the death of a woman he recently employed.

'It's a myth, isn't it?'

'There's stuff about it all over the internet,' he replies. 'We were hoping to see submerged villages from the days when the Scillies were connected to the mainland. We're marine salvage experts. Lorraine's set up a website; divingforgold.com. If we report a find, there's a spike in traffic to our site, but some weeks it's slim pickings.'

'Are many people interested in shipwrecks?' It strikes me as unlikely that the couple can support their ocean-going lifestyle from a website's advertising revenue.

'Tens of thousands follow us, worldwide. Every diver

fantasises about discovering an ancient wreck, and people visit the site who've never boarded a boat in their lives. We're feeding a hungry audience. I suppose you'd call it wish-fulfilment.'

Lorraine touches her husband's shoulder. 'Stop babbling, Steve. DI Kitto doesn't want to know about our business. He's here to talk about Jude.'

'Feel free to shut me up,' Kinver replies. 'Everyone else does.'

'But you always start again, that's the trouble.' Lorraine softens her comment by resting her hand on his shoulder, proving that despite Kinver's bluster, her calm temperament gives her equal power in their relationship. 'We love diving in the Scillies; we've visited Tresco often in the last five years.'

'When were you here last?'

'Last November. The marine survey keeps pulling us back; it lists hundreds of missing ships around the islands' coastlines, dating back hundreds of years. Jude showed us a Spanish galleon and an American tea clipper, but both wrecks had been stripped years ago. We decided to cut our losses and spend a few days fishing, before heading for the States.'

'Do you ever collect things from the seabed?'

'There's no law against it, if you hand over your finds inside twenty-eight days,' Kinver chips in. 'Often we just record the location for our website, instead of bringing stuff to the surface.'

'Doesn't that encourage looters?'

'That's not our problem. We're not breaking any laws.'

'Would you mind showing me below deck?'

His smile vanishes. 'Surely you don't think we hurt Jude? People must have seen us sailing away, after we left Ruin Beach.'

'I'm just interested. I've always been keen on boats.'

'We're citizens of the world, Inspector, we like our freedom. Satisfy your curiosity when you've got a warrant.' He releases a long breath, as if he's blowing out candles on a birthday cake.

I'd like to know more about Jude Trellon's behaviour the day before she died, but Stephen Kinver seems keen for me to leave, and his wife's manner is cooling. Their defensiveness makes me believe the couple could be hiding stolen items in their hold, but the crime of looting is separate from the murder investigation. When it becomes clear that they have nothing more to say about Jude, I instruct them to stay within a three-mile radius of Tresco until they get clearance to leave.

Dusk is thickening as I carry my frustration back to shore. It interests me that Tom Heligan went along for the ride, but Stephen Kinver's attitude could be more relevant. He's got the kind of ego that has to score points in every situation. Maybe Jude's greater expertise grated on him, but it's hard to believe the man could have persuaded his wife to circle back to Piper's Hole to kill a woman they barely knew. He could easily have attacked Eddie this morning, by mooring their boat in one of Tresco's coves then rowing ashore to follow him around the island. Kinver's abrupt manner has set my alarm bells ringing, but there's no obvious reason why he would attack two islanders in quick succession, unless the guy's a psychopath.

I moor the launch by the quay at Ruin Beach, then take a final walk south, with stars overhead already piercing the sky, the sun dipping below the horizon. I want a last look at the stretch of beach where Elinor Jago found Eddie floating lifelessly in the water; she was delivering post to the cottages on Rowesfield Lane when she caught sight of him. The killer would have to be organised and physically fit to carry out the attack. But which islander is warped enough to leave a sailor's prayer attached to a cop's body before condemning him to drown?

The lights are on in Pentle Cottage when I reach the far end of the bay. Sophie Browarth must have returned from her home visits, but when I look through her living room window, a new piece of information falls into place. She's standing in the middle of her lounge, with her arms locked around Shane Trellon's neck, kissing him like he's her new source of oxygen. The scene I witnessed this morning must have been part of a lovers' tiff, while her husband's away. I'm surprised by their carelessness; even though the cottage is remote, anyone could spot them while the curtains hang open. Their kiss lasts for another minute and shows no sign of ending. Adultery isn't a crime, but I'd like to know whether Shane Trellon's affair with his sister's best friend has any bearing on her death.

Darkness has dropped over the beach like a black-out curtain when I finally get home to Bryher. Shadow curls up on the sofa once he's fed, but my own appe-tite is harder to satisfy. Eddie is alive due to a piece of good luck; if circumstances had been different, the vicar would be writing another eulogy to deliver at his funeral. Going to the pub while my mind is so preoc-cupied doesn't appeal, so I toast a bagel, then use the entire contents of my fridge to construct a cheese ome-lette. Once my makeshift meal is eaten I sift through notes on my laptop. Three days have passed since Jude Trellon's death, facts about her personality slowly emerging. She was a thrill-seeker who suppressed her love of danger once she had a child, but may have found other risks to satisfy her thirst for excitement. I'm even more certain that whoever killed the young mother knew of her failings, and had no qualms about subject-ing her to a terrifying death. It would take cold, intense rage to force an object into someone's mouth then watch her drown. The killer's method needs to be taken into account, as well as motivation. Whoever murdered Jude must have had access to a boat and strong sailing skills to escape the incoming tide, so every vessel that has visited Tresco recently needs to be searched.

I scroll through the details of each interview, review-ing each one in turn. Ivar Larsson has revealed little about his relationship with Jude, but the couple appear to be polar opposites, which may have created conflict. He could have left his child asleep at home, then used one of the diving school's hire boats to motor round to Piper's Hole and attack her. Jude would have been disoriented from surfacing in the dark cave, allowing him to rip away her breathing gear. Or it might have been a simple case of fraternal jealousy. Jude led a glamorous life through her teens and early twenties, travelling all over the world, while her brother propped up the family business. Maybe Shane killed his sister after a lifetime of feeling second best. There's an outside chance that one of Jude's acquaintances like the historian David Polrew or the Kinvers harmed her, but the only other interviewee to ring my alarm bells is her ex, Jamie Petherton. The museum keeper could be nursing a long-standing grudge over the knock to his ego when she ended their relationship, or the insults she threw at him a few weeks ago.

I complete a progress report for Madron, then flick through David Polrew's book, oblivious to time passing. The man seems to have an encyclopaedic knowledge of local shipwrecks, including ones not yet discovered. The one that seems to have excited Jude Trellon's interest is a Roman vessel called the *Minerva*, reputed to have foundered off the Eastern Isles in the sixth century, with a cargo of precious metal. The ship's name is familiar from my father's tales of a vessel that lay far below the waves, laden with treasure, but I didn't realise the stories were based on truth. The page that describes the myth of the *Minerva* is covered in diagrams and indecipherable scrawl.

It's only when my phone buzzes that I realise it's almost midnight. A text has arrived from Zoe, inviting me for a nightcap. Shadow lets me exit the house alone for once, lifting his head from the sofa to give me a disapproving look as I slip away. Leaving the house without him feels like an odd kind of liberation. The tide is so far out, the sound of the waves is no more than a whisper, the hotel's white outline glistening on the horizon. There are so few outdoor lights here, the constellations are free to dazzle, the North Star burning a hole in the sky.

When I trot up the steps to the bar, the panoramic window shines like a film set, but the place appears deserted. Only Zoe stands behind the bar, with her platinum blonde hair slicked back, a crimson top hugging her curves, looking like an old-time movie star. I would never dream of passing on the compliment; Zoe and I stopped flattering each other years ago. If I told her she looked like Marilyn Monroe's younger sister, she'd laugh in my face.

'No guests tonight?' I ask.

'They're in the film room, watching *Jamaica Inn*.'

'Lucky them. I could use some escapism.'

'I got a new delivery of vodka today. Fancy a tasting session?'

'Okay, but not too much. I need to be up bright and early tomorrow.'

'How's the case going?' She's too busy filling shot glasses to meet my eye.

'Progress is slower than I'd like.'

She sashays out from behind the bar, a silver tray balanced on her fingertips. 'Come and tell me about it. We can exchange sob stories.'

We settle at a corner table, the place silent apart from a hum of voices in the distance, as the last kitchen staff depart. 'You go first,' I say. 'I'm sick of thinking about it.'

'I'm planning some changes, but it's still up in the air.'

'Are we talking about that yellow folder again?'

'You'll know soon enough. Try this one first; it's flavoured with peppercorns.'

I knock the vodka back in one swallow. 'Are you going on a world cruise?'

Her grin is powerful enough to light up the room. 'No, but I'd love a month doing bugger all except sun-bathing and scoffing exquisite food.' When she faces me again, her smile has vanished. 'I'm stuck in a rut, Ben. Sometimes I'll be chatting to guests, but my brain's left the building. I'm thirty-three, with a first-class music degree and a half-decent singing voice. I love it here, but I'm not fulfilling my potential.' She places another glass in my hand. 'Don't you ever fantasise about a parallel life?'

'Not often since I came home. I used to stand on my balcony in London watching pavements full of people, marching to work like they were on a conveyor belt. It made me wonder what the hell I was doing there. The job was exciting, but undercover work got tougher each year.'

'You must think about the future sometimes?'

The question pulls me up short. I've always imagined having a wife and kids one day, but never set myself a deadline. 'I'm better at dealing with the here and now.'

'That's a good philosophy, I knew you'd say something sensible eventually.' Her grin flares back into life again. 'Tell me how the investigation's going.'

'We're interviewing all the islanders, but Jude's family are suffering. They need answers before they can rest.' I swallow another shot, and by now I'm comfortably numb. It crosses my mind to tell her about the kiss I witnessed between Shane and Sophie, but discretion is not one of Zoe's virtues. 'What's your take on extramarital affairs, if one of the partners is away for a long time?'

'If someone cheated on me, it would be game over.' She gives me a puzzled look, then shrugs her shoulders. 'But infidelity's a fact of life, I suppose; absence doesn't always make the heart grow fonder.'

'You're the last of the great romantics, Zoe.'

'Life cured me of it, big time.' She studies me more closely. 'I know you're working hard, but that's no excuse for a horrible beard.'

I rub my hand across my jaw. 'It gives me a distinguished air.'

'You're just too lazy to shave.'

'I need to find the bastard who drowned Jude Trellon and attacked Eddie. My appearance is the last thing on my mind.'

'Promise to let me drag you round the shops in Penzance when the case closes.'

'You're worse than my boss.' I knock back a shot of cranberry-flavoured vodka that tastes like cough mixture, the alcohol making my vision blur. 'Do you know much about Jamie Petherton?'

'The guy's fragile, and those David Bowie eyes of his have always freaked me out.' Zoe's glass hovers in the air. 'It must be tough living with your mum and dad at his age; I don't think he's been in a relationship for years. Jamie reacted badly when Jude dropped him for Ivar, years ago.'

'How do you mean?'

'It all got a bit *Fatal Attraction*. Jamie kept going round to her house, even when Ivar had moved in.'

'But he got over it?'

'He must have done, it was years ago.' She offers me another shot. 'The aniseed one's best. It's so strong, my tongue's gone numb.'

My head's spinning with vodka and conflicting information when I walk back across the beach, so I sit on a boulder to clear my thoughts. The Plough, Orion, and the Seven Sisters glitter overhead like strands in a pearl necklace as my ideas slowly reposition. It's obvious that Jude Trellon inspired strong passions in everyone she knew: Ivar's low mutterings over her dead body sounded like a love song, and her ex-boyfriend was too fixated to let her go without a fight. But the question I still need to answer is which islander held such deep feelings that they were driven to take her life.

18

It's after midnight when Tom slips downstairs for his final cigarette. His mother is asleep already, lights out in her small room beside the kitchen. He tiptoes down the hallway, closing the door gently behind him, to avoid waking her. When he glances at the houses nearby, only their outlines are visible in the dark. His resentment builds with each mouthful of smoke. Maybe he'll waste years like this, while his mates party the night away at university. He shuts his eyes and tries not to imagine years slipping past while he scrubs tables at the café. Now that Jude's gone, there will be no more trips on the dive boat when the summer days lengthen.

Tom grinds the embers of his cigarette into dust with the heel of his trainer. He wants to yell curses at the night sky but doesn't make a sound. Jude would tell him to forget his self-pity and find a solution, but the answer lies beyond his reach. He carries on staring out to sea. The immensity of the flat plain of water is a reminder that his worries are insignificant. One day things will improve and he'll forget about being trapped here, like a castaway, with no means of escape.

Something flickers in the corner of his eye as he turns back to the house. There's a cracking sound before shock overwhelms him, then a sharp burst of pain between his shoulder blades. He tries to cry out, but his tongue refuses to move. Someone pushes him to the ground, his cheek scraping over raw granite. Now the pain in his back is so blinding he loses consciousness. When his eyes open again, footsteps crunch on the shingle as he's dragged across the shore, the taste of salt water filling his mouth. The boy's arms twitch feebly at his sides until pain sends him under again.

PART TWO

'Still unresistingly heaved the black sea, as if its vast tides were a conscience; and the great mundane soul were in anguish and remorse for the long sin and suffering it had bred.'

MOBY DICK,
Herman Melville, 1851

19

Thursday May 14

Nausea is threatening to overwhelm me when I return to the New Inn. Booze doesn't normally affect me so badly, but a combination of neat alcohol, too little food and concern about the case has kept me awake into the small hours. At 8 a.m., Will Dawlish is already filling out the menu board beside the bar. The landlord looks ungainly as he wields his chalk, belt tight around his paunch, his bald head shiny in the overhead light.

'Want to try my guaranteed hangover cure?' he asks, with a look of sympathy.

'Is it that obvious?'

His face creases into a smile. 'Only to the trained observer.'

'I'll give anything a go, Will. From now on, I'm sticking to beer.'

I settle on a bar stool and watch him squeezing oranges, then dropping mint leaves into a blender with a chunk of pineapple. The result tastes surprisingly pleasant, the ice-cold liquid settling my stomach.

'That should clear your head.'

'It's doing the trick already. Can I ask you about Jude, while I'm here? I wondered if you'd remembered anything else about Sunday night.'

'Why? Was I one of the last people to speak to her?'

'It looks that way.'

Will frowns down at his hands, splayed across the bar's marble surface. 'Jude sat where you are now, with her brother. They seemed fine until the row kicked off. I was collecting glasses when I heard them yelling. She was out of here in a blink, slamming the door behind her.'

'Do you know what started it?'

'I was getting ready to close, but earlier on I heard them talking about money problems. She said something about how she was going to sort it by herself, then he called her an arrogant bitch.'

'Did you see anyone leave straight after Jude?'

Dawlish frowns. 'One of the younger lads went a few minutes later, but he was probably just going home. He'd been playing darts with some regulars.'

'Who was that?'

'Tom Heligan. A nice lad, from Merchant's Point, wouldn't say boo to a goose. He was first to leave, then people drifted away. I locked the doors soon after midnight.'

'That's helpful, Will, and thanks again for lending

us the attic. You're doing us a big favour.' That's the second time that the Heligan boy has been mentioned, first as Jude's diving assistant and now because he could have followed her to Piper's Hole. I'll have to interview him as soon as possible. When I look at Dawlish again, he's observing me more closely than before. 'I never told you how sorry I was about Anna. I would have come to her funeral if I'd heard in time.'

'Don't apologise, you were working away. I still can't believe it happened.' His eyes blink shut for a second. 'Anna went out for an evening walk; she must have slipped on the rocks and knocked herself out. She had a head wound when I found her in Piper's Hole the next day. It was the only place we couldn't search the night it happened, because of the tides.' The landlord's voice falters to a stop. 'The whole island wants Jude's killer found, Ben. If you need anything, just let me know.'

Dawlish's raw tone sounds completely sincere. Jude's death seems to have amplified his own grief, the loss of another young woman at Piper's Hole affecting him deeply, yet I can't suppress a flicker of suspicion. The man appears steady and dependable, running his business while attempting to reconstruct his life, but I've been an investigator long enough to know that anyone can commit murder. It's an odd coincidence that his wife and the latest victim both died in exactly the same place, six months apart. We talk for another few minutes before I thank Dawlish again, then head upstairs to the incident room, with the dog already whimpering at the prospect of being cooped up indoors. I expect to find the hotel's shabby attic empty, but Eddie is gazing owlishly at his computer; a white bandage is taped to his forehead, midnight-blue bruises circling one of his eyes. His appearance is frail enough to put my hangover in perspective.

'I told you to take sick leave till you recovered, Eddie.'

'Good luck with that. I'm staying here,' my deputy snaps.

I stare at him in amazement, before letting myself grin. His choirboy face may be pale, but it's fierce with determination. The attack he suffered yesterday seems to have cured his politeness once and for all.

'If you keel over, don't blame me.'

'I want to find the vicious bastard, before he hurts someone else,' he mutters.

I let him complete his work in silence, his features stony with concentration. The first document my eyes light on is the post-mortem report I ordered from the coroner's office, neatly printed out. It gives a long account of Anna Dawlish's injuries, but I flick forwards to the summary paragraph, which confirms that she was thirty-eight years old and three months pregnant at time of death. It supports her husband's claim that she died by accidental drowning, with no mention of foul play. I finish scanning the report with a sense of relief: Will Dawlish strikes me as a decent guy, unlikely to harm anyone.

My phone buzzes in my pocket just as I'm sliding

the report back into its wallet, the answering service delivering a short voice message. Linda Heligan is requesting an urgent home visit, the rest of her speech too garbled to make out. The visit should give me the chance to learn more about her son and why he accompanied Jude Trellon on her last diving trip.

I set off for Merchant's Point at a rapid march, the dog following a scent trail in the opposite direction, muzzle glued to the ground as he tracks imaginary prey. I think about Linda Heligan as I cut north across the island, the path winding over the rocky headland. She was younger than the other teachers, pretty, and bubbling with enthusiasm; her English lessons were all that interested me at school, apart from rugby. I found myself going to the library each lunch break to read the American novels she recommended, much to my mates' amusement. Under ordinary circumstances it would be a pleasure to see her again, but the tension in her voice indicates that she's in difficulty.

Merchant's Point is beautiful but bleak, the shore a raw waste of granite, with shards of stone rising from the sea like ancient swords. The Heligans' cottage is the only property in sight, a small, two-storey property that's seen better days. From a distance, it looks like a piece of flotsam brought in by the tide, with no garden separating it from the shore.

A woman gazes up at me from a wheelchair when I approach the house. I do a double take before recognising my old teacher. Pain has turned her into an old woman, even though she can't be much past forty; her thin form is hunched over, shoulder-length dark hair streaked with grey. She has lost so much weight since she kept my class entertained, there are hollows under her cheekbones, her eyes set too deeply into their sockets.

'Don't look so shocked, Ben. Didn't you hear I'd broken my back? I can walk a few steps, but that's my limit.'

'I'm sorry to hear it, Linda.'

'It's not important now. My son's been missing all night; I have to find him.' Her voice is a low murmur.

'Why don't we talk inside?'

She wheels her chair into a small living room, lined from floor to ceiling with books, the air smelling of dried paper and firewood. 'Tom left the front door open last night. He works at Ruin Beach café, but they haven't seen him.'

'Try not to worry. Most times when someone goes missing, they're back the same day, safe and sound. Could he be visiting someone?'

'There's no way he'd just leave, my son's incredibly responsible.' She swipes a tear from her cheek as if she's removing a troublesome fly. 'It's my fault he's gone.'

'How do you mean?'

'Tom's got no life of his own. He's spent all year looking after me.'

'Don't think about that now. Can I look in his room?'

'Go ahead, if it helps.'

Mrs Heligan wheels her chair back into the hallway, waiting expectantly while I jog upstairs. The boy's room is the opposite of his mother's bookish lounge. It looks like a monument to the sea, with charts of marine creatures and pictures of a diving bell hovering over a coral reef plastered to the walls. The shelves are crowded with mollusc shells, pebbles and polished chunks of amber. His pinboard shows photos taken with an underwater camera, but it's the biggest image that catches my attention. The dark-haired lad I saw outside the New Inn swims towards the camera, beside the woman I found dead by Piper's Hole, her smile visible through her oxygen mask. The lad's friendship with Jude Trellon could have exposed him to the same dangers. His phone is lying on his desk, beside his wallet, even though he's been gone for hours. I'd like to search the room more thoroughly, but Linda's voice drifts upstairs, checking whether I've found anything. I put through an alert call to Eddie before facing her again.

'Tom's probably just popped out to see someone, Linda, but we'll do a search anyway.'

'My son hasn't been himself lately, that's why I'm worried. He cancelled his place at uni at the last minute, and Jude Trellon's death has affected him terribly.'

'Were they close?'

She gives a vigorous nod. 'Tom worked as a crew member in exchange for free diving lessons; it's been his favourite hobby since his dad left. Jude let him hang around the diving school whenever he had spare time.'

'How's he been since she died?'

'He's stopped talking to me.' She presses her hand to her mouth. 'I'm sorry to burden you with this, Ben. I don't know what I'll do if he isn't found.'

'When's the last time you saw him?'

'I heard him go outside, around midnight, but I thought he'd come back.'

'We'll find him.' I touch her arm. 'Is there anyone to help you, till Tom gets home?'

'Plenty of people, that's the irony. My friends here will give me a hand: Diane Trellon, Elinor Jago, Sylvia Cardew. I'd have managed if he'd gone away to uni, but his sense of duty kept him here.'

'You're sure he isn't with a friend?'

'They all left the island last autumn, except Gemma Polrew.'

'She's his girlfriend?'

Linda releases a broken laugh. 'My son's in love with the sea, nothing else.'

I check the shingle in front of the house before I leave. A few cigarette butts lie between stones near the entrance, but there are no visible footprints running down to the beach, the tide wiping away evidence of the boy's movements. I only spot something in the middle of the path as I straighten up. It's another plastic water bottle, and at first I assume it's been washed up with the latest tide, but the slip of paper inside makes my heart rate double. The killer is savvy enough to wear gloves when he leaves his taunts, so I don't bother to use an evidence bag to pick it up: this time the writing on the scrap of paper inside is bigger than before, but still using the same block capitals, designed to mask his handwriting. I shove the bottle into my pocket before looking back at the house. Linda Heligan is stationed by her living room window, but she's not watching me. Her eyes are fixed on the horizon, as if her son's boat is due home from a long sea voyage.

20

I wait until I'm a safe distance away before reading the message:

FORGET THE TRAITORS, THE LIARS
    AND CHEATS,
LEAVE THEM ALL BEHIND, BOYS,
LET THEM LANGUISH ON THE SHORE,
THEY'LL SUFFER AND DIE WHILE
    WE'RE FREE AS BIRDS,
LEAVE THEM ON THE SHORE.

The cryptic message makes the muscles tighten inside my chest. The odd chant sounds like another verse from a sea shanty, and it must have a meaning for the killer, but who would harm an eighteen-year-old boy that never hurt anyone in his life? It must be linked to Jude and the diving expedition they took together on the day she died, although the connection will be hard to prove. There's no way of knowing whether the boy has been abducted or killed, his body tethered to a rock somewhere, while the killer remains at liberty, like the birds in his message.

My heart sinks when I see DCI Madron in the incident room; his grey mackintosh is buttoned to his throat, as if he fears contamination. My deputy pulls an apologetic face as Shadow bounds through the door.

'That dog should be leashed, Kitto,' the DCI says. 'You're not permitted to bring him on police business.'

'Sorry, sir, we weren't expecting you.'

'That makes no difference. I expect my orders to be carried out, whether I'm here or not.'

'I'll keep that in mind, sir. Did you get my report?'

'I prefer to be updated in person, and I wanted to check that Eddie's recovering.'

Madron's expression hardens when I explain Tom Heligan's absence. He peers at the verse from the sea shanty, before looking at me again.

'Jude Trellon's killer was on the island the night of the murder, Kitto. You must have a list of suspects by now. These messages are no more than distraction.'

'The killer knew she would go to Piper's Hole, then left the crime scene by boat. It was premeditated murder, carefully organised. I've asked Lawrie Deane to search all the vessels in New Grimsby Harbour today.'

'What makes you so certain the attacker used a boat?'

'It would have been impossible to escape by land. Whoever killed her would need to be an experienced sailor to get round the headland with the tide rushing in. I still think they had a personal grudge, to end Jude's life so violently. We know she'd argued with her brother Shane the night she died, so he's our best suspect. He's having an affair with a married woman, but I don't see why that would send him on the attack.'

'Why not bring him in for questioning?'

'There's no hard evidence to implicate him, sir. Jude spent her final day with Tom Heligan and two professional wreck divers, but neither of them have a record. It's still possible that her boyfriend killed her after an argument. He wasn't surprised that she'd died at Piper's Hole, and he's had plenty of sailing experience. Maybe he attacked Heligan because he believes the boy knows he's the killer.'

Madron looks sceptical. 'Is a university academic likely to commit murder?'

'Anyone can turn violent. And he has enough physical strength to force an object into a victim's mouth, then let her choke.'

'I want to see more progress by the end of the week.'

'So do I, sir, but we can't make arrests without evidence.'

'You realise the press will be all over this? If you don't find the killer soon, you'll have an invasion.'

I feel like explaining that getting under the skin of an island community is like piercing the surface of a diamond. The islanders' lives are so tightly connected, it can take months to uncover secrets. Madron doesn't

seem to realise that no one is more motivated than me
to find Jude Trellon's killer; the need for justice has
nagged at me ever since I saw Frida clinging to her
father's side, and it's grown even keener since Eddie
was attacked.

'Get this place cleaned up,' Madron snaps. 'Those
windows are a public disgrace, and why not smarten
your appearance while you're at it, Kitto? You look like
a castaway.'

The DCI marches away at a rapid pace, while I grit
my teeth. Eddie merely rolls his eyes, then continues
to phone around for sightings of Tom Heligan, but my
irritation lingers. Madron has grated on me from the
start. His long spell as chief of police of the island force
has been uneventful, apart from one murder case and
the usual round of petty crimes. Fatalities make him
panic, yet he's wary of handing over the reins. He'll
carry on criticising everything I do until the case closes,
making me even keener to find the killer fast.

I put the mermaid figurine from Jude's attack in my
pocket, then leave the dog with Eddie. Shadow gives
a howl of disapproval, but David Polrew's Persian
rugs and antique furniture wouldn't stand a prayer
if he broke loose. I have no idea whether the historian's daughter will be at home, but Tom Heligan's one
remaining friend on the island might know where he's
hiding.

This time Dr Polrew answers the door himself,
dressed in old-fashioned corduroy trousers, his checked

shirt open at the neck. The academic's expression is animated, as if he's looking forward to discussing his book.

'Could I speak to your daughter please, Dr Polrew?'

His smile is replaced by disapproval. 'I don't allow Gemma to have visitors during the day, it disrupts her study programme.'

'This is a police matter. It won't take long.'

The historian chunters under his breath before climbing the stairs, leaving me to study the decor again. The grandfather clock, parquet floor and subdued oil paintings suit the age of the house but make its atmosphere oppressive. Beeswax lingers on the air, cloying and oversweet. When David Polrew returns, a slim teenaged girl follows in his wake, face veiled by a sweep of blonde hair. Despite the warm weather she's dressed in jeans, boots and a baggy jumper. I smile in her direction but she doesn't meet my eye.

'I'll stay, if you don't mind,' Polrew says. 'Gemma doesn't like meeting strangers on her own.'

The Polrews' living room combines grandeur with ostentation, a chandelier hanging above the inglenook fire. The historian stands sentry by the door while the girl perches on the settee, hands clasped in her lap. She's got a pretty, heart-shaped face, but her expression is wary.

'Have you heard from Tom Heligan recently, Gemma?' I ask.

'Not lately. I've been busy revising.'

'But you're friends, aren't you?'

'We went to school together, that's all.' Her gaze shifts towards her father.

'Your friends didn't help you much last year, did they?' Polrew snaps. 'Tell the inspector why you're still at home.'

The girl's voice drops to a mumble. 'Dad wants me to retake my A levels, to get better grades.'

'She wasted her time socialising. We're having to pay a tutor to coach her, two days a week online,' says Polrew. 'Her brother, Kieran, never caused us this kind of trouble; he's at Oxford, reading chemistry.'

I return my attention to the girl. 'I need you to check whether Tom texted or called you in the last few days, please.'

'I'll get my phone.' Gemma is already on her feet, skirting past her father to retrieve her mobile.

'My daughter fights me every step of the way,' Polrew mutters. 'She's got the concentration span of a goldfish.'

'All teenagers are the same.'

'She needs three A's to study psychology at Bristol, but missed the target, thanks to her hectic social life. She's only got herself to blame.'

Polrew sounds sublimely certain that he's correct, but I have my doubts. His bullying manner leads me to believe that the girl could have been trapped indoors for weeks, the dark paint on the walls making the room feel as oppressive as a prison cell.

'Tom sent a few texts, but nothing unusual,' Gemma

says when she returns, her phone clutched in her hand.

'Could I see his messages please?'

She looks awkward as she hands over the mobile, and the texts between her and Tom Heligan explain why. Hers are a litany of despair about being trapped indoors, haranguing her parents, the boy's answers reassuring her that she'll soon be free again.

'Thanks, Gemma, that's fine.' I pass the phone back. 'How did Tom act, last time you spoke?'

'He seemed worried about something, but we didn't talk for long.'

Polrew glares at his daughter, as if a brief chat with a boy is a hanging offence. It's clear she won't open up in his presence, her expression tense with anxiety, so I give her my card instead of asking another question.

'If you remember anything, please call me straight away.' The girl vanishes from the room, her father still wearing an irritable frown. 'Could you identify an item for me, while I'm here, Dr Polrew?'

I produce the mermaid figurine and the coin from Jude Trellon's kitbag, wrapped in separate evidence bags. Polrew carries them over to the window to inspect them in clear light. He keeps his back turned, exclaiming under his breath. When he finally turns round, the disapproval he showed his daughter has been replaced by excitement, his eyes glittering.

'Jamie Petherton can verify my opinion, but I believe the figure dates from the Roman era, fifth or sixth century. It's an amulet, cast from silver – high-ranking sailors carried them on long voyages for good luck. Where did you find it?'

'At the scene of Jude Trellon's murder.'

His stare intensifies. 'A cache of Roman items was found in a field near here years ago, but none this well preserved.' He examines the figurine again, poring over every detail. 'Historical records talk about a Roman vessel foundering on its way to Tresco. It was called the *Minerva*, loaded with artefacts made from precious metals. Have you heard of it?'

'I read about it in your book. Do you think the amulet's from the *Minerva*?'

'It's the right age, but I've been scouring the seabed for ten years. I doubt a casual amateur would find it before me.'

The anger on Polrew's face proves that his passion for undiscovered wrecks is more than academic. I'm almost certain that he employed Jude Trellon to help him search for a ship that's featured in local folklore for generations.

'What about the coin?'

He shakes his head dismissively. 'They're not my speciality, but Petherton will know; he's a self-taught expert on all things Roman. Now, if you'll excuse me, I have a chapter to complete.'

The historian's tone is sour as he hurries me along the corridor, then barks out a hasty goodbye.

21

Pain throbs at the base of Tom's spine when he comes round. Someone has placed him on his side, the taste of salt lingering on his tongue, panic making his breathing ragged. All he can see is blackness, a blindfold obscuring his vision. He could be trapped in a nightmare, but the ache between his shoulders is too sharp to be imaginary. It's impossible to move; his hands have been bound tightly behind his back, ankles lashed together with rope. He cries out at the top of his voice, his body squirming against its constraints like a fish on a line. When his strength finally fails, the silence deepens. The room must be tiny: if he swings his legs, he can touch walls on either side, the air thick with condensation.

Tom gulps in a long breath, but it's impossible to calm down. He can taste the reek of fish guts, and a smell he recognises from the diving shop: the synthetic odour of wetsuits and diving gear. At first there are no sounds at all, until he hears the murmur of waves hitting a hard surface. When the floor beneath him shifts in a rolling motion, the truth hits home. Someone has sealed him in the hold of a boat, a piece of human cargo with no value, and before long his oxygen supply will run out. He releases another yell, but no reply comes back, not even an echo.

22

Eddie looks surprised by the idea that David Polrew is as keen to locate the Roman cargo ship as the Kinvers. Unlike the professional wreck divers, his motive is likely to be academic acclaim, not money, but the prospect still appears to have gripped his imagination. A few checks on the internet confirm the historian's claims about the area's maritime history. The islands were an important Roman trading post; ships carrying valuable goods often foundered on the rocks, until pilots were paid to guide them through the danger zone to St Mary's harbour. Reading about maritime history makes me follow my suspicions about the Kinvers, to see how they've spent the last year. There's nothing to incriminate the couple in either Jude's murder or Tom's disappearance, apart from the fact that they both spent the day of Jude's death on the Kinvers' yacht. When I run searches through the Police National Computer, neither of them have records, but they've been travelling at a frantic pace, flitting from Indonesia to the

West Indies, then back to the Mediterranean. I'm certain they're involved in illegal trade, but following my instinct about the couple's activities would only distract me from finding the missing boy.

When I call Linda Heligan at 3 p.m., anxiety has sharpened her tone of voice. No one on the island will admit to seeing her son since yesterday, the message left outside her house making me concerned that Tom may have met the same fate as Jude Trellon. Our best chance of finding him alive lies in understanding the link between them.

'We need to interview Jude's parents again,' I tell Eddie. 'Shadow can come with us.'

'The DCI will go mad if he hears.'

'He'll chew up the floorboards if we leave him behind.'

The dog launches himself outside in a wild bid for freedom, leaving us free to walk to Ruin Beach alone. Clouds gather as we head north, shadows rolling across Vane Hill, while sheep cluster under elm trees.

'Do you know how Ruin Beach got its name?' I ask.

'Because so many ships were destroyed here,' Eddie replies. 'Wreckers lured boats onto the shore, then stole their cargo. The offshore rocks claimed plenty of lives too. By the way, Lawrie didn't find anything on the boats in harbour today. I can give you a list of the ones he searched.'

'Bloody marvellous.'

Now that the sun has disappeared, the view is

ominous. A vast expanse of grey ocean lies under a pallid sky, with spikes of granite piercing the waters at the mouth of the inlet, ready to capsize all but the most experienced mariners. It's perfectly possible that Jude Trellon's attacker used a boat moored in a marina on one of the other inhabited islands, and hunting for him is starting to feel like searching for a single fragment of amber on a mile-long beach.

Diane and Mike are alone when we reach their house, the kitchen littered with sympathy cards. The couple look worse than last time, as if the reality of their daughter's death has finally registered. They listen in silence to the news that Tom Heligan has been missing since dawn. The hope on Diane's face has been replaced by grim determination to keep going, while Mike glowers at me, his arms folded.

'What's that got to do with Jude?' He gives me a bloodshot stare.

'It was the same attacker. We need to understand the connection.'

'Tom's a sweet kid. Jude taught him to dive when he was about twelve, and he's hung around the boats ever since,' Diane says. 'He's had a tough time since his dad left last year. The bastard scarpered a few months after Linda fell on the rocks outside their house.'

Mike shifts forwards in his chair. 'I told Jude he had a crush on her, but she didn't listen. He's keen on all the same things: boats, wrecks and diving. The lad followed her around every day last summer.'

'Can I check your logbook again, Mike? I need to see how often Tom crewed for her recently.'

'I'll get it from the shop.' He hurries away, with Eddie in tow, clearly glad to be given a task.

'That boy would have done anything for Jude,' says Diane. 'You don't think he's been hurt, do you?'

'With luck he'll be home soon,' I reply, with a calm smile. 'Have you ever heard about a Roman shipwreck, off the Eastern Isles, called the *Minerva*?'

'It's a myth, isn't it?' Her eyes blink rapidly. 'People have talked about it for generations, saying it's packed with silver and gold. No one really believes it exists.'

'Not even Jude?'

'She would have told us if she'd seen anything.'

I lower my cup onto the table. 'Has Ivar come round much over the last few days?'

Her expression sours. 'Not once; it wouldn't surprise me if he took Frida back to Sweden. We've seen more of Jude's ex since we lost her.'

'Jamie Petherton?'

'He called round the day after we heard; he seems more upset than Ivar.'

'How's Shane coping?'

'It's easier for him to get angry than grieve. He stores it all inside, like Mike.' She stares down at her hands. 'You will find the bastard that killed Jude, won't you? I couldn't bear it if he walked away.'

'We'll do everything we can.'

It crosses my mind to ask if she knows about her

181

son's affair with Sophie Browarth, but it's not likely to be connected with the case. Her green eyes pin me to the chair until Mike and Eddie return, carrying the ledger that holds details of recent diving trips, then we say our goodbyes.

When we return to the incident room, the logbook proves that Tom Heligan crewed for Jude on almost every trip last summer, cutting down to once a week when he started work at the café. The pair must have talked for hours during those long voyages. For a kid obsessed by the sea, Jude's job would have seemed the ideal occupation. It's impossible to know whether he volunteered on board for free diving lessons or because he was gripped by infatuation. When I scan the pages of the record again, it looks like the diving business survives by offering a range of services: seal-watching trips, scuba diving lessons, and wreck dives for groups of holidaymakers. Business dwindles when the season ends, but Jude found work from yachtsmen that visit the islands all year round, taking over her father's role as a personal diving guide, with customers like the Kinvers employing her for days at a time. She spent most of the autumn taking groups out to the wrecks that lie beyond St Agnes. I feel more certain than ever that the answer to her death and Heligan's disappearance lies under the sea, not on dry land.

'Let me see the list of islanders who own boats again, Eddie.'

He shunts the paper across the table, but the names

fail to narrow the field. Lawrie Deane has only searched the boats that were in the main harbour today, and the killer has had plenty of time to hide any signs that his vessel is being used to carry out attacks. Most families own a dinghy for travelling between the islands, and more than half have cabin cruisers. Boats are like taxis here, kids learning to row as soon as they're big enough to hold an oar. The ocean is everywhere you look, tempting people to swim, dive and sail all year round, but I can't forget the certainty on my uncle's face when he claimed that the killer used a boat with a powerful engine to escape from Piper's Hole.

When I look out of the window again, clouds are blocking the late afternoon light as Arthur Penwithick's ferry cuts across the sound. The fact that Tom Heligan has been missing all day nags at me on a personal level as I reach for my jacket. His mother relies on him for company and help around the house. No one has reported seeing a body, which must be a good sign, and my spirits lift further when I see more than forty people gathering outside, ready to scour the island for signs of the boy.

Most of the search party are locals, but a few have made the short journey from Bryher, including Maggie and Ray, with Zoe giving a thumbs up from the back of the crowd. I divide them into small groups, offering specific instructions about where to look, and making a point of thanking Denny Cardew for coming to help, aware that he's been working since dawn. The fisherman shakes his head at the mention of his name, embarrassed to be singled out. The islanders listen intently as I ask them to search outbuildings and caves, as well as the shoreline. There's no sign of Ivar Larsson; it concerns me that he has shunned social contact since Jude died, the rest of the islanders banding together to help find her killer.

My search group includes members of staff from the New Inn, including Will Dawlish, and the postmistress, Elinor Jago. But when I glance around, several families are missing, including the Polrews. It doesn't surprise me that the historian is keeping his daughter closeted away, instead of letting her join the search. I catch sight of Shane Trellon in the distance talking to Justin Bellamy, whose scruffy jeans and summer shirt look out of kilter with his dog collar. Mike and Diane are nowhere to be seen.

Zoe falls into step beside me once we set off. 'Where are you taking us?'

'North along the shore, to Piper's Hole.'

'Do you expect to find him alive?' she asks in a whisper.

'He hasn't been missing long, so his chances are good.' I keep my voice level, in case anyone hears. I learned long ago that an investigation soon fragments if the lead officer shows signs of uncertainty.

The tide is out as we follow the eastern shore. On any other day, I'd enjoy strolling with Zoe while my dog sprints ahead. The landscape is at its best today, waves cresting against the granite slabs of Braiden

Steps, and yachts bobbing past Frenchman's Point like a shoal of minnows, yet my thoughts refuse to settle. Tom Heligan could already have met with the same violence that ended Jude Trellon's life, but the message the killer left behind must have a meaning. I'm struggling to understand the symbolism of leaving lines from old sea shanties and sailors' prayers at each scene; the only suspects with a clear interest in history are Jamie Petherton and David Polrew, but no hard evidence links either of them to the crimes.

The group walks in silence at first. Elinor Jago is to my left, stopping regularly to inspect thickets of brambles and peer through the windows of outhouses. The woman tackles the search with the same thoroughness she brings to her role as the island's postmistress, completing every task with brisk efficiency. But when I try to make conversation, she replies in monosyllables, all of her attention focused on finding the missing boy. Justin Bellamy appears more relaxed while he chats to Zoe. The priest seems to relish the opportunity to rub shoulders with a stunning blonde, his expression animated as they talk.

David Polrew's words return to me when we climb Tregarthen Hill. The incline looks ghost-ridden today, the grass strewn with rocks that look like they've lain there for thousands of years, the terrain studded with entry tombs. But there's no sign of their original purpose; the graves appear to be empty, apart from a few sweet packets and Coke cans left by local kids.

The vicar approaches me outside the deepest cave. 'Weird to think that Neolithic families held funerals here.' He stops to peer up at the sky. 'I can see why they chose the highest land for their burial sites. It must have felt like God was close enough to touch.'

The rocky walls are grooved by the flint tools used to widen the entrance several thousand years ago. The island's kids might be less keen to eat their picnics here if they knew it had once been a resting place for the dead. Elinor Jago is standing outside when I emerge, her expression pensive.

'I remembered something about Jude,' she says. 'I saw her and Denny Cardew talking, about a week before she died. They were outside the diving shop when I delivered some letters. It sounded pretty heated.'

'Did you hear what it was about?'

'I was too far away. Jude was giving Denny a hard time about something, but he kept his cool.'

'How did it end?'

'I didn't stay to watch.' She looks awkward. 'It was none of my business, and it didn't seem important at the time.'

'But it does now?'

'Jude could be hot-headed, but I've never seen Denny argue with anyone.'

'Thanks, I'll keep it in mind. I never thanked you properly for rescuing Eddie. You deserve a medal.'

'I'm just glad he's safe.' Elinor seems flustered as she gives a quick smile then backs away.

I'm still wondering why the fisherman failed to mention his argument with Jude when we reach the island's northern tip. There's no chance of climbing down to Piper's Hole today. The sea is at high tide, waves battering the base of the cliffs, the wind coming off the Atlantic cooler than before. Someone could have marched Tom Heligan up here, then cast him onto the rocks below, the sea claiming him before anyone noticed he was gone, but the idea soon fades. Instinct tells me he's still alive, even though I prefer not to rely on hunches. The killer left Jude Trellon's body tethered to the rocks, to make sure it was found, the messages in bottles part of a symbolic conversation that I need to decode. If he's using the same MO, he'll preserve the boy's life until he's ready to return the body. My best chance of finding the boy alive is to act fast, before the killer has finished with him.

Shane Trellon is by himself when the search party heads back inland, so I fall into step beside him. My presence makes him bristle, but the reason for his dislike remains unclear. I can tell from his scowl that there's no point in making small talk, so I ask the question that's bothered me since Eddie's attack.

'How long have you and Sophie Browarth been involved, Shane?'

Shock makes his shoulders jerk before he checks if anyone's heard. 'What do you mean?'

'I saw you together last night. Shut the curtains, if you want it kept secret.'

His frown deepens. 'She hasn't told her husband yet. It's been a difficult time for both of us; I went round there to comfort her.'

'That sounds like more than a casual fling.'

'I'd appreciate it if you'd keep it quiet.'

'Why would I tell anyone? I've got an investigation to run.'

He gives a curt nod, then strides away at a furious pace, like a soldier on a route march.

23

Dusk is falling when I call off the search. The crowd look tired as we return to the New Inn after searching woodland, fields and the Abbey Gardens. Every shed, fish hut and barn has been checked, yet I haven't abandoned hope of finding Tom Heligan alive. The search party is still loitering outside the inn, waiting for my verdict.

'Thanks, everyone, I appreciate you giving up your time,' I tell them. 'Please let us know if you remember anything that could help us find Tom.'

They drift away, leaving Eddie and I to our own devices. Will Dawlish appears from the hotel's fire doors with some meat scraps for Shadow, disappearing inside again before I can thank him. The action is a typical piece of island behaviour. Living in such a small community forces people to be generous; the unwritten code has existed here ever since families shared food during lean winters in order to survive. I'm still preoccupied when we climb back to the attic, trying to second-guess the killer's next move, until I notice a slight stagger in my deputy's walk, the bruising round his eye darker than before.

'Get yourself home now, Eddie. Are you okay?'

'I just want him found, boss.' The tension in his voice has sharpened since yesterday's attack.

'That won't happen if you wear yourself out. Go and get some rest.'

Eddie has thrown himself into the day's tasks with so much energy, it's easy to forget that he narrowly missed becoming the killer's second victim. I stand by the window after he leaves, trying to imagine where Tom Heligan could be. The killer has increased his pace, delivering two attacks in forty-eight hours, increasingly desperate to ram his message home. Our search has revealed that Heligan is no longer on the island; the boy must be at sea, whether he's alive or dead. If he's lost his battle already, it seems a cruel fate for a kid who has made big sacrifices to care for his mother.

The channel between Tresco and Bryher is turning to graphite as the sun drops behind Shipman Head. My gaze skims the boats floating in the harbour: dinghies, cabin cruisers and fishing smacks jostle together, as colourful as children's toys. Denny Cardew is loading lobster creels back onto the deck of his boat, ready for morning, no one else in sight.

It doesn't take me long to walk to Merchant's Point, a dim light glowing from Linda Heligan's living room. My old teacher must have been keeping watch, because the door swings open before I reach the porch. She manoeuvres her wheelchair back so I can step into the hall.

'Tom's still missing, isn't he? Justin told me, half an hour ago.'

'The vicar phoned you?' I ask.

'He called here, after the search. Justin spent time in Tom's room, saying a blessing.' Her face brightens slightly. 'We're lucky to have such a good priest.'

I nod in agreement, even though religion never convinces me. 'Would you like someone to stay here with you tonight, Linda?'

'People have been dropping in all day. I'll be fine, till Tom comes home.' She gestures towards the shelves lining the room. 'I've got these stories to keep me company. I'll read *The Shipping News* tonight, to remind myself that people can come back from the sea unharmed.'

'Did I ever thank you, for keeping me on the straight and narrow? Without you, I'd probably be in jail.'

'I doubt it, Ben. You were your own man, even then. But I bet you never finished *The Canterbury Tales*.'

'Guilty as charged.' When she manages a smile, I see a trace of the young woman who ignited my passion for books. 'We'll carry on looking tomorrow. I need to go up and search Tom's things properly this time, is that okay?'

'Be careful, won't you? Some of his stuff is fragile. He'd hate it if anything got damaged.'

'Don't worry, I'm less clumsy than I look.'

'Sorry, I'm being paranoid. Take as long as you need.'

I spend an hour in Tom Heligan's room, the search giving me an insight into the boy's personality. Zoe would approve of the few clothes that hang in his wardrobe: classic jeans and plaid shirts from Zara and Superdry. He must have saved hard for each item since he started work, making sure he picked things to last. The room is far tidier than mine at his age, only a few discarded T-shirts lying on the floor. There are hardly any books, except a few thick volumes on marine biology and environmental science. The only typically teenaged thing about Tom Heligan is his taste in music; his iPod is full of American thrash and metal bands. I search every nook and cranny, but find nothing. The boy must have intended to return soon – his phone is still lying on his desk, beside his laptop. I'll have to wait for the IT team on the mainland to hack into his email.

My eyes scour the room again for clues, settling on a calendar pinned above his desk. Tom has marked his diving trips with red crosses, all the other days blank, as if nothing else mattered. It surprises me that there are no photos of his absent father, while there are half a dozen of Jude Trellon. His feelings for her seem to have been close to an obsession, since he took responsibility for his mother's care. If people are fixated, they keep mementoes, yet I can't see any items belonging to the woman Tom Heligan revered.

'He must have kept something,' I mutter to myself.

There's little in the other upstairs rooms, except discarded furniture and old clothes stacked on beds, proving that it has been a long time since Linda could access the first floor of her house. I'm about to return downstairs when I spot that the loft hatch is ajar and pull down the ladder. The attic smells of mothballs and damp newspaper, dozens of cardboard boxes lying side by side. I follow the outline of fresh boot prints through the dust, until I spot a piece of yellow insulating foam that sits higher than the rest. When I pull the material back, my eyes catch on a brown paper package and my pulse quickens. It contains another figurine, but this one is larger and less tarnished than the mermaid. It shows a man with a trident gripped in his hand, the laurel wreath in his hair picked out in gold. The discovery proves that Tom Heligan was lying when he claimed not to have seen anything like the mermaid amulet that caused Jude Trellon's death. Not only had he seen the ancient figurines before, he chose to hide one in his attic. His mother would never have found it if he'd left the package in his room, but he must have feared that someone else might break into the house. The question I need to answer is why Jude would give him something so valuable.

It's 10 p.m. when I return downstairs. Linda listens in silence as I explain that her son's phone and computer need to be analysed. When I show her the figurine, she shakes her head blankly, stating that she has never seen it before. She looks frailer than ever, refusing again to let me take her to a friend's house. I wish her goodnight, then carry her son's belongings with me, wrapped in evidence bags.

Shadow has found company while I've been indoors. Someone is sitting on a rock at the far end of the beach, the dog lying at their feet. As I draw closer, a young woman scrambles to her feet and starts to run.

'Wait!' I call out.

Gemma Polrew looks like a startled deer when I catch up with her, anxiety etched across her face, straight blonde hair shifting in the breeze.

'This is a surprise. Do your parents know you're here, Gemma?'

'They didn't see me leave. I often wait on the rocks, till Tom comes out to see me. We've depended on each other since our other mates left.'

'Why don't you sit down for a minute?'

'I can't stay long.' The girl perches on a boulder, body language so tense it looks like she's about to flee.

'The best way to help Tom is to share his secrets, Gemma.'

'I came here, the night before he went missing. He told me someone was following him.' A tear rolls down her cheek. 'If I'd made him report it he'd still be safe.'

'You had no idea the threat was serious. Don't blame yourself.'

Some of the tension slips from her face. 'Tom thought he was in danger because he knew too much.'

194

'About what?'

'He didn't say, and I can't think of anyone who hated him. He wasn't keen on Shane Trellon, but never said why. He got on fine with everyone else.'

'Let me walk you home.'

Panic crosses her face. 'My dad mustn't know I've been out, he'd be so angry.'

'I won't tell anyone, but you must stay indoors at night, until the island's safe again.'

She gives a rapid nod, and more details slip out as we head inland. Her father's bullying seems to be psychological, not physical, but it still makes me angry. His disapproval lasts for days, if she breaks the rules. He has always been ambitious for her future, and won't accept second best; the man doesn't listen when she pleads to stay on the island. I understand her friendship with Tom Heligan better as she speaks. Both teenagers are carrying heavy burdens, the boy overloaded with duty, the girl by the weight of her father's expectations. It must have been a relief to compare notes. I tell her to call me with any concerns when we come to a halt near her house, then watch her slim silhouette vanish through the gate, her bedroom light flicking on when she gets upstairs.

There's no sign of life when I reach the harbour. The ferry is moored for the night on the opposite shore. Shadow at my side, sniffing the air. I borrow one of the dinghies that floats by the jetty, the dog jumping onto the prow as I begin to row. The boat will be back on its mooring so early tomorrow, no one will notice the temporary theft. When I drag the oars through the water, discs of moonlight float on the current, while the lost boy fills my thoughts.

24

Tom can't tell whether it's day or night, no light penetrating his blindfold. His throat is dry with thirst, tongue sticking to the roof of his mouth, his body aching from hours of confinement. His jeans are saturated with his own urine, the stink of piss adding to other foul smells that taint the air. The one thing he knows for sure is that the sea is calm. The boat is motionless, no movement beyond the rise and fall of his own breathing. He flexes his hands, but the rope binding his wrists is so tight that his fingers are numb. Thoughts of his mother struggling alone keep filling his mind, but he bats them away. All he can do now is fight to stay alive.

The boy drifts into a fitful sleep. Nightmares flow through his imagination, until a sound startles him awake, the pain in his back sharper than before. He focuses his energy on identifying new sounds. The high-pitched whine of a mosquito is growing louder; it could be a dinghy's outboard motor. When the noise rises to a roar, it sounds close by, his hopes rocketing. A rescue party from Tresco must be coming to take him home. He raises his voice to yell out, but his throat is so parched, only a dull murmur emerges. There's a thud as the two boats rub together, then the heavy sound of feet landing on the deck overhead. When he calls out again, there's no reply; someone is standing directly above, ignoring his shouts for help. Tom's whole body tenses as darkness presses against him, the thick air making his lungs ache. Then he hears a woman's voice babbling out a long speech, her tone sour with anger. When he hears footsteps pounding towards him, he can only wait in silence for his next punishment.

25

Friday 15 May

I should have realised that my crime would be discovered. Living in a tiny community means that someone always has your back in times of need, but there's no hiding when you break the rules. Elinor Jago is standing on the quay when I row across the sound, just after 7 a.m. The postmistress watches me moor the borrowed dinghy with a hawk-like gaze. Her expression suggests that she would give me a tongue-lashing if I were a teenager, only my status as deputy chief of police protecting me from her wrath. It's a surprise when her face breaks into a smile.

'Feel free to use my dinghy any time, Ben. I was wondering where it had gone. Fancy a coffee before I open up?'

'You're a lifesaver, I never refuse caffeine.'

It's only a short walk up the quay to the post office, following in Elinor's brisk stride. She's dressed in her usual androgynous clothes: chinos, boat shoes and a crisp white shirt, her grey hair cropped shorter than mine. If the woman has had any romances recently, it's a well-kept secret. I remember her living with a girlfriend when I was in my teens, and the woman leaving Tresco a few years later, yet Elinor doesn't seem bitter about her solitude. She doesn't say a word as she unlocks the post office. The space is tiny but well-organised, from a display of special edition stamps to miniature scales for weighing parcels. She flicks on the kettle and measures instant coffee into mugs so clean they glitter, all of her movements precise. Even though her distress is obvious, I know from experience that it would be pointless to press an islander to talk until she's ready. My only option is to wait for her to open up.

'How's the investigation going, Ben?'

'Tom Heligan's disappearance has thrown us off track, but we're making progress.'

'Diane and Mike are two of my oldest friends. It's hard, watching them suffer.'

'I'm sure they appreciate your support.'

'At least they've got each other. It's Ivar I'm worried about; I keep popping round, but he never invites me in.'

'Everyone deals with loss differently. He's just focused on his daughter.'

She shakes her head. 'It's wrong to keep Frida away from everyone, she must be missing her grandparents terribly. Can you remind Ivar that I'm keen to help? You're one of the few people he's spoken to since Jude died, apart from the vicar.'

'I'm going there later today; I'll talk to him then.' Elinor gives a grateful nod. Knowing that she's a repository for local knowledge makes me throw out a question that's been playing on my mind.

'What do you know about the *Minerva*?'

She looks startled. 'I dreamed of finding it on swimming expeditions when I was a girl. A film crew scoured the seabed years ago, but if it exists, it must be very deep. It still comes into my head sometimes when I'm out on my boat.'

'Do you think Jude Trellon could have found it, on a diving trip?'

'Her dad's the one to ask. Mike's been deep-water swimming for forty years; if anyone knows the local wrecks, it's him.'

'That's good advice.'

'Has the *Minerva* got something to do with Jude's death?'

'Probably not, Elinor. I could be barking up the wrong tree.'

Her gaze is so thoughtful it's tempting to offload my theory that Jude and Tom may have discovered something that put them both in danger, including the mermaid amulet that ended her life, but I can't share details from the case, even with the island's most trustworthy residents. I'm about to leave when I spot some books on a shelf above the door. I scan the titles rapidly and see that she has a taste for tales and poems with a maritime twist: *Moby Dick*, *The Old Man and the Sea*, *The Rime of the Ancient Mariner*. When I spot a hardback entitled *Sea Shanties from the Isles of Scilly*, I pluck it from the shelf, then thumb through it rapidly, but fail to find either of the verses left at the crime scenes.

'That was my father's,' Elinor says quietly. 'Men used to sing shanties in the pub after a few pints when I was young. I haven't looked at it for years. I like a good novel on a winter evening, but I normally read on my tablet these days.'

It may be imaginary, but the postmistress seems to blush as she says goodbye, embarrassed that her intellectual pursuits have been exposed when she prides herself on practicality. It interests me that the killer shares her passion for old literature, but Elinor's innocence has been proved by saving Eddie's life. I doubt that she's strong enough to have overpowered him, and it's unlikely that a killer would haul a man into the sea, only to pluck him out again and call the police. Anyone could have downloaded the verses of local sea shanties from the internet.

There's no sign of Eddie when I drag Shadow over the threshold of the New Inn's attic. I scan the list of boat owners again, already aware that David Polrew owns a small yacht, fully equipped for diving trips. Sophie Browarth uses a restored fishing smack to travel between the islands to visit her patients, instead of relying on ferries, and the museum manager Jamie Petherton co-owns a converted lifeboat with his parents. When I scan the rest of the list, my frustration increases. The killer could have changed his modus operandi, abandoning Tom Heligan's body to the waves without a second thought.

It's mid-morning when I set off to see Denny Cardew again, to check the story Elinor told me yesterday afternoon. It's only a short walk to the fisherman's home in Dolphin Town, at the opposite end of the hamlet from Ivar's house, but his cottage is in better condition. The window frames gleam with fresh white paint, brass letter box shining as I walk through the front garden. Denny's smile takes time to unfold when he finally appears. His big frame is dressed in ancient jeans and an oil-stained shirt, as if he has just returned from today's fishing trip. His ancient black Labrador sniffs at my shoes, before waddling back to his basket.

'Coming in for a cuppa, Ben?'

'That would be great, thanks.' I could explain that Elinor has already given me coffee, but island hospitality dictates that every visitor must accept food and drink, even if they've just finished a three-course meal.

Denny's home is far tidier than his appearance as I follow him down the hall. The wooden floor is polished to a high shine, doilies protecting the hall table from stains, the chemical sweetness of air freshener lingering on the air. The fisherman hums quietly as he makes our drinks. Through the open doorway I can see into his lounge, which is shabby but pristine, dominated by a widescreen TV beside his wood-burning stove. He sets down mugs filled with tea that looks strong enough to strip the enamel from my teeth.

'This place is spotless, Denny. Been having a spring clean?'

'That's Sylvia's work. Cleaning's her favourite hobby.'

'Send her round to mine, will you? It could use an overhaul.'

'That won't happen any time soon. My wife hasn't left the island in months.'

'Never mind, the dust won't kill me.' My first gulp of tea sears the back of my throat. 'Did Sylvia's illness stop her working at the inn?'

'She fell sick with stress after losing her job last autumn.' His face clouds over. 'There was a misunderstanding with Will Dawlish about some missing money. We should have taken legal advice, but in the end she preferred to walk away. She's still bothered by the upset.'

'I don't want to pry, Denny. I just need to ask about Jude Trellon; I hear you had some heated words on Ruin Beach before she died.'

The fisherman's gaze falters. 'I was walking the dog and we got talking. Jude apologised for mouthing off at me the next day, but I wasn't bothered. It takes more than a few swear words to get me riled.'

'What triggered it?'

'She asked to borrow my boat, but it's not insured for third-party use, so I refused. Jude said she'd only need it for a few hours, and went on about some wreck dive she wanted to make. In the end I walked away.'

'Why didn't you tell me the other day?'

Denny's face grows sober. 'Jude was a complicated girl, but she didn't mean any harm. I'd almost forgotten about it. I've got bigger worries, to be honest; it's getting harder each year to make a living from the sea.'

'I'm sorry to hear that.'

'We'll get through it, me and Sylvia. We always do.'

The fisherman lapses into silence, but at least the conversation has confirmed that Jude Trellon believed she knew the location of a valuable wreck. She asked her father to lend her the *Fair Diane*, then Denny for his fishing boat, without success. The fisherman ploughs through a handful of biscuits while our talk continues, answering in monosyllables as I tease out details. Denny is reticent when I ask whether he had seen Jude lose her temper before, unwilling to bad-mouth another islander, even posthumously.

'Is Sylvia here, Denny? I haven't seen her in years.'

'She's outside, gardening,' he says quietly. 'My wife spends time in the garden, but that's her limit. Agoraphobia, the doctor calls it. It's played havoc with her nerves; she's afraid I'll drown every time I take the boat out.'

'That must be tough on both of you.'

'Harder for her.' He turns his back to dump our

mugs in the sink. 'She lives with it every day, not me. Go and say hello if you want. It might cheer her up.'

It's easy to spot his wife when I walk through the French doors. She still looks like the outgoing barmaid I remember from the New Inn: Sylvia's short hair is bleached to a brassy blonde, her electric-blue top standing out against the muted shades of her garden. She's kneeling beside a border, digging weeds from between tidy rows of geraniums with a trowel. The panic that crosses her face when she finally spots me is unexpected. She rises to her feet and backs away, as if she would prefer to bolt back inside the house. It takes time for her to gather enough confidence to muster a smile.

'Benesek Kitto, I heard you were back.' She plants a quick kiss on my cheek. Her round face is calm again, but her hand trembles when she touches my arm.

'I've been here nearly six months, Sylvia. It's good to see you again.'

'You too, I hate it when our best young people desert us for the mainland. I'm glad you're looking for who-ever killed Jude. It still doesn't feel real that she's gone.' She studies me again, her watery blue eyes assessing my face. 'You're so like your dad, it's uncanny.'

'So they say.'

'But not a fisherman, thank God. Keep your feet on dry land, won't you?'

'Don't worry, I never had the knack for it.' I scan the array of flowers blooming at her feet. 'You're performing miracles out here, but I'm sorry you've been ill. Denny says you're having a hard time.'

'It's a stupid disease.' She gives a fierce headshake. 'But it won't defeat me. I'll beat it in the end.'

We carry on talking a while longer, anxiety in her voice when she asks whether Tom Heligan has been found, so I do my best to reassure her. When I leave the house, the couple's eccentricities linger in my mind. Sylvia doesn't strike me as the type to cheat anyone out of money, but her easy-going confidence has disappeared. Denny seems to spend his spare time comfort eating, while his wife tries to dispel her fears by dressing in the brightest colours of the rainbow.

26

Shadow races ahead when we get back to the New Inn. He's barking at full volume as I round the corner, jaws snapping at someone cowering against the wall. Even from this distance I can identify Stephen Kinver's bulky figure. The boat owner looks like a different man on dry land; there's no sign of his brash confidence as he flattens himself against the bricks.

'Come here, Shadow,' I call out. The dog slinks towards me, teeth still bared. 'Sorry about that, he's got no manners.'

Kinver glowers at me, his eyes hidden by opaque sunglasses. 'That dog's a menace. It should be muzzled.'

'He's never bitten anyone yet, Mr Kinver. How can I help you?'

'I want to discuss your investigation.'

'Come inside, we can talk more easily there.'

Shadow is still agitated, so I tie him up in the hotel's yard, his barks pursuing us upstairs. Kinver appears tenser when we enter the incident room. His rigid body language seems at odds with his relaxed clothes; the hemline of his denim shorts drops past his knees, coupled with a bright green T-shirt, his sun-bleached curls in need of a comb.

'Is this the best accommodation you can find, Inspector? Your headquarters need an upgrade.'

'The inn's just a temporary base. Would you like to sit down?'

'I just want to know when we can leave.'

'Not yet, I'm afraid.'

His mouth sets in an ugly sneer. 'Our website depends on us doing new dives. We have to keep moving; the Florida Keys are our next destination.'

'The case is ongoing, so I can't—'

Before my sentence ends, Kinver rounds on me. 'Jude's death is nothing to do with us. We'd be halfway to Key West by now, if you hadn't hauled us back.' The words hiss from his mouth, dark eyes snapping with anger.

'This is a murder investigation, Mr Kinver. Everyone who spent time with Jude Trellon recently must stay here until her killer's found. And now that Tom Heligan's missing too, the case is even more urgent.' My stern tone has an immediate effect, his voice softening.

'Look, Inspector, if me and Lorraine waste any more time, our finances are screwed. Why not just search our boat then let us go? We've got nothing to hide.'

'I may do, Mr Kinver. In the meantime, stay within a three-mile radius.'

'How come you're taking so long to catch the killer?'

'Murderers are good at covering their tracks. It may surprise you to know that they don't enjoy being caught.'

His hard gaze levels with mine. 'What was Jude's bloke doing the night she died?'

'Sorry?'

'She seemed uptight about something. In cop shows it's always the boyfriend, isn't it?'

'I suggest you go back to your boat, Mr Kinver. I'll call you if another interview is required.'

He marches out, slamming the door for good measure. When I watch from the window, Shadow barks furiously as he passes, straining at his leash. The dog's behaviour proves he's smarter than he looks, able to spot an idiot from fifty metres. Kinver's thin veneer of charm evaporated during our conversation, angry statements spilling from his mouth; his reaction makes me wonder if some grievance could have made him sail his boat back to Piper's Hole after parting company with Jude, forcing his wife to cover for his violence. The only statement that rang true during his tirade was his claim that she seemed unhappy. Whether Kinver is guilty or innocent, finding out who killed Jude will lead me to the truth about Tom Heligan.

I remember the vicar telling me that he dived with Jude two days before she died. He might be able to cast more light on her state of mind, but there's no sign of Justin Bellamy when I reach the vicarage, so I walk to the church next door, even though the place carries too many memories. I've attended dozens of weddings and christenings there, but the service that stands out most clearly is my father's funeral when I was fourteen. It resonates in my mind as I enter the chancel; there was no coffin to mourn over after my father drowned, my mother's grief unending. The memory fuels my determination to find out what's happened to the Heligan boy, to give Linda peace of mind. Mahogany pews fill the nave, a commemorative list of lost mariners on the wall, my father's name inscribed halfway down.

'Looking for me?' The priest emerges from the vestry, stepping into a shaft of sunlight. He's wearing formal black vestments for once, the light settling on the puckered skin of his scar.

'Can I ask some questions about Jude?'

'Fire away, I'm glad to help.' He settles his lanky form on one of the pews.

'You were with her not long before she died. How would you describe her mental state?'

Bellamy replies slowly, as if he's hunting for details. 'She seemed a bit stressed, but soon relaxed out on the water. The dive seemed to lift her spirits.'

'Did Jude mention what was bothering her?'

'Only that her parents were having difficulties. I tried to draw her out, but she never said if their problems were financial or emotional.' His face clouds. 'Jude wanted more time with Ivar and Frida, but she had to work long hours most weeks. She seemed frustrated more than anything.' The priest's maimed face carries so much understanding, I doubt whether any human act could shock him. 'Did she mention anything about a shipwreck called the *Minerva*?'

'To be honest, I've forgotten most of our discussion. I was focused on our dive; I still struggle to get depth timings right.'

'But you'd remember if she'd talked about underwater treasure?'

'Who wouldn't? I loved watching Jacques Cousteau when I was a boy.' He glances down at his hands. 'We chatted about everyday stuff: places we'd travelled, jobs we'd done. We even shared details about our body art.'

'I can't imagine you in a tattoo parlour, Justin.'

'Don't judge a book by its cover. I spent five years in the army.'

'Is that where you got your scar?'

'I'll tell you about it sometime over a pint, but now I should get the church ready for Jude's memorial. Forgive me for being a bit keyed up. It's easy to say the wrong thing when the family are so vulnerable.'

'You always strike the right note. I'll see you at the service.'

Justin Bellamy gives a thoughtful smile as he rises to his feet. I leave him placing leaflets in each pew, preparing for the ceremony in a few hours' time.

My next port of call is Ivar Larsson's home at the end of the village, where Shadow is waiting on the doorstep. I swear the creature is clairvoyant, always certain where I'm going before I've decided, but his company will be useful today. Larsson is more likely to welcome me once he sees the dog. The man only opens the door by a fraction, his eyes round with suspicion, until he leans down to stroke Shadow's fur.

'I'd rather be alone, until after Jude's service.'

'I'm just checking you're both okay, Ivar. By the way, Elinor Jago says she's happy to help, if you need anything.'

'I hardly know her. I don't know why she keeps snooping around here.'

'She's just being supportive.' When I look at him again, his mouth is set in a rigid line. 'I'll walk with you to the church, if that's okay.'

He doesn't reply, his expression non-committal. Ivar seems to be coping with his loss by pulling up the drawbridge, reluctant to accept support from anyone. The state of his kitchen shows that he's struggling, an overflowing rubbish bin waiting to be emptied, the air tainted by sour milk, stains darkening the tiled floor. A new set of photos has appeared beside his fridge. They show the mother of his child in a low-backed top, expression relaxed as she tosses Frida into the air. My eyes linger on the blue-black illustrations that scroll down from the nape of her neck.

'I'm still trying to get a clear understanding of Jude.' The dog edges closer to Larsson, pressing his muzzle against his hand. 'Have you thought of anyone who behaved aggressively towards her since you met?'

He shakes his head. 'The threats were aimed at me, not Jude.'

'How do you mean?'

'Jamie Petherton hated my guts when we first got together. He made phone calls, then paid us late-night visits. It got worse after he found out she was pregnant. It felt like a hate campaign.'

'What did he do?'

'He waited till Jude went out to work, then put a brick through our window. The guy screamed abuse at me.' His voice falls to a murmur. 'Jude begged me not to report it, saying it was our fault he was suffering.'

It's hard to believe that the museum manager is capable of direct confrontation, but everyone has a snapping point. 'That was years ago, Ivar. Petherton's not the reason why you hate opening your front door.'

He lifts his chin in defiance. 'No one can make me leave this place before my work here finishes.'

'What did Jude tell you about Tom Heligan?'

'She liked having someone who shared her passion. Jude was happiest on the water, or under it. It thrilled her to find like-minded people.' Something about the way his gaze evades mine makes me certain he's hiding the truth.

'Did you know he had a crush on her?'

A narrow smile appears on his face. 'A lot of men felt that way about Jude. It doesn't surprise me.'

'Tom went missing from his home on Wednesday night.'

A wave of shock crosses his face. 'No one told me.'

'You want the boy found, don't you?'

'If I knew where he was, I'd say.'

My gaze lands on the photos of his girlfriend, the images printed on her body too small to interpret. 'What do Jude's tattoos mean?'

Ivar touches one of the photos with his fingertip. 'Every time she found a new wreck, she had it drawn on her body. It was one of the first things that attracted me to her when I saw her changing for a diving trip.' He rises to his feet suddenly. 'I need to get Frida ready for the memorial.'

I scan the pictures again after he leaves the room, focusing on one taken aboard the *Fair Diane* on a hot summer day. Jude Trellon is at the helm, her skin baked golden brown, standing beside Tom Heligan, her long hair draped over one shoulder. The image has caught the young mother and her teenaged friend in relaxed mood, grinning at the camera like nothing could ever go wrong.

27

The sounds have fallen silent again. Tom can no longer hear the outboard motor, or the woman's voice. Maybe she doesn't realise that he's trapped below decks, unable to move? The oxygen is dwindling, the air tasting of boat diesel and his own stink. The pain in his back is impossible to ignore. When his mind clears again, footsteps tap across the floor above his head. Tom's thoughts veer between panic and relief. His body stiffens at the sound of someone clattering down a ladder, then a door clicks open and shreds of light filter through his blindfold. It's too dark to make out where he's being held, but he can see a shadow rushing closer.

'Who's there? Help me, please.' His words emerge as a dull croak.

A hand pulls his head backwards, and liquid floods his mouth, too fast to swallow. He manages to gulp down some water, before dry bread is crammed between his lips. Tom can hear laboured breathing as someone stands over him, tightening the ropes around his ankles.

'Why are you keeping me here?'

'I'm not meant to do this, but I can't let you starve.' The woman's voice is a dull monotone, as if she's trying to disguise it. 'He's angry that Jude stole from him. If you tell the truth, he'll let you go. If you don't, he'll kill you tomorrow, or the day after.'

Shadows cross Tom's blindfold, followed by a searing flash of light, then the door clicks shut and silence settles over his world again. Moments later he hears the outboard motor roar into the distance. The woman that came to feed him is leaving in a hurry, his body tenses with the knowledge that she may not return. He might be left to rot in this filthy place, without ever seeing daylight again.

28

Half an hour passes before Ivar and Frida are ready for
the memorial service. Ivar's suit is a sombre grey, but
Frida wears a scarlet party dress. The child's eyes are
huge and unfocused when she gazes up at me, as if she's
unable to fathom so much adult confusion. It strikes
me as cruel that the Trellon family have left the pair to
walk to the memorial service alone.

Ivar doesn't speak as we cover the short distance
from his house to the church. The man's hand is clutching his daughter's so tightly, his knuckles are turning
white. I can tell it's more than a normal grief reaction,
the man is afraid of something, but he's unwilling to
share his secrets. The only way to make him open up
will be to spend more time in his company, until he
lowers his guard.

Justin Bellamy is waiting by the door of the church.
The priest welcomes Ivar warmly, before crouching
down to speak to Frida, then ushering us inside. The
air smells different since I came here a few hours ago,

incense and the sickly sweetness of cut flowers catching the back of my throat. The nave is packed with families from Tresco, Bryher and St Mary's, keen to support Jude Trellon's family, even though her body can't be buried until the case is closed. People's faces contain judgement as well as sympathy when they see Ivar arrive. Some still seem to view him as an outsider who has failed to adapt to island ways. My suspicions are confirmed when we reach the front of the church. Mike, Diane and Shane are huddled together, the last seat on their pew occupied by Jamie Petherton. An outsider would assume that he was the grieving boyfriend, his face blank with misery, dressed in an elegant black suit. We sit across the aisle from Jude's family as the service starts.

The vicar's face is pale as he welcomes us all to the service, his voice cracking with distress. The strain of losing a young, charismatic member of this tiny community seems to be affecting everyone deeply. When I glance across at the Trellons, Mike's eyes are fixed on the stained-glass window above the altar, and Diane's face is buried in a tissue, while her son clasps her hand.

The highlight of the ceremony is when Zoe walks to the front of the church. Her great singing voice is a blessing and a curse in such a small place, with islanders begging her to perform at every wedding, anniversary party and funeral. She looks stunning as usual, a gorgeous, Amazonian blonde, showing no sign of stage fright. When she begins to sing 'Beyond the Sea', her unaccompanied voice soars to the rafters. Zoe's version of the old tune is so loaded with emotion, people are dabbing their eyes before the first verse finishes. My old friend is a grown woman now, not the skinny kid I once chased across the sand, and she has a gift that deserves to be shared more widely. Back then I could second-guess her moods, but now she leaves me baffled. I'm still reeling from the power of her rendition as the song ends, a murmur of appreciation rippling through the congregation.

Diane stands up to deliver her eulogy once the last note fades. She's swaying on her feet, as if a hard wind is blowing through the aisles.

'My daughter wasn't the easiest woman in the world, but easiness is overrated. Jude loved challenges, and she was never afraid. She was built for the sea, not the land – a genuine free spirit. She didn't deserve to die at twenty-nine.' Diane's expression changes in an instant, from grief to accusation as she surveys the crowd. 'One of you must know who killed Jude. I'm begging you to tell someone, or send a letter. We can't move on until we know.' She manages to sit down again before lapsing back into tears.

The rest of the ceremony passes without incident. The vicar's speech reminds me that Jude packed a lot into her three decades; competing internationally in free-diving competitions, before settling down. I glance at Ivar while the details of his partner's life unfold. Only a skilled observer could tell that he's suffering as badly as Diane, even though his face is impassive. His hands are braced in his lap, like a mountaineer clutching a guide rope. Frida seems oblivious to her father's sadness, bouncing a painted wooden boat on her knee, as if it's battling a fierce storm.

I stand in the churchyard when the service ends. The cemetery is packed with gravestones, dating back 200 years, names erased long ago by the hard rain that falls each winter. I know from years of undercover work that the best way to avoid attracting attention is to blend into the background, so I lean against the drystone wall that encloses the churchyard. The killer is likely to be among the hundred people who have spent the last hour cooped up inside. Murderers love returning to the scene of their crime, to remember the power of sacrificing someone's life, and see the relatives' devastation, but no one is behaving suspiciously today. Diane and Ivar are making awkward conversation, while Frida plays with two other kids among the gravestones, clearly thrilled to be outdoors. Ten metres away, Mike Trellon is comforting his daughter's best friend, Sophie Browarth, the nurse's face pressed against his shoulder. No one would know that she's having an affair with the victim's brother, because Shane is deep in conversation with Will Dawlish. They stand with their heads down, as if grief is an invisible burden weighing on their backs. The only person wearing a smile is Zoe. She's chatting to one of the waitresses from the New Inn, holding the woman's baby in her arms, oblivious to my stare. In the old days, she claimed that parenthood was a fool's game, but her opinion seems to be changing. I scan people's faces until the crowd disperses, the vicar shaking his parishioners' hands as they leave the churchyard.

I'm about to return to the incident room when DCI Madron steps into my path. He's dressed in full uniform, silver stars on his epaulettes, his cap glittering with brocade. The man's eyes are level with my chest, but his crisp tone is intended to remind me who's in command.

'Good to see you dressed appropriately for once, Kitto. You should wear that suit to your review meeting. Have you got time to update me on the case?'

'Of course, sir.'

'Walk with me to the harbour. The deputy commissioner's coming over to St Mary's for a briefing; I want to tell him about your progress.'

The jetty is deserted when we reach the harbour. The islanders will stay at home until everyone regroups for Jude Trellon's wake tonight at the inn, but her death is a less pressing concern than the missing boy. I've still got a chance of returning him to his mother alive. Madron's grey eyes assess me cautiously as I explain my theory that someone targeted both victims for their knowledge of the sea. The *Minerva* is a local obsession, a fabled ship loaded with cargo that could make a diver rich overnight. Dr Polrew seemed certain that the mermaid amulet is of Roman origin, but I need Jamie Petherton to identify the coin found in Jude's kitbag, and the second figurine from Tom Heligan's loft. The way her body was pinned to the rocks makes me assume that the boy is still alive: if the killer follows the same MO, he'll be returned straight into our hands. Once I fall silent, Madron surprises me with a nod of assent.

'Someone's treating the sea like a roulette wheel, gambling their lives on gaining big rewards.' His face is sober when he turns to me again. 'Keep yourself safe and contact me if you need more officers, Kitto. I can request them from the mainland.'

'Thanks, sir, I'll let you know.'

The DCI gives a nod of dismissal, then walks away, leaving me in shock. For the first time in recorded history, the man listened without prejudice, but there's no point in accepting his offer. A sudden influx of strangers would send the island into lockdown. The police launch disappears into the distance, returning Madron to the desk-bound duties he loves.

I take a slow walk from Dolphin Town to Jamie Petherton's house at the foot of Vane Hill, passing through fields grazed short by generations of sheep. The creatures bleat out protests at my arrival, short tails bouncing as they race to the far side of the field. It's lucky that Shadow is nowhere in sight. One of his favourite pastimes is chasing vulnerable animals while barking at ten decibels. The sky is darkening by the time I approach Petherton's house. It looks like a modern version of a forester's cabin; the two-storey building is insulated with rough-hewn timber, its peaked roof covered with solar panels, half a dozen water butts positioned to collect rain from its gutters. The building looks like it would tick all the boxes in the Green Party's housing manifesto, designed to conserve every natural resource.

Petherton gapes at me when I ring the bell, as if he's trying to decide whether to slam the door in my face. The museum manager is still dressed in the clothes he wore to the memorial: his well-cut suit must have cost him a month's wages, but his face looks thinner than before, ravaged by deep shadows. It seems fitting that one of his eyes is brown, the other blue. His odd gaze makes him look like a changeling, not fully equipped for either land or sea.

'Can I come in please, Jamie? I need a favour.'

'Of course, I'll do my best to help.' The man's courtesy seems to cause him discomfort, his lips forming a narrow smile.

The woodman theme carries on inside Petherton's home. The hall floor is made from scaffold boards planed to a smooth finish; pieces of tie-dyed fabric adorn the walls, and even the lampshades look homemade. Jamie catches me eying the decor as we walk deeper into the house.

'Quite something, isn't it? This is my parents' section of the house; they met at Glastonbury forty years ago, then came here to run a smallholding and live off-grid.'

'Did they achieve their dream?'

'They missed life's luxuries after six months.' He

gives an awkward laugh. 'Dad worked as an account-
ant on St Mary's and Mum wrote children's books.
They just keep a few chickens in the garden these days.'

'Your parents aren't at home?'

'They're travelling round India, to celebrate my
father's retirement. This is my part of the property.'

The man's living room contains two large sofas and
a direct view of Vane Hill, but it's the range of decora-
tive items that catches my eye. Every wall is lined with
shelves to accommodate a vast array of possessions, as
if the man is creating another museum inside his home.
The place is packed to the ceiling with collectibles,
from *Star Wars* figures and Matchbox racing cars to
leather-bound books. I ignore the clutter and place the
evidence bags on his table.

'Can you identify these for me, Jamie?'

He stares at the objects inside their plastic wrapping.
'A professional antiquarian could give you more detail.'

'You know more about history than most people.
Why not just take a look?'

Petherton collects a magnifying glass from a cabinet,
then hunches over the dining table to study the coin.
He inspects the figurine with the same close attention,
shifting it to examine every angle.

'The coin's Roman, from the sixth century, stamped
with the profile of Emperor Anastasius. It must have come
from the sea, because the copper's so heavily oxidised.'

'How do you know all this?'

'Roman society has always fascinated me. They were

barbaric, of course, but some of their systems were more progressive than ours.'

'What about the sculpture?'

'It's the sea god, Neptune. It was cast from bronze, with gold detail added later, made for someone of high status.' His face relaxes as he holds it up to the light. 'The verdigris doesn't spoil its beauty. Roman artists were the first to observe the human form so accurately. I'd say it was the same age as the coin, but you'd need expert confirmation. It's a pity the museum doesn't own anything this fine.'

Petherton's reaction differs from Dr Polrew's. He seems more interested in the aesthetics of each piece than where they were found.

'What if I told you they came from a local wreck?'

'That's not possible. Only one Roman vessel went down near here, and no trace of it has ever been found.'

'Jude discovered it before she died.'

'The *Minerva*?' Petherton's eyelids flutter rapidly. 'How do you know?'

'I think she told the wrong person, and got into trouble.' The man's thin form sways towards me, making me step forwards to help him into a chair. 'Stay there, Jamie. I'll get you a glass of water.'

Petherton is still recovering when I return. 'Jude mattered a great deal to you, didn't she, Jamie?'

'More than I realised,' he murmurs. 'I tried to forget her, but it's impossible in a place like this. She was everywhere I looked.'

'Is it true that you put a brick through her window?'

'I'm not ashamed.' His uneven gaze suddenly comes back into focus. 'We'd still be together if Ivar had left us alone. He has to answer for his own actions.'

The suppressed anger in his voice makes me certain he could have flipped and harmed his ex-girlfriend, despite his mild manners. But I can't accuse him of using his parents' boat to attack her in Piper's Hole without evidence. He has little information to offer when I ask which islander might be so obsessed by finding the *Minerva* that Jude's discovery would put her in danger. By the time I leave, he's reverting to type. There's a lengthy pause before he hands back the coin and figurine, as if relinquishing them causes him physical pain.

29

The New Inn is filling when I return, Shadow keeping watch over the crowd gathering for Jude Trellon's wake. I ignore his protests and leave him tied up in the yard. The Trellons have enough challenges to face without a boisterous dog running amok. There's no sign of Will Dawlish inside; a young bartender stands in his place, pulling pints at a furious rate. The landlord may be absent but his bar has been prepared for a lavish party. The victim's attractive face grins down from a poster-sized photo on the wall, her golden eyes observing the mourners through a cloud of balloons suspended from the ceiling. When I was a child, I never understood why parties were thrown for every birth and death, but it makes better sense now. The end of a life well-lived deserves celebration, but Jude Trellon's murder wiped out her existence decades too soon. It feels wrong to buy drinks for myself and Eddie while Tom Heligan is still missing, but most of the islanders will spend their evening here; if we stay vigilant, the killer may slip up and reveal themselves.

When I turn round again, the bar is packed to capacity, tables and chairs pushed back to the walls. One of the advantages of being the tallest man in any room is the ability to see every face in a crowd, my eyes skimming the new arrivals. Families have travelled from neighbouring islands to raise a glass in the victim's honour, but some are missing from the Tresco community. Sophie Browarth and Shane Trellon haven't arrived yet – probably comforting each other in secret, before arriving separately. Jamie Petherton has stayed at home after our chat, along with the Polrew family, but the dead woman's parents stand by the entrance welcoming guests. People take it in turns to offer sympathy, or press drinks into their hands, but Ivar Larsson is keeping a low profile. I can see Elinor Jago making intense conversation with my deputy on the far side of the room. The postmistress offers me a distracted nod before disappearing into the crowd when I arrive with Eddie's beer. He seems to be recovering from his attack, but the combative look on his face is still in evidence, alongside his black eye. Despite his slight build, he looks ready to beat the killer to a pulp if he should ever cross his path.

'Thanks for the rescue,' he murmurs. 'Elinor was pumping me for information.'

'People are concerned, that's all.'

'I couldn't give her much reassurance.' Frustration sours his tone of voice. 'The forensics lab called earlier to say it could be days before we get results back on

Shane's computer and Tom Heligan's phone. Their senior officer's just resigned and they're short-staffed.'

'Just what we need, but we'll manage somehow. Finish your drink then go home to Michelle.'

He ignores my instructions. 'What will Linda Heligan do if we can't find her son?'

'I don't normally have to tell you to stay positive, Eddie.'

'Sorry, boss, the attack's left me jangled. Michelle's been nagging me to look for a safer job now the baby's coming. Her dad's got a holiday company on the mainland.'

'Would that suit you?'

He shakes his head. 'I'd be bored rigid renting out caravans.'

'Don't even think about resigning. You're my right-hand man.'

The tense set of his shoulders relaxes slightly as someone turns up the music. Otis Redding's 'Sitting on the Dock of the Bay' echoes from the speakers, followed by more vintage Motown ballads. Mike and Diane Trellon rise to their feet to honour an island tradition. They dance together in the centre of the floor, swaying in a slow circle, managing to smile at the crowd. There's a thunder of applause when the song ends, everyone determined to send their daughter off with a riotous celebration.

Ivar is sitting by the door, the man's face austere while Denny Cardew offers words of comfort. Frida is playing with her friends nearby, showing no sign of distress. I get the sense that she may need a counsellor to help her understand that her mother won't return, but for now Frida's innocence is shielding her from the pain of losing Jude.

The evening passes in a flurry of speeches and songs, but I make sure to stay sober. Some of the guests have been drinking hard, talking to all and sundry, confidence raised by an overflow of booze. The party has been going for several hours before I catch sight of Shane and Sophie standing in separate corners of the room. It's 11 p.m. when Zoe takes to the floor with Justin Bellamy, and I have to ignore a stab of envy that lasts until she appears at my side.

'Dance with me, quick, before Justin asks me again.'

'Why? You'd make a great vicar's wife.'

She grabs my hand. 'One dance, big man. Is that too much to ask?'

'Go on then, if you insist.'

The truth is, it's no hardship to feel those hourglass curves pressed against me. It takes effort to keep my attention trained on the room, watching the crowd for any disturbance that could reveal the killer's identity.

'There's something weird about Justin,' Zoe whispers. 'It's like he's going through the motions, but there's nothing inside.'

'He seems okay to me. Don't break his heart, will you?'

Over the top of her head I catch sight of the vicar

heading for the exit. I could tell Zoe that the man she's evading has gone home, but she might cut our dance short, and her cool hand on the back of my neck feels more intoxicating than any amount of alcohol. The music ends too soon. Now the room is emptying, Zoe dashes away to catch the last ferry back to Bryher. It doesn't surprise me that Diane and Mike look the worse for wear, after coping with their daughter's wake with so much dignity. Mike's speech is slurred when he thanks the bar staff for their work. Ivar is sitting at a corner table, with Frida curled up asleep at his side. Diane's eyes are glistening as she reaches down to embrace him.

'Jude would want us to get on better, for Frida's sake, wouldn't she?'

Larsson lets his head rest on the woman's shoulder for a moment, the pair of them united for once. I stand back to let the family say their goodbyes, until just Ivar and Frida remain in the room. The man's face only brightens when he receives an ecstatic greeting from Shadow outside. Frida hums quietly to herself as I accompany them through Dolphin Town, but Ivar says little on the short journey, as if the effort of receiving so much sympathy has drained him of conversation. His relief is obvious when his cottage appears at the end of the hamlet, his footsteps quickening. But when we approach, it's clear that something's wrong: the front door is hanging open. Ivar runs towards his home before I can stop him.

'Stay back,' I call out. 'Look after Frida while I check it's safe.'

He releases a stream of Swedish curses, but waits by the gate as I approach the building, with Shadow's loud bark echoing down the path. The kitchen window has been smashed, shattered glass pooling on the ground outside. When I return to the front door, the lights don't work, so I grab a torch from the hall table to assess the damage. The laptop computer that usually sits on Ivar's kitchen table is missing, a china cup shattered on the floor, coffee splashed across the tiles. It looks like someone has taken a strategic approach, only breaking things in their haste to escape. Drawers hang open, papers littered across the floor, but there appears to be no structural damage. Someone knew what they wanted, and disabling the lights was a clever touch. If Ivar had returned early, darkness would have given the intruder a chance to flee. I check the first floor, but whoever broke in probably left a long time ago. Every cupboard and chest of drawers has been searched, clothes dumped on the floor and books pulled from shelves. Frustration sets in as I show Ivar the damage downstairs. Most of the islanders attended the party, but several arrived late or left early, giving them time to break into the place while everyone else was busy. I use my torch to look inside the fuse box at the top of the stairs, light returning when I flick a few switches. The killer had the presence of mind to cut off the power supply, rather than smashing light bulbs, suggesting a calm, methodical approach.

My anger increases when I watch Ivar surveying the mess in silence, while his daughter clings to his hand. The child is my biggest concern; she's been through enough trauma already, her eyes wide with shock.

'Why not put Frida to bed, Ivar? Her room's untouched. I'll wait for you down here.'

Larsson frowns at me but takes the child upstairs without arguing. I hear him singing a quiet Swedish lullaby to his daughter as I check the property again, trying to work out which islander would be cruel enough to ransack a grieving man's home during his girlfriend's wake. I could go door to door, hunting for the perpetrator, but I'm certain they're smart enough to cover their tracks. Whoever broke in will have buried the missing computer by now, or thrown it into a rock pool. I call the forensics lab on the mainland, leaving a voice message to request a visit, to check for clues that are invisible to the naked eye. The killer may have stayed true to form and worn gloves when he searched the place, but there's a chance he's left a traceable DNA imprint.

Larsson looks drained when he returns downstairs, and I can tell it's the wrong time to quiz him about potential suspects. Instead we stick to practicalities and make an inventory of missing items. The thief has taken his laptop, which Jude only used occasionally, and a few photographs from her diving expeditions. The intruder probably came here looking for information about the *Minerva*, but couldn't resist pocketing some mementoes. Ivar answers my questions in slow mono-syllables, and I sense that he's still guarding a vital piece of information, but he's immune to questions.

'You should go home,' he says in a measured voice. 'Thanks for helping us.'

'I'm staying over, Shadow can keep guard outside. It's not safe for you and Frida to be here alone.'

'There's no need. I don't want her routine upset.'

I stare at him. 'Are you too proud to accept help from anyone?'

There's an edge of fury in his voice when he replies. 'It's so easy for you, isn't it? You were born here and people trust you. I've had nothing but suspicion since I arrived. Jude's family and the whole community wanted me to leave.'

'Is that what happened when you were eighteen?'

'You know about my car accident, do you?' His pale eyes lose focus as he drops onto a chair. 'If I'd gone to prison for dangerous driving, people might have for-given me, but my parents fought to keep me out of jail. Villagers scrawled graffiti on our door and sent us hate mail. It taught me that the only person you can rely on is yourself. The people here are no different to the ones I left behind.'

'If you meet the islanders halfway, they'll accept you.' But there's a grain of truth in what he says. The slow pace of life here makes some people reluctant to adapt. 'I'll go early tomorrow, but for now I'm staying. It's my job to keep you both safe.'

There's a pause before he replies. 'As you wish.'

Ivar brings me a pillow and blankets, then disappears upstairs. The man seems to have buried his feelings so deep, they're impossible to access. I stand by the window, surveying the darkness outside. There are no stars tonight, the moon a haze of brightness behind a veil of clouds. In the dim light I can trace the fields rolling down to Ruin Beach. The Kinvers' boat is lit up brightly in the distance, even though it's the middle of the night. It would have been easy for them to row ashore while the islanders were at the inn, mourning the loss of a woman they'd recently employed. The couple had good reason to want access to Trellon's computer, for information about hidden wrecks. I'm still watching the light shifting over the waves when a sound drifts from upstairs: a man's muffled sobbing, low and grating. Larsson survived his girlfriend's memorial service and wake without shedding a tear, only releasing his sadness in the privacy of his own home. The sound continues long after I lie down and wait for sleep to come.

30

Saturday 16 May

Tom's body flinches when early morning light floods the hold. Brightness seeps through the rough fabric of his blindfold, but all he can hear are waves striking the side of the vessel, and the man tutting to himself.

'You need a shower, boy,' the voice hisses. 'This one will be heavier than normal. You won't forget it in a hurry.'

Fingers tighten around Tom's shins, then without warning he's hauled across the plastic floor. The rapid movement makes the pain in his back throb harder, but he tries not to yell. Someone jerks up his shirt, hands rough as he's stripped bare, then icy liquid floods across his chest. Suddenly a blast of water hits his face so hard, his head jerks backwards. When his airways clear, he releases a scream, until another vicious jet of water silences him again and it's impossible to breathe. The punishment seems to last forever. Tom is left naked and shuddering on the floor, his limbs bound so tightly, sores are forming on his skin. Drowning is the death he fears most, despite his love of the sea. Now a woman's soft murmur reaches him, begging the man to stop, until he tells her to shut up.

'Not very brave, are you, boy?' the man's breath whispers across his face. 'You were squealing like a baby.' There's something fake about his voice, his accent hard to identify.

'Let me go, please. My mum's got no one else.'

'You should have thought of that before, shouldn't you? Give me what I need and you can go.'

'What do you want?'

'The truth.' The man releases a strangulated laugh. 'Jude told you everything, didn't she? The location of the wreck, the depth, and what she found there. I saw her at Piper's Hole, hiding things for others to find.'

'I don't understand.'

The hard jet of liquid strikes Tom's face again, filling his nostrils and mouth until he almost blacks out. When the hose is finally switched off, water spews from his lips as he chokes for breath.

'Stop, please, I'm begging you.'

'Don't treat me like a fool then.'

Before Tom can reply, rough hands drag him across the wet floor again, his limbs battering against obstacles, until he's thrown back into the hold.

31

I wake up, dazed, at 6 a.m. The mountainous landscapes on the wall remind me that I spent the night at
Ivar Larsson's house, his hard sofa leaving a crick in my
neck. Daylight reveals that last night's intruder did a
thorough job of turning the place over. Papers still litter
the floor, some of the pictures hanging askew on the
walls, as if the intruder was searching for a concealed
safe. An unexpected sound makes me swing round
suddenly. Frida has appeared in the doorway, golden-
brown eyes observing my every move. She seems more
interested in her new housemate than the fact that her
home has been ransacked. Her pale-blue pyjamas look
like hand-me-downs from a much larger child, the toy
she played with at the funeral still clutched in her hand.
I haven't had much experience with kids, apart from
occasional visits from my niece, but something about
the girl cuts me to the quick when she fixes me with a
curious stare.

'Do you like it?' She holds out the painted boat.

'It's beautiful. Did your dad make that for you?'

She shakes her head slowly. 'Mummy did. She painted it too.'

When Frida presses the boat into the palm of my hand, it's obvious how much care has gone into each detail. It's a minute replica of an old-fashioned fishing smack, made of balsa wood. Jude must have spent hours gluing the pieces together, which offers a new insight into her character – people say she was impulsive and quick-tempered, but it would have taken patience to craft something so delicate. The girl's smile flares into life when I return her toy.

'Can I have a drink?' she asks.

'Why not ask your dad, sweetheart?'

'He's asleep.' Her direct request won't allow for a refusal, so I reach for my shirt and follow the kid into the kitchen in my boxer shorts, aware that Madron would be appalled by the intimacy of the situation. When I pass her a tumbler of apple juice, she sits on a low bench by the table, legs swinging as she gulps noisily from the glass. I stay in the kitchen to check the tumbler doesn't slip from her hands, her gaze tracking me as I make myself coffee.

'Do you go in the sea every day, like my mum?' she asks.

'Not that often. Most days I'm too busy.'

'She finds things there, to bring home for daddy.'

I crouch down beside her, keeping my smile in place. 'It's still really early. I think you should go back upstairs and play with your toys, until your dad wakes up.'

The kid takes a moment to digest my suggestion, then flits away. I'm left holding her empty glass, aware that I'm out of my depth. Frida is nothing like my exuberant niece; her intense gaze seems to assess the world in forensic detail. Before long she'll be asking questions about her mum's death that her father will struggle to answer, unless I discover the truth.

Larsson still looks pale when he comes downstairs at seven thirty. He hardly speaks as he concentrates on spooning cornflakes into Frida's mouth, while the girl plays with Lego on the tabletop. My attitude towards the man has shifted in the days since I told him of his girlfriend's death. It's growing harder to believe that he could have killed Jude in a fit of passion, when his entire focus seems to be trained on protecting his daughter. Frida has accepted my presence already, humming to herself when the meal ends, then slipping outside to play with Shadow.

'She's a great kid,' I comment. 'It's obvious she's pretty smart.'

Ivar stands by the kitchen window, watching his child play in a small sandpit. 'I hope she'll be a scientist like me, but maybe she'll be athletic like Jude ...' his voice tails into silence.

'Who do you think broke into your house, Ivar?'

He swings round to face me. 'It's obvious, isn't it?'

'How do you mean?'

'Petherton, of course. He's still bitter after all this time.'

'The intruder was looking for something specific. The break-in could be related to Jude's death.'

'Check his place today. I'm telling you, the man's unbalanced.' Ivar's features are hard with certainty.

'I'll look at all the islanders' alibis, but don't spend time alone. Jude's killer may have come here looking for information. I want you to take Frida to Mike and Diane's.'

'We're not being driven out of our home.'

'Then an officer will have to guard your house.'

He shakes his head firmly. 'Frida doesn't need any more strangers coming here, and whoever did it has had their fun. A year of my research was stored on that computer; thank God I backed it up.'

'You're turning down police protection?'

'Leave your dog with us. He'll guard the place well enough.'

'Call me later this morning, when you've checked every room. Let me know if anything else is missing.'

Larsson gives a grudging nod, his manner as tense as a steel trap. My plan to win his trust by spending more time in his company seems to be having little effect, which makes me wonder if his secret is more sinister than I thought. He might be concealing something that could land him in jail. His relief is palpable when I leave the home he protects so fiercely, but Shadow seems thrilled with the new arrangement. The creature

doesn't even blink when I tell him to stay, tongue lolling, not a care in the world as he fetches a tennis ball
Frida has thrown for him.

I call Eddie on my way to see Jamie Petherton again,
informing him of last night's break-in. His voice is disbelieving when he hears that another crime has been
committed in a place that has been law-abiding for
decades. I ask him to follow up my call to forensics,
then walk towards Vane Hill. At 9 a.m. the island is
going about its business as normal, tourists strolling
along inland paths towards the Abbey Gardens, and
a few locals waiting for the ferry to transport them to
St Mary's. The rest of the island's permanent population will be at work already at the inn, or the Abbey
Gardens. The sun is warming the back of my neck
when I return to Jamie Petherton's eco-house, and I'm
sweltering in yesterday's charcoal-grey suit. When I rap
on his door again, he doesn't answer and I assume that
he's at the museum already. I can see evidence that he
spent last night alone through his lounge window: a
single wine glass sitting on his coffee table, waiting to
be washed up. It's only when I approach the back door
that the smell of burned plastic reaches me. The odour
is emanating from a black bin bag, half concealed by
a rose bush. My eyes blink wider when I look inside,
a reek of chemicals rushing out as the bag spills open.
It contains the burned-out remains of a laptop, the
keyboard melted to a congealed lump of plastic, and
it doesn't take a genius to see that Larsson may have

been right about the museum manager breaking into his home, but the reason for his vandalism is harder to understand. The break-in must have been planned carefully. Setting light to the computer would have destroyed fingerprint evidence, but what information was he so desperate to find, and how would he have known the password? I seal the bag shut again, suppressing my disappointment. If Petherton's act was a bid to destroy Ivar's research, as vengeance for a romance that ended years ago, it may have no connection with Jude's death.

32

I place the remains of Larsson's computer on the table at the incident room.

'We need a formal interview with Jamie Petherton today,' I tell Eddie.

My deputy screws up his face at the chemical stink rising from the bag. 'One of the barmaids downstairs told me something about him last night. Apparently he made another girl's life a misery before Jude. The relationship ended badly, but he wouldn't let go. After months of phone calls and accusations, she moved to the mainland.'

'To escape him?'

'Most people would, if some nutter kept hassling them,' he replies.

'He doesn't seem that unstable now, but it could be an act. We need to know his exact movements.'

It takes time to track Petherton down. The museum's answer machine informs me that the place is closed. When he finally answers his mobile, the man claims to be at a meeting in St Mary's, his voice bemused when I ask him to report to the police station. Eddie and I use the force's smallest launch to travel there, the powerboat scudding across shallow waves until we enter Hugh Town harbour, where kids are learning to crew lugsail dinghies, the fair weather tempting people outdoors. One of the boats clips past at a hectic pace, almost causing a collision as we steer towards the jetty, the kids on board hooting with laughter. It's a reminder that most of the population are enjoying a relaxed Saturday, while Eddie and I drive ourselves mad hunting for clues. The boats make an appealing picture as I step onto dry land, dozens of pastel-coloured sails catching the breeze as they drift on the tide.

Lawrie Deane looks relaxed for once when we reach police headquarters. His grievances about my senior position seem to have been forgotten while he completes admin tasks on his computer. The sergeant's expression grows taciturn again when he advises me that Madron's office is available for the interview. The DCI's room is as orderly as the man's uniform, his old-fashioned desk polished to a high shine, ranks of colour-coded folders lining his walls in alphabetical sequence. Jamie Petherton doesn't seem perturbed when he arrives a few minutes later. His funereal suit has been replaced by a grey T-shirt, jeans and trainers, but his expression is sombre when his mismatched eyes meet mine. The man looks surprised when I describe the break-in at Larsson's house last night.

'I'm just checking details at this stage, Jamie,' I explain. 'Can you tell us how you spent last night?'

'I had a quiet evening, watching a DVD and drinking a few glasses of wine.'

'Why didn't you attend the wake?'

'Ivar's not my biggest fan. I didn't want to make Jude's family uncomfortable.' His gaze is so calm, either he's completely innocent or an accomplished actor. 'Why would I go to his house while he was out?'

'You've admitted to having strong feelings for Jude, and you broke in once before, didn't you?'

He looks at me in disbelief. 'That was years ago, for a specific reason.'

'If you could do it then, why not now?'

'Jude and I had just split up; I was at breaking point. Plenty of people would react the same.'

'You harassed another ex-girlfriend for months, didn't you?'

'Are you accusing me because I made mistakes in the past? I've never harmed anyone in my life.' The man's tone is incredulous, not angry.

'The remains of a laptop computer were found outside your house earlier this morning.'

'Anyone could have left it there.' Petherton's body language is tense while he struggles to remain polite. 'It was nothing to do with me. Now, I need to get back to the museum; I'm running late for a meeting with the governors.'

He rises to his feet, but I advise him to stay until

the interview ends. The man retreats into a resentful silence as his fingerprints are taken. Once the formalities are over, Petherton exits the building at a rapid pace. He didn't deny the tension between him and Ivar Larsson, but no one will be able to confirm that he remained at home last night, because his neighbours were at the wake. Even if he did break into Larsson's property, it could have been a simple act of spite. Sergeant Deane gives me a scathing look when we finally leave the station, as if I make a habit of pursuing innocent citizens for my own enjoyment.

The sky is a pallid blue when Eddie and I return to Tresco, a crisp breeze coming off the water, but my thoughts refuse to clear. I'm certain that someone's playing me. One of the islanders knows about the ill feeling between the two men, and they're capitalising on it to buy themselves time.

I'm still tense when I get back to the New Inn alone by mid-morning, after sending Eddie off on house-to-house enquiries about the break-in; it feels like the investigation is veering from one false lead to the next, and I'm powerless to get it back on track. Will Dawlish is in his usual position behind the bar, polishing wine glasses. The innkeeper raises his hand in greeting, but the look on his face is subdued.

'Is something wrong, Will?'

'Not really. I'll be fine once the lunchtime crowd arrives.'

'You were missed at the party last night. It's not like

you to take a night off.' I pull up a stool at the bar.

'I couldn't face another wake, to be honest. You'd laugh if you knew how I spent the day.'

'Try me.'

His gaze fixes on the window. 'Anna and I bought a boat last summer. She loved to swim and dive; being on the water was a passion for her. I've hardly used it since I lost her, but yesterday I went for a sail.'

'You didn't capsize?'

'I didn't even have to call the coastguard. It felt good to turn the engine off and drift.' When he looks at me again, his eyes are out of focus. 'Sometimes life feels like we're heading in the wrong direction, doesn't it? It's hard to justify our actions.'

'You'll feel more confident, next time you sail.'

'Let's hope so.' His smile slowly revives. 'I might do it again this afternoon, just for the hell of it.'

'Lucky you, I'd tag along if I was less busy.'

'Another time, I hope.'

I leave Dawlish whistling in a minor key as I climb the stairs. The view from the attic window is distracting, the channel between Tresco and Bryher glittering like quicksilver, half a dozen boats at anchor, being chivvied by the tide. It's a reminder that someone sailed a boat to Piper's Hole and waited for Jude Trellon, then returned home in the middle of the night after committing murder, without alerting anyone's suspicion. It would take a cool head to behave with so little conscience. The only islander who fits the bill is the historian, David Polrew. The man is hard-hearted enough to turn his daughter into a virtual prisoner, and goad her to fulfil his ambitions. Jude Trellon might have let slip about discovering the *Minerva* on one of their diving expeditions, but refused to disclose its location. Something about his arrogance makes me believe that Polrew would destroy anything that got in his way.

PART 3

'For thou didst cast me into the deep,
Into the heart of the seas,
And the flood was round about me;
All thy waves and thy billows passed over me.'

Jonah 2:3

33

Tom's senses are working overtime. His clothes have been stripped away, apart from his jeans, the damp air making him shiver. The boat's endless rocking increases his nausea, waves slapping against the hull as the sea nudges it from side to side. He can hear seagulls screeching, and hours ago the low-pitched drone of a helicopter that planted dreams of rescue in his mind, only to fall silent again. The boy shakes uncontrollably when someone walks overhead. This time the tread is lighter than before, one person climbing aboard instead of two. When the door clicks open, a woman's voice addresses him. Her tone is familiar, light and breathless, yet he can't place it.

'Can you stand up, if I help you?'

'I'll try,' Tom croaks, his throat raw with thirst.

Her touch is gentle as she loosens the rope around his ankles. He feels as weak as an old man when he finally stands upright, his feet shuffling as the woman guides him along, streaks of sunlight filtering through his blindfold.

'Sit here,' she says. 'That cut on your back's infected. I'll clean it for you.'

Tom sinks onto a padded seat, wincing as the smell of anti-septic fills his airways, the pain sharpening when the woman smears it across his wound. Her touch is brisk and efficient as she seals a bandage to his skin. Afterwards she gives him a water bottle. The boy is so thirsty he lifts it to his mouth too fast, some of the liquid spilling onto his thigh.

'Steady,' the woman murmurs. 'You'll be sick at that rate.'

'You have to help me.' He drains the bottle before speaking again. 'Let me go, please.'

'You know I can't.'

'Have you brought food?'

'A sandwich, but don't tell him, will you?'

'Okay, but why are you keeping me here?'

'I told you, he wants the *Minerva's* co-ordinates, longitude and latitude.'

'I don't know them.'

'The wreck is all he cares about.' There's a tinge of sadness in the woman's voice. 'Tell me, then he'll stop hurting you.'

'It's somewhere past White Island, but that's all I know.'

'You'll have to do better than that.' She gives a mirthless laugh. 'Do you understand how Jude Trellon died?'

'Underwater, at Piper's Hole.'

'Drowning's the worst death, Tom. Your lungs feel like they're on fire, then there are terrible visions as your brain's starved of oxygen. Is that what you want?'

'Please don't let me die like that.'

'Tell the truth then.' The woman grips his arm as he swallows the last mouthful of bread, her touch less gentle than before. 'We're leaving the boat now. Come with me.'

It crosses Tom's mind to lash out, but his hands and feet are still bound. She could easily send him tumbling overboard. Instead she forces him down a short ladder, into a smaller boat. A rough plastic tarpaulin scrapes across his back, hiding him from view, then the outboard motor roars into life. Tiredness and fear overwhelm him, his eyes gritty under the blindfold, as the dinghy scuds over choppy waves.

34

I've spent hours considering every suspect, but the pieces refuse to add up. The violence of the killer's MO and items found at each crime scene make me certain he's obsessed by the *Minerva*, his messages intended to taunt us. I can understand why the prospect of finding the ship could drive someone to madness. If it was loaded with precious artefacts, it could make someone's fortune overnight, and turn the finder into a household name; the discovery of such an ancient wreck would create worldwide media interest. The killer may have found items of cargo hidden by Jude Trellon, his anger growing when she refused to disclose the wreck's location. Tom Heligan has probably been targeted simply because the killer believes he knew her secrets. Despite Shane's aggressive behaviour, there's nothing linking him with either crime. Plenty of people remain on my suspect list, including the Kinvers and David Polrew, but the lack of hard evidence leaves me powerless. My only arrest so far has been Jamie Petherton, who has been freed pending investigation, for the crime of breaking and entering, not murder.

I switch off the computer and head outside. All I can hope is that Shadow is keeping Ivar and Frida safe, while I set off for Merchant's Point to give Linda Heligan an update. I opt for the long walk round the coast, rather than the short cut inland, hoping some exercise will clarify my thoughts. When I follow the track through Dolphin Town, Justin Bellamy stares out from his office window at the vicarage, scrutinising me before he raises his hand in greeting. When I was a boy, it felt like the walls had eyes, the smallest misdemeanour reported back to my parents, and nothing has changed. People are still observing my every move, waiting to see whether I'm capable of finding the killer.

I pause on Ruin Beach to watch the Kinvers' boat. When I pull my binoculars from my pocket, it's anchored further offshore than yesterday; Stephen Kinver is standing on deck, no doubt brooding about being confined to local waters, reminding me that the warrant to search his boat is tucked in my pocket. I'm about to continue my journey when a large wooden-framed dinghy cruises past, with its lugsail folded against its mast. The slim, grey-haired woman at the tiller is unfamiliar until the binoculars bring her features into focus. Miriam Polrew, the historian's long-suffering wife, wears a rapturous look on her face

257

as her boat powers along, its outboard motor whining, clearly enjoying her moment of freedom, even though the open vessel gives no protection from the elements. She sails past the bay at speed, cutting a shallow line in the water as I reach Merchant's Point.

Linda Heligan's house looks bleak even on a sunny day, alone on a wide plane of granite, no other houses in sight. The beach below is rarely used by tourists because it's too exposed for sunbathing, even though the view is majestic. On a clear day the vista seems limitless; you can trace the Atlantic back to the horizon for a hundred miles. I expect to see Linda in her wheelchair when I ring the bell, but Elinor Jago opens the door – the postmistress looks awkward, but soon recovers her composure.

'Good to see you, Ben. Linda's having a nap. Shall I wake her for you?'

'I wanted to give her an update, but I can come back later. Is she okay?'

Elinor's smile fades. 'It's a hellish time for her. I've popped in each day after work, to keep her company.'

'Linda's lucky to have your support.' My eyes scan the living room, catching on a sideboard with its doors hanging open, papers and envelopes stacked in piles on the floor, reminding me of the chaos at Larsson's house.

'We've been having a clear-out. Linda needs to keep her mind occupied.'

My eyes skim the piles of brown envelopes and old

notebooks. 'If you come across any letters to Tom, can you keep them for me?'

Elinor looks puzzled, but nods her head. There's an outside chance that the boy may have received a note from Jude, sharing information about the Minerva that I'm struggling to access.

When I return to Ruin Beach, the Kinvers have saved me the trouble of using the police launch. Their boat, *Golden Diver*, is moored to the jetty, and Stephen Kinver is mopping the deck. He's dressed more conservatively than on previous occasions, in black shorts and a white T-shirt. It's only when I come to a halt three metres down on the quay that he finally abandons his mop.

'Are you giving us permission to leave, Inspector?'

'I'll come on board and take a look around first.'

'Get that search warrant, did you?' The man lounges against the rail, working hard to look nonchalant.

I pull the document from my pocket. 'This gives me the right to seize any item that could be linked to Jude Trellon's death. Feel free to read the small print.'

Kinver snatches the document from my outstretched hand. He scans the details thoroughly, before speaking again. 'If you break anything, I'll call my lawyer.'

'Your valuables are safe with me,' I reply pleasantly. 'Where's your wife today?'

'At the shop. Lorraine likes being on dry land, occasionally.'

'But you'd rather stay at sea?'

'Of course. Shit like this never happens on open water.'

He gives me another fierce glare before allowing me on board, but once I begin to search, he lets me work in peace. The guy may hate external intervention, but he's smart enough to know that the faster I work, the sooner I'll leave. Kinver and his wife have done a comprehensive job of cleaning the boat since my last visit. Ropes and equipment are stowed in storage boxes under seats at the helm, and their living quarters are spotless. I take my time searching cupboards and drawers, peering into the recess behind their bed. My interest rises when I pull up the trapdoor and stare into the hold. The space is confining for a broad man of six feet four, forcing me to bow my head to complete the search. Most sailors fill their holds with junk, but a single storage box in the corner contains fishing rods, nets and twine, a large oxygen tank propped beside it. The smell of fish lingers behind a tang of fresh bleach.

'Something's missing,' I mutter, scanning the hold for a final time, but there's no reason to prevent the Kinvers from continuing their ocean journey. I've found no proof that the couple used their boat to attack Jude Trellon at Piper's Hole, or that they are responsible for Tom Heligan's disappearance, yet discomfort lingers like a bad smell when I grant Kinver permission to leave.

'About bloody time,' he grumbles. 'We've been waiting for days.'

'I apologise if Jude Trellon's murder has slowed you down.'

Kinver ends the conversation by throwing his bucket of water overboard, filthy liquid splashing the jetty. I'd have preferred to be doused from head to toe, then I could lock him up for assaulting an officer. It requires effort to force my dislike of the man back into its box before turning inland.

I've only been walking for a few minutes when my phone buzzes in my pocket.

'Can you go to the Polrews' house, sir? Sophie Browarth's not answering her phone. It's an emergency, their daughter's ill.' Eddie's voice sounds panicked, so I set off at a rapid jog.

Fields pass in a blur of green, a few locals pausing to watch my progress. The spectacle of a big, ungainly man dressed in funeral clothes sprinting through a meadow is what passes for entertainment in a place this quiet. No doubt my haste will prompt a fresh round of gossip about the case before the day ends. When I reach the historian's home, the front door hangs open. David Polrew drops his mobile onto the hall table when he sees me. There's no sign of his usual arrogance; the man's face is as pale as candle wax today.

'Thank God,' he mutters. 'Gemma's sick. I can't bring her round.'

'Where is she?'

Polrew paces up the stairs ahead of me. When the girl's bedroom door swings open, I see her sprawled across her desk, long hair obscuring her face. I make her father stand back, to let me check on her condition. A thin pulse is beating in her wrist, but when I pull back one of her eyelids, her pupil is too wide, a line of saliva running from her mouth. There's only one obvious reason why a healthy young girl would slip into a dead faint, so I haul her to the bathroom. She releases a moan as I force her to vomit, producing a froth of white liquid, a few tablets floating on the surface. I push my fingers down her throat again, until her stomach's empty.

'Call emergency services again,' I yell at her father. 'She's taken an overdose.'

Polrew shakes his head in disbelief before striding away. By now his daughter is coming round, still limp as a rag doll as I lay her on the bed. There's an empty pill bottle on her bedside table bearing her mother's name, the word Diazepam printed on its label. A few words filter from the girl's lips.

'You should have let me go.'

'Don't be ridiculous, you're just getting started. What made you do it?'

A few tears slide down the girl's cheek. 'I can't face my exams. He'll never forgive me.'

'None of that matters.' I give her hand a squeeze. 'Promise not to do anything that stupid again.'

Her gaze slips out of focus. 'Tom said they'll go back to Piper's Hole. They never stay away long.'

'Who, Gemma? What do you mean?'

The girl's eyes are closing again, the sedatives she's taken rendering her unconscious. I splash her face with cold water, barely managing to keep her awake until the flying ambulance's engine roars above the roof. The helicopter lands on the Polrews' wide lawn, two paramedics jumping out with a stretcher to take the girl to hospital on St Mary's. There's a look of calm determination on their faces as they enter the room. They must deal with this kind of crisis often: medical needs can turn into emergencies fast on a small island with limited access to healthcare. They listen in silence to my explanation as they check Gemma's vital signs then lift her onto the stretcher.

I stand beside David Polrew as the helicopter rises above the treeline, then heads south. With luck, the girl's cry for help won't have caused permanent damage. The historian appears to have slipped into a state of shock, shaking his head in numb silence when I ask if he's contacted his wife. I lead him back into his kitchen to make a hot drink. The man's hands are shaking when I place a mug of tea in front of him, so I pick up his phone. Sounds in the background reveal that Miriam Polrew is still out on the water, seagulls screeching as she answers, her voice diluted by the wind. When I pass on the news that her daughter is being hospitalised, there's a crashing sound before the line dies. She must have dropped her phone onto the deck in her hurry to return to harbour. Both mother and daughter have identified ways to evade the historian's bullying. Miriam swallows tranquillisers and goes sailing alone, while her daughter's method was more extreme, believing an overdose could provide the ultimate freedom.

35

My head is still full of Gemma Polrew's attempted suicide when I return to the New Inn. I expect to see Eddie
hunched over the table, filing yet another progress
report, but Will Dawlish is cleaning the windows, using
a duster to shine the glass. Shock sharpens my tone of
voice when he meets my eye.

'You shouldn't be here, Will. The room has to be
kept locked at all times.'

Dawlish blinks at me. 'Sorry, Ben, I just wanted
to tidy up, and bring you some lunch ...' His voice
tails away as he gestures towards a tray filled with
cartons of juice, a thermos of coffee and a platter full
of sandwiches.

'We can order food downstairs, but thanks, it's a
kind thought.'

'I want to help you, Ben. There was no way to save
Anna, but this time's different. Tom Heligan might
still be alive.'

It's only when I step closer that the tension in his face

is visible. The man seems so burdened by his loss, it could have happened yesterday, but sympathy doesn't remove my suspicions. He could easily have left the tray on the landing without setting foot inside. Eddie will have to confirm whether the evidence folders have been tampered with – I can't tell at first sight.

'You've done enough by giving us a base. But I'll need any spare keys until the case closes.'

'No problem,' he replies, dropping a key into the palm of my hand. 'That's the only one, apart from yours.'

Dawlish retreats, leaving me frowning. Instinct tells me to trust a man I've liked for years, but why would he enter a police incident room uninvited? Maybe he was telling the truth about his desire to help, his shock over a murder committed at the site where his wife drowned triggering powerful emotions. Luckily, Eddie has left little information on display, most of it stored on the police laptop which has an encrypted password. Apart from a few interview notes waiting to be entered into the system, there was little to find. Eddie has written me a note saying that Madron called earlier, in a foul mood. There are three voicemail messages from the DCI, which must have arrived while I was helping Gemma Polrew, but answering them will have to wait. If my boss plans to harangue me for breach of protocol, I need to be calm enough not to retaliate. I punch a quick message into my phone, telling Larsson that I'll be staying at his house again tonight. Another sleepover on a lumpy sofa carries little appeal, but there's no choice. The man is too headstrong to accept support unless it's enforced, and there's a chance that patience will win the day. If I spend enough time in his company, maybe he'll break his vow of silence and reveal the secret he's been hiding all along.

My plan is to go home for a quick shower, before returning to perform guard duties. But when I get back to Hell Bay, the hotel lights are sparkling like a Christmas tree, offering a direct invitation. I've worked flat out since the case began five days ago; it wouldn't be a crime to take a short break with Zoe. But Gemma Polrew's odd statement about Piper's Hole fills my mind as I cross the shingle. Eddie and I have both searched the place and found nothing; she may have been confused by the effects of the pills she swallowed, but the urgency in her voice makes me consider returning to the cave one more time.

The hotel looks like a different world when I stand on the decking. I catch sight of my reflection in the panoramic window of the Atlantic Bar; a shambling giant in a cheap suit, black hair unkempt, with a ragged beard. On the other side of the glass, the holidaymakers look glossy with health, couples sitting at tables, sharing pre-dinner cocktails. Zoe gives me a wide grin, then holds up three fingers. It's a familiar signal, but it always takes her longer than three minutes to find a staff member to cover her at the bar.

The door to her flat is unlocked as usual, so I make

myself at home and grab a beer from her fridge. I'm about to flake out on her settee when I spot the yellow folder she's been hiding. It's full of papers, with Post-it notes sticking out from the cover, proving that she's gone through each page with a toothcomb. Curiosity threatens to get the better of me, but I manage not to look. Reading Zoe's private documents would be almost as bad as entering a police incident room without authority. I'm still staring down at the folder when she arrives. My friend's reaction is like a greeting in reverse, her smile slowly souring.

'Have you been snooping, Ben?'

'I resisted, by the skin of my teeth.'

'Just as well. I'd have had to torture you as punishment.'

'That would be fine, if it includes whips and leather.'

Zoe rolls her eyes. 'I suppose everyone has to know, sooner or later.' She hesitates before handing me the folder, but the information inside doesn't make sense. There are some official documents waiting to be signed, the second set of papers covers health insurance, malaria risks and inoculations. I'm still gawping at them when she speaks again. 'Don't just stand there, big man. Say something.'

'You're going to India for a year?'

'I'll be teaching music at a school for street kids in Mumbai, and helping to run the place.'

'You're serious?'

'I need a break from mixing cocktails. All I have to

do now is sign the papers.' She takes back the folder. 'How come you're not congratulating me?'

'You planned all that without saying a word.'

'I couldn't tell anyone. The decision has to be mine.'

'Go ahead and leave then. I won't stop you.'

'Why are you angry?'

'We used to talk to each other. We never had secrets.'

'Until you suddenly buggered off and left me here for years. I'm due a bloody adventure.' Her words come out as a sob, her eyes welling.

'Don't cry, you know I hate it.'

'People have emotions, Ben. Deal with it.' She pulls a tissue from her pocket to blot her eyes.

'You've always loved living on Bryher.'

'This place is amazing, but I need to see the world before I die of old age.' She makes a wild gesture with her hands. 'Let's not talk about it anymore.'

'Do your parents know?'

'I'm telling them tonight. Mum'll be upset, but she'll understand. An interim manager can cover for me while I'm away.'

Zoe's face crumples into tears, so I pull her into my arms. An odd sensation shifts in my chest when she returns the embrace, my feelings repositioning. I should dig deep and find the generosity to admit that she's doing something admirable, but it's easier to keep my mouth shut.

36

Hours have passed since Tom last heard the woman's voice. He's determined not to break down; he will need all his strength to fight, if the chance comes. The boy keeps trying to guess where he's been taken. He's still lying in the hull of a dinghy, the boards pressing against the wound on his back, but at least he's out in the open. He can taste salt on the air, and the boat must be moored somewhere sheltered because it has stopped rocking, protected from the fierce currents. Before he can take another breath, the tarpaulin is yanked back, strands of light penetrating his blindfold.

'Enjoying the change of scene?' The man's harsh voice addresses him.

Tom has no time to reply before the man hauls him from the boat then over jagged granite that tears his skin. The man grabs a clump of his hair, yanking it until his eyes smart.

'Let me go, please. I can't help you.'

'Mark the places where Jude hid things on this map when light comes. It's your last chance.'

Tom keeps his mouth shut as the man ties his hands in front

of him, then drags the blindfold from his eyes. When the torch beam falls on the hand-drawn map, he sees Tresco's curved outline, with every house and field marked in place, and feels a stab of homesickness. The beam of light hits his face again, making his eyes stream until the brightness is extinguished. He can hear the man's footsteps battering across the rock, producing a dull echo, as the shadowy figure disappears.

37

It's 7 p.m. when I use the launch to return to Tresco, dressed in fresh clothes. The walk to Larsson's house gives me time to digest Zoe's revelation. I can see that an exotic adventure is more appealing than serving drinks in a hotel at the edge of the world, but it still hurts that she's prepared to abandon everything here, including me. It's a relief to arrive at Dolphin Town, where Larsson's house is so brightly lit he seems to be using electricity to ward off bad spirits. His face wears its usual fierce expression when he opens the door. It's clear he'd like me to sling my hook, but concern for his daughter's safety wins the day. Shadow's warm welcome offers a direct contrast, the dog's paws landing on my chest as he makes a desperate attempt to lick my face.

'Has he been behaving himself?'

Larsson gives a crisp nod. 'It's Frida who's breaking the rules; she's refusing to go to bed. Maybe you can persuade her it's time to sleep.'

The girl is sitting on the living room floor, dressed in bright-red pyjamas, hunched over a sheet of paper. She continues her frantic scribbling when I drop down beside her, but all I can see are random black lines floating on a swirl of turquoise.

'I'm drawing a boat for mummy,' the kid announces, without looking up.

'That's pretty good, I can tell the sea's at high tide.'

The comment draws a quick smile, then Frida carries on scratching her pen across the page so hard, pressure marks score the paper. I watch until the sheet is almost covered before speaking again.

'You look tired, kiddo. Want me to carry you up to bed?'

The girl shakes her head vehemently, but exhaustion soon topples her. The expression on Larsson's face combines relief with irritation that his unwelcome guest has persuaded his daughter to behave. I feel a stab of pity as I cart the kid upstairs. She smells of soap, lavender shampoo and innocence, but any day now her world will crack apart. The least I can do is find out how her mother died, to protect her from unanswered questions. I wait until she snuggles under the duvet, her eyes closing before I switch off the bedside light.

Larsson is tight-lipped when I return to the kitchen, but keeps his displeasure private. 'We may as well eat,' he says. 'People keep leaving emergency supplies on my doorstep.'

He ladles chicken soup into bowls, then places

them on the table, with wedges of granary bread. The room has been put to rights since last night; surfaces have been cleaned, and the papers that were strewn across the floor filed away. He listens intently when I explain that I found the burned shell of his laptop this morning.

'At Jamie's house?'

I haven't mentioned Petherton's name, but news travels fast here, whether it's good or bad. 'Keep an open mind, Ivar. Someone else could have broken in, then dumped it there.'

'No one else is crazy enough. I don't want that freak anywhere near my daughter.'

The anger on his face reminds me that I intended to get under his defences by establishing common ground, not to upset him further. 'Why not tell me about your research? There's nothing we can do tonight; it might be a good distraction.'

He frowns at me. 'My work's pretty straightforward. I came here to map changes in the marine ecosystem, and the easiest way is to look at wreck sites. Each one's unique, but the seaweeds, plankton and crustaceans are all suffering. Each year I check to see which species are dying out.'

'How do you record all that information?'

'On computerised sketches.' Ivar shows me a wreck site on his phone; the ship's remains are illustrated so accurately, every broken timber is shown in a 3-D diagram. His software could draw the seabed far more clearly than David Polrew's old-fashioned maps. 'If you touch the screen, it brings up lists of species inhabiting that section.'

'It must take hours underwater to collect so much evidence.'

'The job needs doing before the ecosystem reaches a tipping point.' His face hardens again. 'Huge strands of sea kale grew here for thousands of years, but it's almost gone. Acidification's killing it.'

His mournful tone confirms that it's easier to grieve for the polluted sea than for his girlfriend, righteous anger keeping his sadness at bay.

'Does anyone help you with the survey?'

'Jude dived with me sometimes to take photos, and Anna helped me last year.'

My eyes blink open. 'Anna Dawlish?'

'She was a biology teacher before she met Will, so she knew how to record data and identify species. She came diving with me and Jude every week last summer; she was a good friend of ours. It was a terrible shock when she died.'

When I look at Ivar's face again, he seems on the verge of tears, but pulls it together at the last minute. I still don't fully understand the man's reluctance to show emotion, but a raft of feelings swirl across his face: anger and despair, with fear rising to the surface. I know it would be pointless to ask why he's afraid, but at least he's shared some fresh information. Will Dawlish's wife went on diving expeditions to help his research. Despite the coroner's verdict of accidental death, it seems even more likely that Anna was murdered by the same person who killed Jude Trellon.

38

Sunday 17 May

Madron is waiting for me outside the incident room this morning. It's lucky that Shadow is still guarding Larsson's house, because the dog's presence would only increase his bad temper. The DCI must have serious concerns about the case to leave his home on St Mary's so early on a Sunday. His grey eyes are cold as liquid nitrogen when we cross the threshold.

'I thought you had begun acting more professionally, Kitto, but I was wrong. I've a good mind to remove you from the case.'

'Why, sir?'

'You've been staying at the victim's house. That man may have killed his wife; he's one of your chief suspects. An SIO should remain impartial at all times. Why aren't you using a guard from the mainland?'

'I need to win Larsson's trust.' I take a breath, to stop myself exploding. 'He's in a fragile state, and so's his daughter. He wouldn't stay with Jude's family after the house was burgled, so I slept on his sofa. I spent last night there too.'

'I thought as much.' Madron gives a loud sigh.

'Ivar could be next on the killer's list. If you remove me from the case, he'll need round-the-clock protection.'

'What makes you think he's vulnerable?'

'The killer's guarding his patch, stopping other divers from finding the *Minerva*, so he can claim its cargo. He thought Jude Trellon knew the wreck's location, so he's bound to believe Larsson knows it too.'

'Who else is on your suspect list?'

'I've got a warrant to search David Polrew's house. He ticks all the boxes and he's a manipulative bully. You got my report on his daughter's suicide attempt, didn't you?'

'Polrew's never committed a crime in his life.'

'Plenty of murderers have clean records, sir.'

'I thought Shane Trellon was your top suspect?'

'Nothing implicates him, except sibling rivalry. We finally got the lab results on his computer and phone, which came back clean. The only thing his emails and texts prove is that he's having an affair with a married woman. I let the Kinvers go due to lack of evidence too. Forensics are taking days to give us results; I'd be grateful if you could remind them that the murder case should be their top priority.'

'Don't blame them for your mistakes; they've only got five officers to cover all of Cornwall.' Madron fixes me with his icy stare. 'You're impossible to supervise, Kitto. Don't you realise you're risking your future?'

'If Larsson or his daughter had been hurt, it would have been my responsibility.' I keep my gaze steady. 'Why not put some faith in me, sir? It would make both our lives easier.'

'Faith has to be earned, Kitto. It's time you started following orders.'

'I can't leave Ivar and his daughter unprotected.'

'An SIO must keep his professional distance. I'm ordering you to put appropriate security in place.'

'Larsson wouldn't tolerate a stranger in his home, sir, and I'm close to a breakthrough.'

Eddie barges in at the perfect moment. I suspect that he's been on the landing with his ear to the door, waiting for the row to end. His presence soon disperses Madron's rage. The DCI praises his hard work and immaculate uniform, before giving me a meaningful look, indicating that my deputy has outshone me again. Eddie and I both breathe a sigh of relief when he finally leaves. My deputy has begun to relax in my presence, but his eyes widen as I explain that David Polrew might be the killer. His belief in me is flattering, but he will only be disappointed if I fall from my pedestal. Right now, I'd do almost anything to prevent Madron from removing me from the job. Returning to undercover work carries no appeal whatsoever; I've spent enough time pretending to be someone else. It's a relief to be myself again, on familiar ground.

I push my concerns aside to study the coroner's report into Anna Dawlish's death in more detail. The account confirms that her husband discovered her body in the far reaches of Piper's Hole; there were deep wounds to the back of her head, consistent with the tide battering her against the rocks. Her hands sustained injuries too, several fingernails torn away, but it was the bruising to one of her legs that convinced the coroner she had hit her head in a fall, then become unconscious, allowing the tide to sweep her into the cave. I drop the report back onto the table and stare out at the sea. It looks harmless today, stippled by shallow waves, reflecting the sky's tranquil mid-blue, but I've spent enough time here to know that it can turn vicious in an instant. The killer could have targeted Anna Dawlish six months ago, hoping for information about the *Minerva*. If he knows the local waters, he would have realised that by dragging her body into the cave it would remain there until the next high tide. The deep circular currents that Ray described would drown even the strongest swimmer.

'Anna Dawlish was the killer's first victim, Eddie.'

He rocks back in his chair. 'But the MO's different, sir. Jude's body was tied to the rocks.'

'There was no need with Anna. He knew the sea would keep her body exactly where he left it, in Piper's Hole. She put up quite a fight, tearing at him with her hands, but the brine removed every trace of his DNA.'

'Will's going to be upset, if it's true,' Eddie murmurs. 'He's been in a bad way since she died.'

My suspicions about the landlord have faded. No clues connect him to either killing, yet finding him in the incident room has left me concerned, even though Eddie claims that none of our papers were touched. The man fits the job description for a publican perfectly; affable and courteous. It's hard to see how he would profit from the brutal murder of his own wife, followed by the death of a local diving guide. I set off for the Polrews' house with my thoughts spinning. The walk takes me south to the Great Pool, where Canada geese skim the water's surface, webbed feet scrabbling wildly as they land. The Abbey stands on the next rise; the imposing building was designed on a grand scale to remind the local population that Augustus Smith controlled the island 150 years ago. The Polrews' house looks like a shadow of the original mansion, built in darker stone, its mullioned windows like hooded eyes. There's something so gloomy about the place, it doesn't surprise me that Gemma Polrew's mental health is suffering.

The front door takes a long time to open, but eventually Miriam Polrew appears. She's dressed from head to toe in charcoal grey, as if she's wrapped herself in a shroud, silver hair hanging down in lank strands. Her face only brightens by a fraction when she greets me.

'It's good to see you, Ben. I can't thank you enough.' Her words tumble out in a rush. 'Gemma wouldn't be here without your help.'

'I was only doing my job. How's she doing?'

'The doctors had to pump her stomach, but she'll make a full recovery after some rest.' Her gaze slips to the floor. 'I wanted Gemma to see a counsellor, but David doesn't believe in talking cures.'

'Can I come in, Miriam? I need to see your husband.'

'I'm sorry, that's not possible. He told me to keep visitors away.'

Miriam Polrew's tense expression makes me certain that her home life is worse than I imagined. I can sense that her husband has bludgeoned her into submission through endless bullying over the years. Her trembling is visible from ten paces, as if she knows that she'll be punished for holding a conversation without his permission.

39

Little light filters into the cave, but it's better than the absolute dark of the boat's hold. Tom's body feels weak after another night without sleep, the hard stretch of rock allowing only a few hours of rest, his hands chafed raw by the rope around his wrists. The man has left the map of Tresco behind, protected from the damp air by a plastic wallet, but he hasn't touched it. Despite longing to go home, he's not prepared to put another life in danger.

Tom leans forwards, trying to peer past a huge wall of rock. It's impossible to guess where he's being held, but he can no longer be on Tresco; this place is unfamiliar, and he knows every inch of his native island. He tries to imagine what Jude would do in his position. She always knew how to act; even underwater her movements were quick and decisive. The boy stares at the chain tethering his ankle to the rock. If he could free his hands, escape might be possible, and trying will keep him occupied. He drags his wrists across rough stone, hoping to work the rope loose. The motion scrapes his palms until they're covered with blisters, but Tom keeps going. He thinks of his mother waiting at home, and Gemma waving up at him from the shore, as the pain in his wrists sharpens.

40

'I've got a warrant to search your property. I'm afraid you have to let me in, Miriam.'

Mrs Polrew steps back slowly. 'You'd better tell David; I can't get involved.'

When I'm finally permitted to enter, it strikes me again that only a historian would live in a house that favours darkness over light, the walnut panelling and heavy rugs on the floor too oppressive for my taste. If the property was mine, I'd paint the walls white, to accentuate the soaring ceilings and allow the place to breathe.

Miriam Polrew scurries upstairs to check on her daughter, leaving me outside her husband's office. I can hear the man's booming voice giving someone a piece of his mind, but when I knock on the door, the only reply is an outraged grunt. Dr Polrew keeps his back turned, his phone still pressed to his ear. He does a double take when our eyes finally meet, ending the call with a curt goodbye. His arrogant sneer is missing for once; it no longer feels like he's preparing to give me a lecture on marine archaeology.

'Have you come to check on Gemma's recovery, Inspector?'

'Among other things, yes.'

'The psychiatrist claims she's got emotional issues, but the girl only wanted our attention. She thinks she can avoid her exams with a foolish gesture. My daughter's always had a taste for drama.'

'Her attempt was serious, Dr Polrew, it's recorded in my incident report. Gemma waited until her mother left before taking the pills; it was pure luck that you found her, because Miriam normally checks on her during the day, doesn't she?'

'Meaning what, exactly?'

'I lost a colleague to suicide. Your daughter will need professional support to recover.'

'How dare you advise me on her welfare?' Polrew emerges from behind his desk like a veteran boxer lumbering into the ring, but the sight of a taller, heavier man stops him in his tracks. He deflates suddenly, as if someone's pricked his balloon. 'Gemma needs to pull herself together, that's all.'

'I'm not here to discuss her future. I need to search your office, in connection with Jude Trellon's death.'

His mouth gapes open. 'You think I was involved?'

'It has to be ruled out. You dived together plenty of times.'

'I can't believe you're singling me out.'

'This is routine, Dr Polrew. Other properties on Tresco have been searched.'

Like all bullies, he backs away when he's cut down to size. Polrew's presence lingers in the empty room, with an odour of stale cigar smoke, the air still crackling with his bad mood. I put on sterile gloves to sift through the folders stacked on his shelves, pulling down one with the word *Minerva* scrawled on its spine. It's fatter than the others, proving that his interest in it trumps every other shipwreck. The folder contains photos from dives near the Eastern Isles, over the past three years, as well as a ship's log. My eyes blink wider when I see the number of additional crew members scribbled beside the dates of each voyage. Until now, Polrew has claimed that only Jude Trellon accompanied him, but sometimes two or three other islanders were on board, yet none of their names are recorded. I spend an hour combing through Polrew's office, learning more about his passion for maritime history. Photographs on the wall include one of an ancient wreck being winched from the seabed, the wooden outline resembling a whale's skeleton. My irritation builds as I complete the search. I'm sure the office once held items from his dives with Jude Trellon, which he's moved somewhere harder to access. My hunt may have revealed nothing, but I can't give up until Tom Heligan is found.

When I finally emerge, Polrew is waiting in the corridor, arms folded tightly across his chest.

'I need the names of everyone that accompanied you when you looked for the *Minerva*, Dr Polrew.'

'Several people joined me over the years. My wife, Ivar Larsson, Anna Dawlish and Jamie Petherton, but there may have been others. My expeditions tend to blur into one these days.'

'Anna Dawlish crewed for you?'

'She was a keen diver, unlike Jamie. He'd rather sit in his museum than get his skin wet.' Polrew gives a sneering smile. 'At least he's a decent navigator.'

'Where are the keys to your boat?'

'I don't have them.' His words emerge on a hiss of amusement. 'A friend on St Agnes borrowed it yesterday for a family trip.'

I produce my notepad from my pocket. 'Give me his contact details, please.'

The historian scribbles a few words, then hands the pad back with a flourish. 'I'll want a formal apology when you accept that Jude's death is nothing to do with me.'

I keep my eyes level with his. 'Did you ever take Tom Heligan on your boat?'

'Jude brought him along once; the boy was an accomplished diver.' The man's stare is a direct challenge, daring me to call him a liar.

I leave the house with little to show for my visit except the man's dossier on the *Minerva*. Miriam Polrew hurries out to thank me again for helping her daughter. Her expression is so anxious that I press one of my cards into her hand and tell her to ring me if she has any more concerns, even though her husband is eavesdropping by the front door. The atmosphere is leaden when I finally leave the couple to resolve their differences.

I've only been walking for a few minutes when I bump into Justin Bellamy, dressed in jeans and a light-green shirt, his dog collar hidden beneath his jacket. His usual smile of greeting is missing when he hurries along the path.

'I thought I'd call on Gemma. I was hoping to speak with you too, Ben.'

'Now?'

'If you've got time.'

'There are benches by the lake. Why don't we go there?'

Our five-minute walk to the Great Pool reveals that the priest is troubled. His good humour has vanished, and he keeps his hands buried in his pockets, eyes trained on the ground. Justin stays silent as we settle on a bench, giving me time to admire the Sabine gulls hovering over the stretch of water, which reflects the clouded sky with photographic accuracy. The scene looks so tranquil it's hard to believe that a local woman has been brutally murdered and a teenage boy abducted in the past six days.

'I haven't been completely honest with you. I've been wrestling with my conscience since Jude died.' The priest's face is tense when he turns towards me. 'She came to the vicarage soon after our last dive together, in an agitated state. She gave me a package to look after. Jude made me swear to hand the box to her father, if anything bad happened. She promised it wasn't stolen goods, so I agreed, to give her peace of mind.'

'Have you opened it?'

'No, it's still in my cellar.'

'Did you tell anyone else?'

'Of course not, I gave her my word. I should have acted sooner, but my decision-making skills have suffered since this happened.' He points at the scar that bisects his cheek. 'Sometimes the line between right and wrong gets blurred.'

'How do you mean?'

He takes a deep breath, before speaking again. 'I was a chaplain with the Royal Fusiliers. I loved it at first, travelling the world with a great bunch of soldiers, counselling them and praying for their safety. They were the last unit to leave Afghanistan when British troops withdrew ...' His words fade into silence before he can talk again. 'I was in a transport with twenty men when we ran over an IED. Only six of us survived.'

'I'm sorry, Justin.'

'The carnage was terrible, and the waste. All I could do was give them last rites as they died.' He shifts awkwardly in his seat. 'I thought about resigning – a priest needs empathy to do his job.'

'You seem to have plenty.'

'A little more comes back each year, but it's a slow process.' He pauses, lost in thought for a moment. 'If you come to the vicarage now, I'll give you the box.'

A couple of minutes' walk brings us to Bellamy's home, and I glance around as he describes his time in the army. The vicarage is far more orderly than my cottage. Justin Bellamy's front garden proves that he likes a high degree of control over his environment; the grass newly cut, a line of rose bushes trimmed to a uniform height. The interior is equally tidy, proving that his time in the forces taught him to travel light; there are few personal items on display except a wooden crucifix above the fireplace. Justin smiles when he catches me scanning the room.

'The Church of England doesn't do luxury. I'll have to leave this place just as I found it if they move me to another diocese.'

'Is that likely?'

'I hope not, but the islanders will decide. The parish council report to the synod next year.' He's standing with his fingertips pressed together, like he's offering up a prayer. 'I'll get the box for you, Ben.'

The man's loneliness resonates from the walls. He probably didn't even get to choose the furniture in his temporary home, the room awash with beige, a sofa in the corner that's crying out to be replaced. Bellamy has lived through enough violence to turn most people insane, yet he's still ministering to his parishioners. Despite my sympathy for him, it crosses my mind that he could have stolen someone's boat and attacked Jude Trellon in a fit of madness, triggered by post-traumatic stress disorder.

The priest is breathless when he returns, as if he's eager to rid himself of guilt. The package looks innocent enough, a small cardboard box held together with parcel tape. It feels light in my arms, probably no more than a couple of kilos.

'Sorry I took so long to tell you about this,' Justin says.

'Don't worry, whatever's inside may not even be relevant.'

I'm about to return to the incident room when he touches my arm.

'I hope you know how lucky you are, Ben.'

'Sorry?'

'It took me weeks to find enough courage to ask Zoe out.' His smile fades. 'I saw the way she danced with you at Jude's wake. I hope it works out for you, she's a lovely woman.'

'We're just friends, it's not a romantic thing.'

He releases an astonished laugh. 'Situations change, Ben. Use your eyes.'

The man's comment leaves me lost for words, so I raise my hand in a goodbye salute, then head for the New Inn, with a murder victim's last gift tucked under my arm.

41

I've only been walking for a minute when a familiar sensation crosses the back of my neck. I learned to sense when I'm being observed during my time undercover. The feeling never leaves you and medics even have a name for it: hyperawareness. All your senses are so attuned to the next hazard, you notice minute changes in your environment. But all I can see are the granite cottages of Dolphin Town, gardens rioting with late spring flowers, and the spire of St Nicholas's church. I'm standing outside the Cardews' cottage, and when I scan the upstairs windows, Sylvia is gazing down from the top floor. The fisherman's wife offers me a wave, and it seems pitiful that the woman's agoraphobia has reduced her existence so dramatically: apart from time in her garden, her bedroom window must provide her only view of the outside world.

Eddie is in the bar when I return to the New Inn, talking to half a dozen locals, including two of the hotel staff. I put the box down on a table and watch him in action. Madron would be proud of how carefully he fields each question, so no one feels short-changed, the abduction of a second victim raising their anxiety levels. Tresco's community is used to fixing their own problems, but this time they must wait passively for an outcome. Eddie's reassurances soon send them on their way, reminding me again that we're polar opposites. While I set people's nerves on edge, he knows how to pacify them, his manner far more conciliatory.

'You handled that like a pro,' I say, when we reach the incident room.

The praise makes Eddie's smile flare into life. 'They're desperate for the killer to be found, everyone's on edge right now.'

'You did well reassuring them.' I pass him the slip of paper with contact details for the man who has borrowed the Polrews' boat. 'If David Polrew used his cruiser to escape from Piper's Hole, there must be evidence on board. Have the forensics team let you know when they're arriving?'

'The whole team's on an assault case in Truro. They've promised to get back to me by the end of the day.'

'It's bloody ridiculous. The killer's free to go about his business because they're short-staffed.' I use scissors to pry the box open with more force than necessary. 'Let's see why Jude gave this to Justin Bellamy for safekeeping.'

The box is full of shredded paper, with three metal

objects nestled at the bottom: an engraved plate, a square box which fits the palm of my hand and a necklace set with gemstones. All of the pieces are dented and scratched, but there's an elegance to their design, a filigree pattern making the plate shimmer like fish scales.

'This looks like copper, or it could even be gold,' Eddie says, as he rubs the necklace with his sleeve, trying to remove the tarnish.

I'm almost certain the items are precious metal. But did Jude Trellon find them on the seabed or steal them from someone else? I'm not fully convinced by the priest's claim that loyalty made him wait so long to hand over the package. It's possible that she hid cargo from the *Minerva* all over the island, if her life was in danger.

'Can you get Will to put these in his safe? I need to visit Linda Heligan again.'

The walk to Merchant's Point gives me time to process the day's events, from David Polrew's arrogant defence of his daughter's state of mind, to Jude Trellon's box of tarnished treasures. I'd like to go straight to Mike's home to speak with him about the package, but my old teacher is expecting my visit. My head is so full of the investigation, I hardly notice my surroundings until I reach Ruin Beach. The decking outside the café is full of day trippers enjoying the afternoon sun. The island is operating as two parallel worlds; while oblivious tourists tuck into cream teas, the locals are still reeling from the murder case and Tom Heligan's disappearance.

The door is open when I reach Merchant's Point, Linda hunched over a book in her kitchen. Her face fills with hope when she sees me, but I can only shake my head.

'No news yet, Linda, sorry. I just wanted to see how you're doing.'

'I can't concentrate on anything.' There's a tremor in her hands when she shows me the cover of *Little Dorrit*. 'Dickens is all I can face today.'

'He's always good in a crisis.'

I give her a brief version of developments, including finding Jude Trellon's stash of items that may have come from the *Minerva*. Linda's brow rises at the mention of the boat's name.

'Tom was planning a dive with Jude this week. He'd been excited about it for ages; he said it would be his deepest yet.'

'Can you remember the date he mentioned?'

'It'll be on his calendar. Feel free to take a look.'

When I reach Tom's room, the boy's presence is everywhere I look. His denim jacket is hanging from the back of a chair, diving memorabilia still covering the walls, the smell of his hair gel artificially sweet. But when I study his calendar, the date he's circled only holds the words 'White Island, 7 a.m.' The light is murky with the curtains half closed, making it feel like the room is submerged underwater.

'What were you hiding?'

The words slip from my mouth before I can stop them. Tom Heligan's telescopes, maps and sextants stare back at me accusingly, like I should already know.

42

Dim light filters into the cave as Tom wakes up. The only sounds come from the surrounding water: drops of condensation fall onto granite below, like a tap that won't switch off, waves hissing as they caress the mouth of the cave. Something is wrong with his body. It hurts to take a deep breath and the damp air has given him a fever, his heart beating too fast, limbs shaking. When he closes his eyes again, he plummets into ugly dreams where Jude returns to life, only to die again. Suddenly he can hear footsteps, but the cave's echo is deceptive. It's impossible to tell which direction they're coming from.

Tom is rising from sleep once more when someone pulls a blindfold back over his eyes. He hears the man give a grunt of disapproval when he snatches up the map of Tresco.

'You haven't touched it. Still protecting people, are you?'

'Jude never told me anything,' Tom whispers.

The man doesn't reply. There's a clicking sound as the chain round his leg is released, then he's dragged to the water's edge. Before he can say another word his head is plunged underwater. New sounds rush at him as water fills his ears; the sucking noise of the ebbing tide, bubbles of air gushing from his mouth. His lungs are burning now, panic telling him to inhale, even though brine would flood his airways and kill him in moments. Suddenly the man hauls him from the water and dumps him back on the rocks, heaving for oxygen.

'Listen to me, you little shit. Everything Jude took belongs to me. Next time I'll let you drown.'

'How can I tell you, if I don't know?' Tom splutters.

'Still playing the fucking hero.' When the blindfold is ripped away, a harsh light shines into Tom's eyes, his retinas burning. 'Is the stuff she found at your mum's house?'

'She never left anything there.'

'Ivar's got it then?'

'Jude wouldn't put her family in danger.'

'You're lying; I can see it in your face. I'll ask him myself.' The chain tightens round Tom's ankle again, but this time he's closer to the water's edge. 'If the next tide's high, you'll drown. Better start praying it stays at low ebb.'

43

It's 7 p.m. by the time I call Gemma Polrew, to check how she's coping. The girl's voice still sounds shaky, and there's silence at the end of the line when I remind her to call me if her father's behaviour ever becomes threatening. Once the call's over I head for Ivar Larsson's house. Nothing about the case feels straightforward, except my certainty that he and his daughter need protection. Going against Madron's orders is putting my job in danger, but Larsson is reluctant to admit anyone else to his house. Shadow seems to be enjoying his role as guard dog when I arrive. He's lying across the threshold by the back door, rising to his feet with a snarl until he recognises me.

'Impressive,' I tell him. 'I thought you might take me down.'

The dog licks my hand before returning to his sentry duties. Ivar and his daughter are sitting at the kitchen table, the child absorbed in another drawing while her father sorts through correspondence. Larsson barely raises his head, but Frida offers a wide smile, as if she's been waiting for my return. When her father's mobile rings, he snatches it up immediately, a rush of Swedish words flowing from his lips as he carries the phone into the living room.

'Do you like my picture?' Frida asks.

A woman stands by herself at the centre of the page, brown hair flaring like a hedgehog's quills, her feet encased in lopsided red shoes.

'It's really good. Who is she?'

The kid looks surprised. 'Mummy, of course. Can't you see her tattoos?'

'Of course I can. You're doing a good job.'

I sit back to let her continue drawing. The girl is concentrating so hard, her fist bunches tight around her felt-tip pen, as if she's conjuring her mother back to life. I'm so far out of my comfort zone that the right response is out of reach. I've never witnessed the collateral damage from a murder case at such close range before; normally I'm several steps removed from the victim's family, but this time there's no hiding. At least the kid seems calm while she completes her picture, humming quietly as she scrawls lines of blue sea across the background.

'Come and have your bath now, Frida,' Larsson says when he reappears in the doorway.

'Not yet, Daddy, please.'

'You've already had an extra half-hour.'

Frida gazes up at me, eyes beseeching. 'I want to stay here.'

'Your dad's in charge, kiddo,' I say. 'I'll still be around when you get out.'

The girl abandons her drawing reluctantly, but I soon hear her laughing in the bathroom, her emotions still flexible enough to change direction in an instant. My attitude towards her father has shifted since we first met; spending time in the house has shown me the depth of his affection for his daughter. The islanders who view him as cold and unfeeling would be amazed by his parenting skills, even in an advanced state of grief. It's becoming harder each day to believe that the man could have killed his girlfriend in a crime of passion.

I take the opportunity to flick through the papers on the table while they're gone. Jude's credit card bills and subscriptions lie in a messy pile. I've already seen her bank statement, but it must have been an earlier version: the balance is far higher than I remembered. Five thousand pounds was paid into her account the day after she died, the donor's name unfamiliar. Why would someone pay her a large lump sum when her family have been struggling for money? I'm keen to find out what Larsson knows, but my questions will have to wait until his daughter is in bed.

Frida seems more relaxed when she returns from her bath, dressed again in her scarlet pyjamas. The girl settles on the bench beside me while her father warms milk in a pan, but when he puts a cup in front of her, she pushes it away.

'Mummy puts cinnamon on top. Will she be home tomorrow?' She directs the question to her father.

'No, Frida. Do you remember what I said? She went into the sea and can't come back to us.'

'Ever?'

Larsson shakes her head. 'She wanted to, but it's not possible. She'll be peaceful now, nothing can hurt her.'

The child studies her father's face, then mine, before picking up her milk, humming quietly between each sip. My admiration for Larsson rises by several notches; he has managed to explain Jude's death to his daughter in the simplest terms, but the exchange still unsettles me. The kid's shoulder presses against my side, as if she's seeking an extra layer of comfort while her world adjusts. The milk works its magic fast, Frida's eyes closing as her father carries her upstairs. I take the opportunity to look around the room again. Something here must explain Jude Trellon's death and the reason why Tom Heligan is missing, but all I see is a chaos of dirty dishes and laundry waiting to go into the tumble dryer. Larsson is more likely to open up if I make myself useful, so I fill the washing-up bowl and set to work. I'm putting the last glass away when he returns downstairs, looking drained.

'You don't have to do my chores,' he says.

'I like to keep busy.' When I turn to him again, he's sitting at the table, head in hands. 'Do you want a drink?'

'More than oxygen.'

KATE RHODES

There's a bottle of Merlot on the counter, so I pour him a large glass. He holds it between both hands, as if the liquid is warming them, then knocks the wine back in a couple of swallows.

'Frida keeps asking about Jude,' he says. 'It seems like she's understood, then she rejects the idea, and the questions start all over again.'

'It's a lot for a four-year-old to digest.'

'She's not the only one.'

'This could explain what happened.' I point at the bank statement. 'Do you know why someone paid Jude five grand, just after she died? It's from a foreign bank account.'

His tone sharpens. 'You went through her papers without my permission?'

'We're on the same side, remember? If you tell me everything, you could save Tom Heligan's life. Jude was leaving valuable objects with people she trusted; she must have had a reason.'

'If I knew, I'd say.'

'Tell me what's scaring you, Ivar.'

He hesitates before replying. 'Jude had been getting death threats. They were left on the boat, in plastic bottles, with her name on them. She thought someone was playing a stupid joke at first.'

'Why didn't you tell me?'

'The messages said all three of us would be killed if the police found out.'

'Did you keep them?'

'Jude burned them. They were these odd rhymes, full of threatening words about the sea. Then she got a note telling her to put everything she'd found on her dives in the highest grave on Tregarthen Hill. She refused of course – Jude never backed down. She said the less I knew, the safer we'd all be.'

The highest peak on Tresco would be an ideal place to collect a package in secrecy at night. The killer could check for onlookers in every direction while hiding in one of the graves below.

'Whoever killed Jude must think you know the location of the *Minerva*. I want you to take Frida to the mainland, or back to Sweden for a while.'

'I told you before, this place is all my daughter knows. I'm not uprooting her.' He drains his second glass of wine, then goes upstairs in silence, dismissing my efforts to keep them safe. I breathe out a string of expletives, but at least I know more than before: Jude understood that her family's lives were under threat, yet still dived in Piper's Hole late at night, despite the risks. She must have had a good reason to court that kind of danger.

It's only 9 p.m., so I spend the next hour checking Jude's papers. Her credit card statements are a reminder that she spent every penny she earned, with the mortgage, bills and a few treats for Frida consuming her monthly wage. No wonder she clung so tightly to the dream of a pot of gold at the end of the rainbow. I'm still studying the documents when the priest's face

305

appears at the window, his skin white with panic. When I open the door, he stumbles across the threshold.

'What's wrong, Justin? You look like you've seen a ghost.'

'Are Ivar and Frida safe?' The man's breathing hard, as if he's run a race.

'They're upstairs, in bed. Try to calm down, then tell me what's wrong.'

Bellamy takes a long time to relax. He rubs his hands across his face, then sits opposite me, doing his best to look composed. 'You'll think I'm mad, if I explain.'

'Try me anyway.'

'I fell asleep after evensong. I had a dream that blood was running down the walls of this place, body parts on the floor. I couldn't do anything . . .' His voice ebbs away.

'That sounds more like a memory than a dream. I can ask Ivar to come down if you want reassurance.'

His eyes blink shut. 'My nightmares are sometimes so vivid, it's hard to tell where reality starts and fin-ishes. I made a mistake coming here.' He reaches for his jacket. 'I apologise for wasting your time, Ben. I'd better get back.'

'Don't rush off. Why not stay for a glass of wine?'

'I should sleep. A good night's rest will sort me out.'

The man hurries away before I can explain that he's not interrupting anything except my attempts to unpick Jude Trellon's past. His odd speech is a reminder that plenty of people seek emotional stability on the islands, but peace is a rare form of treasure; past troubles are often too deeply engrained to shake off, like the priest's PTSD.

I carry on sifting records of Jude's life: old passports, letters and final demands. It's late by the time I lie down on the rock-hard sofa, searching my brain for images to lull me to sleep. Oddly enough, it's Zoe that springs to mind, standing behind the hotel bar, laughing at me. I wipe my hand across my face to erase the picture, but it stays there, even when I shut my eyes.

44

Monday 18 May

Shadow whines loudly when I leave him at Larsson's house early next morning. I can tell he'd rather be chasing seagulls across Pentle Beach than performing guard duties again.

'I'll take you for a run later,' I promise, but he whines in disgust.

Eddie is waiting when I reach the New Inn. Our makeshift incident room looks tidier than before, as if he's spent hours wiping grime from the walls, but his expression is tense.

'This was hanging from the door when I arrived,' he says.

A bottle stands on the table. It's smaller than the last one, probably used originally for vinegar or cooking oil, and made of glass. I curse under my breath as I hunt for sterile gloves, then shake the slip of paper onto the table. The message is written in black ink, in crude block capitals.

> SINCE ROMAN DAYS WE'VE SAILED
>   THESE SEAS,
> FULL OF PIRATES, ROGUES
>   AND SLAVES.
> MEN THAT ROB FROM US WILL DIE
>   IN CAVES,
> WITH THE OLD GRAVES
>   LOOKING DOWN.
> WHEN THE TIDE'S HIGH WE'LL
>   FINISH THEM
> AND THEY WILL SAIL NO MORE.

The killer must have been in a rush this time, taking less care to disguise his handwriting, and his message is more overt. I could be clutching at straws, but for the first time he seems to be giving a direct clue to where Tom Heligan is being held: in a cave, near ancient graves, due to drown with the next high tide.

'Ask Will for a tide table, can you, Eddie?'

My deputy sets off at a sprint, even though the message could be leading us in the wrong direction. I'm prepared to scour every beach while there's a chance that Tom Heligan's alive, but it's clear that we'll need help. I swallow my pride and call Madron to request every available officer to search Tresco's coast by boat and land.

'Shall I tell the boy's mother we're looking for him, boss?' Eddie asks when he reappears.

'Not yet. There's no point in worrying Linda until we've got an outcome. The next high tide is at midday: I want all the caves searched on foot, we'll use boats to check the shoreline.'

It's just before ten o'clock, leaving two hours before the tide peaks at noon. The island is only two miles long, so the search should be an easy task, whether the boy is dead or alive. I pull on my jacket and collect a torch from the table, then hurry back downstairs. Will Dawlish is whistling to himself while he polishes the mirror behind the bar, movements slow and deliberate as he brings the glass to a high shine.

'Someone left a message for us upstairs, Will. Who could have reached the top floor last night?'

'We don't lock the fire escape until closing time, so someone could have sneaked in the back way without being seen. Then there's me and the kitchen staff, of course.' His small eyes blink at me. 'Is something wrong?'

'There's no time to explain; I need you to take me out in your boat. Bring a jacket and binoculars, we'll have to move fast.'

The innkeeper looks startled but seems glad to be involved. We'll need plenty of boats to scour the island's inlets and caves, even though more officers are coming from St Mary's to search on foot. Setting off early will give me a head start.

Dawlish is panting hard as we jog to the harbour, bald head gleaming with perspiration by the time we reach New Grimsby Sound. His boat is a modest thirty-foot cabin cruiser made of white fibreglass, with curtains obscuring its small portholes, the name *Anna May* printed on its side. When I ask him to head round the coast, staying close to the shore, he runs the motor hard to clear brine from its system before setting off. Dawlish is surprisingly adept for a man who claims to spend little time on the water. He eases his boat between vessels that pack the small harbour, then lets the tide carry it into the sound. We don't speak much as he picks up speed to chase the coastline south. It infuriates me that some bastard is using this idyllic place to commit terrible acts. Sunlight glints from the sea's face as we pass the sandbanks of Saffron Cove, with Abbey Hill rising in the background, seamed with narrow pathways. The landscape looks incorruptible, yet the killer is staining it with his deeds. There's nothing unusual on Appletree Bay's long stretch of sand when I peer through the binoculars, except some middle-aged holidaymakers rekindling their childhoods by flying a massive kite.

Our journey becomes more treacherous as we reach a notorious shipping hazard; the Chinks are needle-fine spikes of granite that are invisible at high tide, but this morning their tips stand proud of the water as we reach the island's southernmost point. Oliver's Battery looms over the headland, even though its glory days of firing cannons during the English Civil War ended centuries ago; the rock-strewn beach below is littered with masonry from the ruined building, but no signs of the missing boy. I keep hoping to see a figure bobbing on the waves, but all I can make out is a cluster of dinghies rising and falling with the currents. An old man fishing from one of the boats gives us a jaunty salute, as if we're day trippers enjoying a pleasure cruise.

By the time we reach Pentle Bay, my eyes are throbbing from scrutinising every detail. Will remains focused on steering his boat near to the shore, without running it aground. He's an unlikely skipper, portly in his smart trousers and Oxford brogues, windcheater zipped high to protect himself from the elements, but his expression is determined. We skim the eastern coast of Tresco at speed, with the Heligans' house rising from its rocky foundation on Merchant's Point. When we reach the northern tip of the island, conditions worsen. The breeze rolling in from the Atlantic is producing ragged waves that threaten to push the boat off course. I ignore its hectic rocking, keeping my spyglasses glued to the coast, where the beach is being consumed by the tide.

Eddie is no bigger than a toy soldier when he emerges from Piper's Hole, to give me a thumbs down, his search party following behind. I don't know whether to be angry or relieved that the killer hasn't left Tom Heligan's body in the same cave as the last two victims. My heart sinks as we pass Kettle Island, where currents boil across the rocks. It feels like a rerun of events from exactly a week ago, when Denny Cardew took me to Jude Trellon's body. The boy could be anywhere, but all I can do is scour each beach in turn.

45

Water is lapping over Tom's feet. The temperature feels colder than before, his skin icy. His system is shutting down, fever and thirst conquering him at last. The woman's voice swims at him, softer and less frightening than before.

'You look feverish, Tom. Do you want a drink?' She presses a bottle to his lips and he tastes the sweetness of lemonade, the liquid easing his parched throat.

'Let me go, please. Don't let me die here.'

'Tell us about the *Minerva*, then you can go home.'

'I don't believe you.'

Tom purses his lips, to stop words slipping out. If he says the names of people guarding the pieces Jude found, they'll be killed too, and it will make no difference. The sweetness in the woman's voice is too saccharine to be real.

'If I knew where it lay, I'd never tell you.'

'You arrogant little bastard.'

The blow comes without warning, an explosion of pain against his temple, then the sound of glass fracturing. When his head lolls back, the blindfold falls away, and he sees his captor clearly for the first time. Surprise overwhelms him as his vision dies: the woman's face is familiar. The shock lingers, even as he loses consciousness, and the tide rises further up his body.

46

I jog back to the incident room after circling the island with Will Dawlish. My stress levels are skyrocketing after wasting an hour on a fruitless search. If the boy is alive, my mistakes are condemning him to a slow drowning. I have under two hours to find him, but the men searching the coastline on foot have had no luck. Lawrie Deane arrives just as I'm about to call Eddie for another update. The sergeant offers a sneer instead of a smile, his red hair neatly combed, top button fastened despite the warm weather, as if he's hoping for a neatness award from DCI Madron.

'I've searched all the inlets and caves, from Gimble Point to Rushy Porth, and found nothing,' he says. 'Looks like you made another wrong call.'

'Leave your problems with me out of this, Lawrie. An eighteen-year-old boy will be dead by noon if we don't find him.'

'The same age as my son,' he mutters. 'Can I see the killer's note?'

'It's pretty cryptic; he's a man of few words.'

Deane frowns at the slip of paper. 'It doesn't make sense. The old graves on Tresco are dug high into the hills, not directly above the shore.'

'Maybe we should look elsewhere.' I scan a map of the Isles of Scilly on my computer, hundreds of islets and rocky outcrops littered across the screen. Many of them are riddled with tiny bays, making them a smuggler's paradise, and ideal for a killer's purposes. The boy could be hidden somewhere too remote to find. The only factor narrowing the field is the killer's reference to old graves, but a quick scan of the internet shows that many of the islands contain burial sites from Neolithic times onwards.

When I look out of the window again, the other officers from St Mary's are returning, with a gaggle of islanders in tow. Eddie's call for volunteers has drawn dozens of people to the inn, including Mike and Diane Trellon and Elinor Jago, the island's families turning out in force. My uncle has made the crossing from Bryher too, which lifts my spirits. Ray can always be relied on in a crisis, his constitution as solid as the fishing boats he builds, designed to roll in a hard storm, then bob back to the surface.

I jog downstairs to speak to the search party, with Deane keeping pace. For the time being the sergeant seems prepared to shelve our differences and focus on the missing boy. The small crowd looks expectant when I reach the hotel's yard, which often happens, whether or not I'm in uniform. Being the biggest man in a crowd always makes people turn to me for leadership, even when I'm grasping for solutions. I conjure a calm smile to address them.

'Thanks for helping us again. We still think Tom Heligan's being held near an ancient gravesite, but I need you to search the other four inhabited islands. Look in every cave, as well as on the beaches. Call me please, once you've finished.'

It takes Eddie and I moments to sort the group into teams that know each island intimately. I watch them set off in an assortment of dinghies and sloops, like the rescue boats of Dunkirk, each with a mission to fulfil. The only person left on the quay is my uncle Ray, and the cedar lapstrake boat he built himself is still moored on the jetty. His vessel is a thing of beauty, but it has no cabin to protect him from the elements, so I'm reluctant to send him too far from Tresco.

'Where would you hide someone, near an old burial ground?' I ask.

Ray's reply arrives faster than his usual drawl, as if the pressure of time is affecting him too. 'The Eastern Isles all have them. He could be on Round Island, Northwethel, Tean or St Helen's.'

'Can you check Northwethel? I'll take the rest.'

Ray gives a brisk nod, before stepping into his boat and casting off.

I can feel the minutes passing as I fire up the motor on the small police launch, then set off at maximum speed.

I wish I had a more powerful boat at my disposal, but will have to make do with an ancient speedboat, its white polymer sides turning yellow with age, only the police crest on its prow distinguishing it from the boats kids mess around in at St Mary's harbour all summer long. Its low plastic screen fails to protect me from the surf, leaving me soaked by the time Round Island rises on the horizon. The origin of its name is easy to understand as my boat scuds closer: a lighthouse stands at the centre of its domed outline, like a candle on a birthday cake. I use my binoculars to study its rocky coast, then steer the boat ashore, beaching it on the sand. The island has just one deep cave, with an entrance wide enough to admit a dinghy. Like Piper's Hole its floor drops downwards as it narrows, the fissure extending for ten metres. But all it contains this morning is an assortment of torn plastic bags, piles of seaweed and flotsam delivered by the last tide.

My next destination is Tean. The island's craggy outline looks stark as it juts from the water. I know little about its history except that a religious order lived there centuries ago, the remains of St Theona's chapel still visible at the centre of the island. When I pull out my binoculars again, I can see the decaying walls of ancient farmhouses and barns. All the island contains now is overgrown brambles that choke its fields. I test the boat's motor to its limit as I sail closer, until something catches my eye: a boat is moored in a cove, bobbing on the water. When I draw closer, it's the

Kinvers' yacht, but there's no sign of them on board; the couple's dinghy is missing from the bow, and my suspicions are rising. Why did they lie about their plans to cross the Atlantic? They must have been hiding here ever since I gave them permission to leave.

The Kinvers have left their boat at anchor, protected from the rising tide. When I climb on board, it seems they've been enjoying themselves – empty beer cans stacked in a bin, this morning's breakfast plates left on their table – but when I try to go below decks, the door is locked. It can't be a coincidence that they've returned the day after the killer made contact again. The couple could easily have sailed to Tresco at night, then come ashore unnoticed to leave their message. I scan the water for a sign of their dinghy, but see only the mouth of the cove, enclosing the sea in a perfect horseshoe, its surface glittering. The scene looks tranquil enough to adorn a postcard, but my frustration is reaching boiling point.

47

Tom is alone when his eyes blink open again. Pain throbs above his temple, a line of blood dripping down his cheek, the cold weakening him. The woman hasn't bothered to retie his blindfold and he can see the cave slowly filling, water lapping at his waist. A fresh surge of panic hits him as he scans the surface. Soon it will pass his chest and he will have to strain his neck to keep his head above water.

'I can't die like that,' he mutters.

His hands are still tied behind his back, the rope saturated. He tries to loosen the knots by rubbing his wrists against the stone, with no success. Frustration makes the boy take a deep breath then yank one of his fists upwards. The pain is bad enough to make his vision blur. He makes repeated attempts to free his hand, not caring about the pain as his knuckles are bruised to the bone. Waves are rising higher when he finally drags his right hand clear, muscles aching from being bound for so long, but his relief is temporary. A chain still binds his ankle to the rock, and the sea is inching nearer all the time.

Tom looks around for anything that could help, but finds

only a fist-sized rock. After days without movement, his fingers are too stiff to flex effectively. Once he can grasp the stone, he smashes it against the links of the chain. He carries on using the rock as a hammer, the action producing a tinny sound that echoes back from the roof of the cave.

48

There's no time to look for the Kinvers, but I drag my phone from my pocket and alert the coastguard, asking them to impound the couple's boat. I need to ensure they don't escape before being questioned again. I've just circled Tean's rocky coastline when a dilapidated fishing boat chugs across the water, a telltale plume of black smoke spewing from its engine. It's a relief to catch sight of Denny Cardew, who wears a tense expression when he pulls up beside my launch, two waiters from the New Inn peering at me from the bow. Cardew squints into the sun, his tar-stained fishing overalls full of holes.

'Eddie asked me to pick up some helpers from the quay. What can we do?'

'Check Ganilly and the islands east of there please, Denny. The boy could be at the mouth of a cave, like Jude Trellon.'

A spasm of anxiety crosses his weather-beaten face. 'But he's still alive?'

'I hope so. We've got less than an hour to find him.'

The fisherman gives an abrupt nod before spinning his boat east, cutting a broad line of wash across the waves. It's reassuring to know that men like Denny, Mike and Ray are all involved in the search. The old-timers have spent their lives on local waters, giving the boy his best chance of survival.

St Helen's is less than half a mile to the west, but its atmosphere is darker than Tean's. The island was once a quarantine; sailors with infectious diseases languished in its Pest House 300 years ago, to keep the inhabited islands free from contagion. The place spooked me as a boy, and it still looks haunted today. St Helen's is the bleakest island on the archipelago, shores strewn with huge boulders, hardly any trees or vegetation to disguise the barren rock. The ruins of the Pest House are still visible as I approach the southern shore, stones blackened by time and the elements. Ray told me once that the Romans used the island as a cemetery. It's easy to see why the place has often accommodated the sick and dying; with no fresh water supply, castaways would soon lose their battle to survive, in the days before powerboats existed. My vision blurs as I focus on the shore, hunting for signs of Tom Heligan, and it feels like I'm getting closer. The island is riddled with historic graves; its dark past would appeal to the type of vicious killer who could choke a woman to death, or leave a teenaged boy to drown. But it's home only to rats and shearwaters now, the birds cawing louder at my approach. It doesn't take much imagination to picture sailors dying here of leprosy and cholera, with no medicine to ease their suffering. The birds' cries grow shriller as my boat hugs the shore, a few terns dive-bombing the deck, intent on scaring me away.

There's no sign of Tom Heligan as I circle the island. The tide will soon reach its peak, and none of the search parties have found a trace of him yet. The coastguard's helicopter buzzes low overhead, flying over the island at its slowest speed, then hanging motionless before sweeping away to the west. Waves almost cover the shore, and the boy may have lost his battle already. If the killer tied him to the rocks closest to the sea, he will be a metre underwater already, but I let the tide carry me further inland. I want to search the island's caves before rejoining the main search party.

It's a hazardous journey to bring the launch ashore, with a vicious riptide straining the boat's engine. My father brought my brother and me to these caves as children, thrilling us with their murkiness and slime-covered walls, but they're a tough proposition at high tide. I steer the launch between two high outcrops, until a wall of granite shelters me from the worst currents. The entrance to the widest cave is already flooded as the passage recedes underground, the temperature dropping to a subterranean chill once the light fades. I'm about to admit defeat when my torch beam catches a piece of rope resting on a ledge. My eyes blink wider when I approach for a closer look. Blood is smeared across the rock, beside a piece of broken chain. For the first time since the search began, I can see clear evidence that Tom Heligan was held here; the blood looks fresh, so he may still be alive.

49

After so long without food, Tom has little energy left to fight the currents. They're threatening to pull him below the surface, cold water numbing his skin as the turning tide drags him out to sea. The sunlight is blinding after so long in the dark, the islands rising ahead no more than blurred outlines. Tom's diving training echoes in his mind. Instinct tells him to use his last reserves of energy to swim towards land, but it's best to float until a passing boat spots him. He recognises familiar landmarks: the lighthouse on Round Island, and the black coastline of Tean. Their positions tell him that the current is bearing him past the Eastern Isles towards open sea. It requires effort to remain above water, his limbs are barely moving, the broken chain around his ankle weighing him down. Suddenly a tall wave crests over his head, and he rises to the surface, spluttering for air. The open sea may finish his life faster than if he'd stayed in the cave.

Tom struggles to roll onto his back, arms lolling uselessly at his sides. He concentrates on staying afloat, sun beating down on his face, even though the water's chill makes him shiver.

Gulls wing overhead, considering him as a new source of prey, and from the corner of his eye, Tom sees the yellow outline of the rescue helicopter. His arms are too weak to lift, his panic replaced by exhaustion. It's tempting to let the sea's endless rocking take him under at last. When he shuts his eyes, he can picture the wrecks waiting for him on the seabed below: frigates, Victorian freighters, high-masted schooners that lost their bearings.

The islands are smaller now, as he's carried east. He can feel the sea wrapping him in its tight embrace, his eyes refusing to stay open, until something nudges against his side. A big piece of driftwood is bobbing on the surface. He conjures enough strength to climb onto it, before passing out. His face is shielded from the waves as he drifts further out to sea.

50

I call the coastguard again, to summon the rescue helicopter back to St Helen's, but there's no sign of it as my launch clears the mouth of the cave. I scan the sea's face in every direction as the high tide retreats, looking for a sign of the boy. The only way he could have escaped the flooded cave is by swimming, and there's no sign of him on the beach, so the riptide may already have ended his life. I turn off the engine and let the boat drift, hoping the sea will have dragged the boy in the same direction, even though there's little hope of finding him alive. The undercurrent is so powerful, it would be impossible to swim back to shore. The boat is being carried past Round Island, towards the edge of the archipelago. If the boy is still alive, he's at the mercy of the Atlantic; he could already be miles away. There's a chance the rescue helicopter will spot him, but finding a single body in an ocean full of waves is a tall order.

I follow my instinct and motor at full speed in the same direction as the current, over endless ragged waves. There's nothing marking the horizon ahead except the low outline of White Island, a grass-covered mound that breaks the surface for a final time before the Atlantic unfolds for 2000 miles. If the boy has lost his battle, it seems the loneliest death imaginable, like being catapulted into outer space with no hope of return. I'm about to abandon my search when I see something floating on the water, and my heart thuds against my ribs. The dark spot on the field of green liquid is unmistakeable; a human head cresting the waves. But when I get closer, a grey seal swims up to inspect my boat. It's only as I swing the wheel in the opposite direction that another bump appears on the horizon. I keep my hopes in check; a colony of seals could be circling me for entertainment. But this time I'm in luck. The boy is fifty metres away, draped across a plank of wood, his body motionless. I yell out to him as the boat draws nearer, but there's no sign of movement, making me curse out loud. I don't want to find Tom Heligan's corpse lying on a piece of driftwood after so much effort. When I get close enough to haul him onto the deck, his skin is freezing; there's a deep gash on his back, and a line of midnight blue bruises running from his temple to his jaw. His only item of clothing is a ragged pair of jeans, a piece of chain looped around his ankle.

Tom Heligan doesn't respond when I pummel his stomach, sending a stream of brine gushing from his mouth, then lie him in the rescue position. When I press two fingers against his throat, his pulse is faint, but at least he's alive. I grab the boat's emergency pack and wrap him in a thermal blanket, before calling search and rescue again. The boy is hollow-cheeked with exhaustion when I look down at him, swaddled in silver plastic that billows in the breeze. The rattling sound in his chest increases my panic, until the chopper reappears. The sound is deafening as it hovers overhead, the downdraught flattening the waves, but it only takes a few minutes for a paramedic to strap the boy into a harness, then disappear back into the sky. For some reason, I feel hollow as the helicopter buzzes west, carrying him to St Mary's hospital. Relief almost levels me when I think of my old English teacher retreating into stories ever since her son was taken. I blink hard to pull myself together before circling back towards Tresco. Eddie's voice is shrill with excitement when I call to explain that Tom Heligan is being airlifted away, even though there's no way of knowing how long he's been in the water, or the severity of his injuries.

A welcome committee is waiting on the quay when I get back to Tresco. Elinor Jago has erected a picnic table outside the post office, where she is handing out mugs of tea to the search team, islanders milling around with broad smiles on their faces. The sight of them makes me relax by a fraction: Tom Heligan is in safe hands, the medics will be pulling out all the stops to keep him alive.

'I called the boy's mum, boss,' Eddie says. 'She's being taken to the hospital now.'

My deputy's face is flushed with excitement, and even Lawrie Deane looks less taciturn. He's not quite managing to smile, but his scowl is missing for once. The rest of the islanders are in high spirits, people coming forwards to congratulate me. DCI Madron appears to be enjoying the celebration too, but the crowd are ignoring an obvious fact: Heligan may be back on dry land, but the killer that held him captive for five days is still on the loose.

'Have the Kinvers been found yet, Eddie?' I ask.

'We picked them up near their boat. They said they were out on their dinghy, taking pictures for their website. They'll be at the station till you want to interview them.'

'Let's see what they've got to say.' It still seems too coincidental that the couple stayed here after claiming to be desperate to leave.

I'm about to jump back into the boat when a familiar noise rings across the bay. I'd recognise Shadow's howl anywhere; the high-pitched sound reminds me of Canadian forests at midnight, when wolves are on the prowl. He's standing at the edge of the crowd, the fur on his hindquarters so saturated with blood it looks like he's been caught in a trap. I tell Eddie to wait for me, then head in Shadow's direction, but the dog skulks away; he's limping badly, but still moves too fast for me to catch him.

'Come here, you stupid hound.'

He runs as far as Dolphin Town, scattering drops of

blood on the path, only slowing down outside Larsson's house. He stations himself by the open back door and pants for breath, low growls issuing from his mouth. When I squat beside him, there's a raw wound on his left flank. I try to grab his collar, but he snarls at me, then runs inside. The house feels too silent; there's no reply when I call Larsson's name, and I can sense that something's wrong. The man is too wary to leave his back door unlocked.

'Not you too,' I mutter under my breath.

There's no sign of the father and daughter, apart from two long smears of blood on the kitchen floor. Shadow could have left a trail from his wound, but my tension increases when I spot a red-stained handprint on the living room door. Apart from that, the downstairs rooms look undisturbed. The sheets on Ivar's bed lie in a tangle, his duvet heaped on the floor, suggesting that he sprang up suddenly sometime after I left this morning. There are dried smears of blood on the bathroom sink, as if the attacker stopped to rinse away evidence. I call Frida's name when I enter her room, but my only reply is silence. The bastard must have taken both of them. I slump onto the edge of the child's bed and let my head drop into my hands. The killer can have no conscience at all: he struck again during the rescue mission, while many of the islanders were hunting for the lost boy. I'm still sitting motionless when I hear a noise that sounds like mice scrabbling under the floorboards. I keep my voice as calm as possible when I address the empty room.

'It's safe to come out now, Frida.'

There's a soft click, then a section of the floor rises, and the child steps into the open. Her pyjamas are covered in dust, her face tear-stained. When I hold out my hand, she runs straight to me, her small face pressed against my shoulder while she sobs.

'I hid, where Mummy puts her things.'

'Clever girl. Will you show me?'

She rubs tears from her face, then leads me to the opening. It's a metre wide and about half as deep; plenty of clear space concealed under the floorboards. The house must be almost as old as Smuggler's Cottage; it makes sense that it would also have a false floor, at a time when smuggling contraband was the islands' main source of income. I find a small lever by the skirting board, and another section of flooring lifts to reveal a box packed with items of the kind Jude's friends have been safeguarding: figurines, coins and pieces of jewellery. Frida must have curled up beside the *Minerva*'s treasures to escape the killer, but the objects are unimportant compared to her safety. When I look at the child again, her eyes are wide with shock.

'Let's go downstairs, Frida, I bet you're starving. We'll get you some food, then go and see grandma.'

'Where's Daddy?'

'He'll be back soon, sweetheart.'

When we return to the kitchen, Shadow has finally calmed down. He's lying on the blanket Larsson found for him, carefully licking his wound. He shoots me a sceptical look, reminding me to listen next time he's accused of crying wolf. I make toast and jam for Frida, then pour her a glass of milk. Diane Trellon says little when I make my call, before begging me to bring her granddaughter round straight away. My next call is to Eddie, who appears a few minutes later. He looks amazed when he sees the box concealed under the bedroom floorboards, before carting it back to the incident room. There's no way of knowing how many hours Frida spent hiding under the floorboards, too terrified to lift the hatch.

When I sit down at the kitchen table again, the kid has abandoned her snack.

'What's wrong, Frida?'

'Can I take my crayons to Granny's house?'

'Of course. I bet she'd love one of your drawings.' She manages a smile, before taking another bite of toast. 'Did you see who came here this morning?'

She shakes her head. 'A man was yelling at Daddy, so I ran away.'

'Did you hear his voice?'

'The lady was shouting too. Daddy told them to go away.' The girl's eyes are full of fear.

'Let's pack some stuff, then get moving; Granny's going to spoil you rotten.'

I fill two carrier bags with toys and clothes, then lead the girl outside, considering her statement. If she really heard a man and a woman, it could have been the Kinvers, intent on finding out what Ivar knew about the *Minerva*.

The dog makes no attempt to follow us, too weak for another excursion. Frida accompanies me to her grandmother's house with a coat over her pyjamas to keep her warm. Apart from her tight grip on my hand, there's no sign that she's distressed, humming quietly as we follow the track to Ruin Beach. She even stops to pick wild flowers for her grandmother, but I can't guess how much psychological damage has been done. I hope her grandparents can steer her thoughts away from her father's absence, limiting any trauma that could emerge later.

Diane doesn't say a word when we arrive, already standing by her gate. She swoops down to hug her granddaughter, then gives me a look of gratitude. Mike hasn't yet returned from the search for Tom Heligan, which strikes me as odd, when all the other boats were moored by the time I got back, apart from the innkeeper's. When we go indoors, Frida wastes no time in pulling her box of crayons from one of the bags, then settling on the living room floor with her drawing pad, her dark hair veiling her face. The kid has developed strong coping mechanisms since her mother died, but she looks more fragile than before. There's no way of knowing how she'll manage if her father never comes home.

51

I tell Eddie to meet me back at Larsson's cottage, where Shadow is fast asleep, still recovering from his adventure. When the forensics officers arrive, they are bound to criticise me for trampling over the crime scene, but at least the girl is safe. My mind spins from one regret to the next; I should have insisted that Ivar took Frida to a safe house on the mainland, but he was so determined to stay, it would have been like trying to shift a mountain. It strikes me as odd that the killers haven't left me another taunting message – perhaps they were so anxious about being caught, they abandoned their MO.

My heart sinks when DCI Madron arrives instead of Eddie. He's glowing from the morning's outcome, and it's clear that my deputy has left me to explain Larsson's disappearance. Madron is still beaming when he steps forwards to shake my hand.

'Your methods are unconventional, Kitto, but they seem to work. How did you know the boy had been taken to St Helen's?'

'A mixture of luck and common sense, sir.'

'You seem very downbeat. Why not show some professional pride?'

'Events have moved on since then.'

The DCI's tone grows bitter when he hears that Larsson is missing, his approval turning to censure. 'You knew he was in danger but never requested a guard. Now we're back to square one, and this puts the Kinvers in the clear, doesn't it?'

'No, sir. They could have come ashore last night, left the message, then carried out the abduction.'

'I ordered you to arrange appropriate security.' His grey eyes have frosted over.

'I tried, sir, but Larsson refused police protection.'

'Save that for your review meeting,' he snaps. 'Now get on and find him.'

'I'll interview the Kinvers first, sir. They must be involved.'

I almost bump into Sophie Browarth outside Larsson's cottage. She's dressed in her nurse's uniform and carrying her medical bag, which explains why she didn't take part in our search for the missing boy. She couldn't cancel appointments and let her patients down. Browarth's flame-red hair is pulled back in a sleek ponytail today, her face as pale as milk. There's a lost look on her face, as if she'd rather be standing in someone else's shoes. It's the first time I've seen definite proof that her complicated home life is weighing on her. She seems startled when I ask for a favour.

'My dog's injured, could you check him over?'

'Humans are my speciality, Ben, not animals. I'm on my way to see Sylvia Cardew.'

'The vet on St Mary's can't see him today.'

The nurse tuts under her breath, complaining that she's running late, but her manner softens when she hears Shadow whining. Normally he's reluctant to let strangers touch him, but he doesn't flinch when Sophie examines his wound. Her voice is matter-of-fact when she explains that his wound needs stitches.

'The painkiller in my bag may not be suitable for animals,' she says.

'He'll risk it.'

The dog moans pitifully when he sees the hypodermic, but tolerates the injection, as if he realises there's no other choice. My attitude towards Sophie changes as she comforts the dog. It's impossible to believe that someone capable of such gentleness could cause anyone harm. She waves my thanks away as she straightens up, telling me to let him sleep for the rest of the day, but I follow her outside with Shadow in my arms, hoping that Sylvia Cardew will be prepared to look after him. Sophie seems uncomfortable as we walk the short distance, and we must make an odd sight: a big man lumbering along with a wounded dog in his arms, beside a petite nurse, dressed in her navy-blue uniform. She turns to me before we reach the Cardews' house.

'You know about me and Shane, don't you?' she says. 'We're waiting till Phil gets home to tell him. It's not

something we planned, I tried to fight it for months.'
Her gaze drops to the ground.

'Will you stay on Tresco?'

She nods her head firmly. 'We both love it here;
nothing could drive us away. You won't tell anyone,
will you?'

'It's none of my business, Sophie. Why would I mention it?'

The nurse looks relieved as we reach the Cardews'
front door. She stops to brush some stray locks of
hair back from her forehead, before ringing the bell,
preparing herself for duty. Sylvia Cardew looks even
more anxious than last time we met, cowering behind
the door, but she promises to look after Shadow for
the rest of the day. The couple's old Labrador comes
to sniff at the new arrival, then wanders away again,
his curiosity satisfied. It's a relief to know that the
dog's welfare is guaranteed while I chase details about
Larsson's abduction.

I scan the boats in the harbour when I get back to
New Grimsby Sound, noticing that Will Dawlish's
cruiser is still missing, even though he must be needed
at the New Inn by now. After the help he's given me,
I hope his engine hasn't broken down, but there's no
time to check he's safe, so I push his absence to the back
of my mind. Eddie spends most of the twenty-minute
journey to St Mary's talking at top speed, his excitement dispersing in loud bursts of chatter. He gives me
a full update on Tom Heligan's condition, and the fact

that Lawrie Deane has stopped moaning for once. The sergeant is phoning round to see if any islanders can explain Larsson's absence.

The Kinvers are an unlikely sight when we reach the police station; their cut-off shorts and brightly coloured T-shirts make a striking contrast with the reception area's drab furniture. They both glower at me when Eddie and I walk through the door.

'You're wasting our time again, Inspector,' Stephen Kinver snaps.

'Not from my point of view. Come to the interview room, please.'

I take the Kinvers to the small anteroom off DCI Madron's office. Once Eddie has set up the recorder, I explain that they will be questioned in connection with the abduction of Tom Heligan and Ivar Larsson.

'That's ridiculous. We've never hurt anyone in our lives,' Lorraine interjects before I can finish.

'Can you explain why you stayed here, after getting permission to leave?'

'The weather was against us, so we decided to give the Scillies a few more days before leaving for the summer,' she replies, in a sullen voice. 'Our website shows what we've been doing. We've dived near a different island every day, and we haven't been secretive about it. We ate at the pub on Bryher last night, and before that we moored in St Mary's harbour. Loads of people must have seen us.'

'I've had your website checked out. There's no way

you're making enough money to finance your lifestyle, so how are you managing it?'

'We tick over,' her voice is quieter now. 'Our savings cover anything that goes wrong with the boat.'

'Tell me why you anchored near where the boy was found.'

Stephen Kinver stares at me. 'What are you saying?'

'We'll be checking whether you kept Tom Heligan on board.'

'Jude brought the lad out to dive with us, that's the only time we saw him,' he says. 'We've never even met Ivar Larsson.'

'Where have you hidden him? In another cave?'

'You're not making sense,' Kinver replies.

Lorraine leans forwards in her chair. 'Why not ask the boy? Tom Heligan will tell you the truth about us.'

'I shall, once he's stronger. You both had reason to carry out the attacks. Jude wouldn't tell you about the *Minerva* and the boy didn't know; that's why you took Ivar Larsson last night, hoping for more information. You could have made a fortune if you claimed to be the discoverers. And you were here last November; maybe you attacked Anna Dawlish too.'

'If Jude had found the *Minerva*, she wouldn't have kept it to herself,' Kinver replies. 'I bet her whole family knows.'

'I'm arresting you on suspicion of Jude Trellon's murder, and Tom Heligan and Ivar Larsson's abductions. We'll be checking your backgrounds carefully, so tell us now if you've ever been convicted of any crimes. I want to know exactly what you've been buying and selling on your travels.'

The Kinvers waste no time in requesting a lawyer before they're interviewed again, and the rest of the interview is an exercise in frustration. Their story about remaining in the Scillies because of poor weather on the Atlantic Strait seems unlikely, but it will have to be verified. The couple complain bitterly when I explain that they must spend the night in custody. Lorraine gives a squeal of protest when she sees that her holding cell is the size of a broom cupboard, with a narrow bed and a toilet tucked in the corner. Her husband remains silent until his cell door is locked, but curses at high volume as we walk away. I leave Eddie to guard them; on such a small island the police force doubles as jailors, with three small holding cells at our disposal.

I take a brisk walk along the harbour, with locals stopping me several times to ask questions. The news of Tom Heligan's rescue has already spread between the islands like wildfire. I keep my answers brief, then complete the short journey to the island's hospital. The boy's room is closed to visitors when I arrive, but I can see him through the window in the door. His mother's wheelchair is pressed against the bed so she can hold his hand. I stare at Heligan's thin form outlined under a blue blanket, his face gaunt as he sleeps. Watching the boy reminds me that I should call his closest friend on Tresco, to let her know he's safe.

Gemma Polrew's voice lifts as she hears the news; there's relief in every syllable, even though I warn her that he's dangerously ill. Her tone is full of quiet determination when she explains that she won't be retaking her A levels. She plans to stay on the island to pursue a career in garden design, and will soon have to give her father the bad news.

I'm still peering through the window of Heligan's room when a doctor comes to a halt at my side. She must be close to retirement age, with grey hair cropped close to her skull; the name badge on her lapel states that she's called Sheila Barrett, her expression kindly when she peers up at me through steel-framed glasses.

'He's very weak, I'm afraid,' she murmurs. 'Two broken ribs and pleurisy in his left lung, not to mention a fractured jaw.' She reels off his injuries at speed, as if the victim of a car accident has just arrived on her ward.

'But he'll survive?'

Dr Barrett holds my gaze. 'He's got a good chance. We won't know the full extent of his injuries until he comes round; with luck that will be tomorrow. I've given him a sedative to let him sleep in peace. We'll have him airlifted to Penzance Hospital once he's strong enough for the ride.'

'Thanks for helping him.'

She touches my arm. 'The boy's fought hard to stay alive. He's unlikely to give up now.'

The doctor leaves me observing Heligan through the

window, but my mind shifts towards Ivar Larsson. I can do nothing else for the boy, except keep my fingers crossed until he regains consciousness. Now my energies have to focus on finding the missing man, before he receives the same brutal treatment.

52

Tom drifts, far below the surface. He can hear the bleep of a monitor, his mother's voice telling him he's safe, footsteps drumming down a corridor, but none of it seems real. Time is slipping back to his last dive alone with Jude. The cold spring day rises from his memory in prismatic detail. Jude laughs as she steers the boat east from Ruin Beach, promising to show him something amazing, if he has the nerve to look. It's in a secret location, and he must promise never to tell. Tom shifts restlessly on the hospital bed while his imagination spins time into reverse. He's back on the *Fair Diane*, bumping over choppy waves, the sun clear overhead as the boat passes the edge of the archipelago.

Tom's sleeping body twitches as he watches Jude throw the lead weight overboard, securing the shot line to the seabed, while White Island shifts on the horizon. Nerves and antici-pation tingle through his system as he dives backwards into water that dazzles with sunlight, fronds of seagrass floating on the currents. Jude is descending already, her body spearing through the water, supple as an eel. He has never followed her so deep into the ocean before, his lungs constricting as light fades. The water turns dark green as they sink fifty metres below the surface. Far below them, wreckage is strewn across a sandbank. Tom's gaze scans broken timbers encrusted with barnacles, the outline of a longship's hull, its mast almost buried by sand. Hundreds of pieces of metal cover the ocean floor, glittering in the dull light, too many to count. He wants to carry on diving, so he can touch the treasures with his own hands, but Jude is tapping her watch already. It's time to ascend, or they won't have enough air to surface. They rise slowly, stopping to acclimatise every twenty metres, hands clutching the shot line.

Tom's fingers flex tight around dry air in his hospital bedroom. He wants to swim back to the light, so he can tell the police about the woman that hurt him, but the distance is too great. His mother's voice sounds in his ears. He listens to her calling out his name, until pain drags him under again.

53

Darkness has fallen by the time I trudge back to Larsson's house. Two forensics officers are packing equipment into a black metal box, full of brushes, torches and bottles of chemicals, as if they've been conducting an elaborate chemistry experiment. The older officer is around fifty, his jaded expression proving he's witnessed plenty of murder scenes. His female colleague looks much less worldly, giving me a fresh-faced smile, her light brown hair tied in pigtails. The pair look like an ex-con and a nursery school teacher, but they seem united in their desire to chase every detail.

'It's a pleasure to have your company at last,' I say.

The older guy seems immune to irony. 'We're finished in here. We've taken blood samples from the floor, walls and ceiling,' he says, in a gruff smoker's baritone.

'Would someone have to be badly injured for it to travel that far?'

'Not necessarily,' the young woman replies. 'Droplets

from a small cut can spread over a metre. Our UV lamp picks up single molecules.'

It's 8 p.m. by the time they leave the house, the dry smell of chemicals still filling each room. They will stay at the New Inn until tomorrow, then search the Polrews' and the Kinvers' boats, before carrying evidence back to Land's End. It could take days before their test results explain how Larsson was taken, and fingerprints are unlikely to help. Every member of Jude Trellon's family has visited the house recently, and plenty more islanders have spent time here, making the evidence trail difficult to read.

It's 9 p.m. before I return to the Cardews' house. Denny and his wife both greet me when I arrive; the fisherman looks exhausted from his day's work, but it's obvious that Shadow has been receiving excellent care. Toys are strewn across his blanket and there's a bowl full of dog biscuits at his side. I thank them for giving him so much attention, but Sylvia looks embarrassed. She makes no attempt to cross the threshold when I say goodbye, as if the outside world might damage her if she breathes fresh air. Shadow tries to wriggle out of my arms, but I refuse to put him down.

'You're not walking, buddy. That leg needs to heal before you go running across the fields.'

He whimpers in protest but lets me carry him back to Larsson's house and make him comfortable on a pile of towels. Now that the day's duties are over, my thoughts spin back over a day that started with a successful rescue and ended in failure. I felt elated when I hauled Tom Heligan from the sea, only to be knocked flat by Ivar going missing. Whoever the killer is, his obsession with the *Minerva* seems relentless; no sooner than he loses one victim, he acquires another, determined to discover the ship's location before the chance slips from his hands.

I cast my mind over the suspect list again, focusing on who could have left the message at the inn, then taken Ivar Larsson in the middle of the night. My main focus is on the Kinvers, but they're still protesting their innocence. Jamie Petherton's reluctance to let things go keeps him at the front of my mind too; his passion for glittering antiques could easily have become an obsession. The same theory applies to David Polrew. The historian loves the glamour of the past, yet spends the present day tormenting his family. The man's bullying personality could easily cross the line into violence.

I'm still sitting at Ivar Larsson's kitchen table when a text arrives from Zoe.

Are you hungry?

Always, meet me on the quay, I reply.

My mind is still chasing in circles, aware that Larsson could be tied to a rock with the sea level rising, but there's nothing I can do until morning, so I walk down to the harbour. Zoe is crossing New Grimsby Sound in the hotel's launch. Her shock of platinum blonde hair stands out against the dark; she's wearing skintight jeans, a scarlet jumper that accentuates her curves, her lips painted the same vivid red.

'Don't just gawp at me, big man,' she says, stepping onto the jetty. 'This hamper weighs a ton.'

It's relaxing to let her boss me around on the five-minute walk back to Larsson's cottage, neither of us discussing her plans to work abroad. She's raided the hotel's kitchen to provide a high-class picnic. Her hamper contains smoked salmon, potato salad, quiche, a punnet full of ripe strawberries and a bottle of Prosecco.

'You deserve it, Ben. Tom Heligan would have drowned without your help.'

'I was feeling pretty good about it until Ivar was taken.'

Her dark gaze is unblinking. 'You'll find him.'

'How come you're so sure?'

'Because you're smart, Ben, you always have been.'

'So I'm ideal boyfriend material?'

'Not with that beard.' She looks amused. 'Only Ryan Gosling is allowed facial hair.'

The rest of the evening passes in a flurry of conversation. She listens to my story of finding the missing boy floating a mile from shore, even though the islands' gossip factory will already have circulated every detail. Our talk returns to childhood exploits, when we used to canoe around Bryher's coves, forgetting to go home for meals, until our parents sent out search parties. When she gets up to leave at midnight, her job in India still hasn't been mentioned.

'I've been meaning to say well done, Zoe.'

'Is that your sad attempt at congratulations?'

'I'm proud of you, but it's all you're getting.'

'How come it's okay for you to leave the island for years, but when I go travelling, you act like I'm deserting you?'

'I'm a selfish bastard, obviously.'

'You've got plenty of friends here.'

'Have you signed the contract yet?'

'I've got three more days to make up my mind.'

'If I kissed you, would you stay?'

Her gaze locks onto mine. 'We agreed that would never happen, remember? You made a promise.'

'That was twenty years ago, Zoe.'

'Nothing's changed.'

'Bollocks.'

'And that's my cue to say goodnight.' She gives one of her lightning grins that sends sparks around the room, then heads for the door.

We trudge back to the harbour in silence, and I settle for a hug, before she steps back into the boat. She could be right about a kiss being a bad idea, because it would cross a line we drew to protect ourselves long ago. It preserved our friendship through our teens and twenties, as our friends fell in and out of love, sometimes doing each other brutal damage. I've kept my relationships short and sweet, and so has she, but the bond between us only gets stronger. Now that we're adults the attraction is harder to ignore. Maybe by the time we hit our forties it will fizzle out, if it hasn't driven me crazy by then.

I stand on the quay, staring across 500 metres of water to the island where I was born. Bryher looks mysterious in the dark, even though I know every inch of its terrain. The steep hill of Shipman Head looms in the distance, and the light inside my uncle's living room pulses above the entrance to his boatyard. I could follow Ray's example and spend the rest of my life alone, but permanent solitude doesn't appeal. My only option is to remain on Tresco until I find Ivar Larsson, forgetting about personal concerns until Frida is reunited with her father.

54

It's midnight before I bunk down again on Larsson's settee, but sleep seems unlikely. Starlight floods through the thin curtains, and when I look outside, there's an unbroken view of the galaxies. Stars are visible here from dusk till dawn because there's so little light pollution, the Milky Way wreathing the horizon. But the long view can't help me tonight. My mistake could cost Larsson his life; I should have ignored his objections and put a permanent guard outside his door. The girl will be inconsolable if she's orphaned.

My body feels stiff with tension as I twist and turn. I can't forget Frida telling me that she heard a woman's voice as well as a man's when her father was taken, but the Kinvers may be innocent, even though few people on the island have reason to behave with such violence. I flick through the names of couples I've interviewed during the investigation: the Polrews, Mike and Diane Trellon, Sophie and Shane. Only the historian and his wife seem likely candidates, keeping their daughter trapped in their stultifying house, imprisoned like Tom Heligan, yet no hard proof links them to the crimes, unless the forensics officers find evidence on their boat. It's a relief when exhaustion finally forces me into a shallow sleep.

When I wake up, a ray of moonlight has pierced the curtains, illuminating the room, while Shadow barks at the top of his voice. I curse out loud when I check my watch and see that it's 4 a.m., Shadow's recent heroics forcing me to my feet. The creature often indulges in random fits of barking when he hears cats prowling at night, but experience has proved that his alarm calls are sometimes valid. Shadow is scratching the back door when I go into the kitchen dressed in boxer shorts and a T-shirt, my arrival silencing him. I peer through the window, but Dolphin Town seems to be sleeping peacefully, the lane empty. The vicarage and neighbouring houses are all in darkness.

'You're imagining things,' I say, but the dog refuses to lie down.

It's only when I open the back door that the reason for his alarm call becomes clear. A plastic bottle is suspended from the porch beam by garden twine at eye level, fresh sand still crusting its surface. The killer probably collected it from the rubbish that washes ashore with every high tide, using gloves to keep it free of fingerprints. I carry the bottle inside, desperate for information about Larsson. It dawns on me that the killer's latest taunt puts the Kinvers in the clear; they may be smuggling goods between countries, but whoever left the latest message is still wandering the island at liberty, having the time of his life. Anger rises in my throat when I read the words printed on the usual slip of white paper:

> WHERE THE WIND CARRIES US, YOU
> WILL NOT KNOW,
> ACROSS OCEANS WIDE, WHERE
> BREEZES BLOW,
> WE ARE FREE AS THE GULLS IN THE
> HEAVENS ABOVE,
> WHERE THE WIND CARRIES US, YOU
> WILL NOT KNOW.

I screw the paper up, then hurl the bottle at the wall. The killer is literally free as a bird while I flounder in mistakes, and it's clear that he's a risk-taker; he was prepared to rise before dawn to leave his message, despite the danger of being caught. The gesture echoes the recklessness of his other attacks. But which islander is fearless or angry enough to assault a police officer and drag his lifeless body into the sea, or abduct a grieving father from his home? He must be physically strong to carry out such violence. Shane Trellon seems the most likely suspect. The man's temper and physical strength make him the right type to perform the attacks, but why would he and Sophie want to hurt Jude, when they both claimed to love her?

It's still dark outside, but sleep is impossible now the killer has paid his visit. There's no point in chasing across the island looking for the culprit; he'll be back in his home by now, reliving his latest exploits. I make a pot of coffee, then sit at Larsson's kitchen table going through evidence files on my laptop until my eyes blur.

I open David Polrew's book and stare at an illustration of a Roman longship built in the same era as the *Minerva*. It was a *navis oneraria*, a merchant ship with a square main sail. There's something familiar about its curved prow and high mast rising from the centre of the deck, with dozens of long oars protruding from its sides. I have to concentrate hard before remembering where the image comes from.

When I open the encrypted photographs from Jude Trellon's autopsy, the same boat is inked on her upper arm: the tattooist must have used the illustration as a template, but it's the vessel jostling beside it that catches my attention. Jude chose to have the *Minerva* drawn on her skin beside her father's boat, the *Fair Diane*, and there must be a reason. Mike has spent his life diving in the local waters, so passionate about his hobby that he set up his own school, teaching his kids to scuba while they were small. Jude had the image of the *Minerva* etched on her body alongside her father's boat because it was him that found the wreck, not her. The theory would explain his guilt on the day of Jude's death, when he claimed that he could have prevented it, without saying why.

357

55

Tuesday 19 May

It's still early when I set off for Ruin Beach, with
Shadow limping behind. Despite my best efforts to
lock the creature indoors, he managed to sneak past
me, and I don't have time to drag him back to the
house. Mike Trellon looks like he's dressed in a hurry
when he appears at the door, his shirt unbuttoned,
eyes bleary.

'Why didn't you tell me you'd found the *Minerva*?'
Tension makes me fire the question at him.

His face is sober as he leads me inside. There's no
sign of Diane in the kitchen when Mike settles on
a stool, keeping his back as straight as a soldier on
parade, his expression defiant.

'It's been a curse, not a blessing,' he says quietly.
'Some marine biologists booked a deep-sea dive last
autumn; I took them past the Eastern Isles, and we
went down to forty metres. I saw an outline on the

seabed, but it was too deep to reach without specialist equipment.'

'You didn't tell anyone?'

'The other divers didn't notice, and I wasn't even sure it was a wreck, but I took photos on my next visit. When I enlarged them on the computer, I knew it was a Roman longship straight away.'

'How could you tell?'

'From the width of the deck and curved prow; it's incredibly well preserved. Once I figured it out, I was frozen in the headlights. The discovery might change our lives, but my hands were full, raising capital to keep the business going. It was November before I told Diane, Shane and Jude. They agreed we should keep it quiet. By then it was too late in the season to dive again; we decided to wait until spring.'

'Who else knew?'

'No one, it was our secret. The *Minerva*'s part of diving folklore, and there's serious money attached to marine salvage. Two guys got killed in Greece last year when a gang thought they knew the location of a valuable wreck.'

'Could the Kinvers have guessed?'

'Jude was too smart to tell anyone.'

'Did you know she'd been getting death threats?'

He gives a slow headshake. 'She never said.'

'Anna Dawlish and Jude both lost their lives because of the *Minerva*. We can't let Ivar die as well. Tell me exactly what happened.'

He grimaces. 'I planned to do it all legally. I was going to call the Maritime and Coastguard Agency, then go down with a salvage team in a hired submersible. I didn't tell my family the exact location, but Jude found it in one of my notebooks. I warned her not to tell anyone, even Shane.'

'That's why they argued in the pub?'

Mike screws his eyes shut. 'She was afraid someone would beat us to it. Jude knew my business was in trouble and thought the wreck could save it; she believed the profits were ours by right, because divers like us take all the risk. I refused to let her use the boat, but that didn't stop her.'

'How did she get down there?'

'I don't know. It drove a wedge between us; I hated her diving there and selling what she found. She gave Diane money for the business, because she knew I wouldn't accept it.'

'How much did Jude give her?'

'A couple of grand, in cash, to buy stock for the shop.'

'Some of the things she found were hidden in her house, the rest given to friends for safekeeping; Jude even left pieces at the vicarage. She told Justin to take them to you if anything bad happened.'

His hands rise to cover his face. 'I wish I'd never seen the bloody wreck.'

'How would she have made such a deep dive?'

'By breaking all the rules. The sea's a hundred and fifty metres deep at the wreck site; she couldn't have done it alone. She'd have needed a rebreather and circular bailout equipment, to avoid narcosis.'

'Tell me what that means in layman's terms, Mike.'

'If you dive below thirty metres, nitrogen builds up in your bloodstream; you have to stop regularly on your way back, to acclimatise. Hundreds of divers die each year by surfacing too fast. The rebreather gives you a mix of compressed gases that helps the pressure in your body stabilise. You need someone on the dive boat monitoring you every step of the way.'

'A friend would have been above water, giving her technical backup?'

'She should have had a diving buddy too, but Jude didn't care about safety.' His voice contains a mix of bitterness and regret.

'Whose boat could she have borrowed, Mike? Whoever lent it to her knew what she'd found; I think we're looking for a couple.'

'I refused and so did Denny. No one in their right mind would let someone take that much risk.'

'What if they didn't fully understand the dangers?'

Mike stares back at me, and for the first time since Jude's death, his gaze is animated. The prospect of finding his daughter's killer is bringing him back to life.

56

Tom is lying on his side in a hospital bed when he comes round. The mattress seems to rock from side to side, like a ship fighting a hard storm, and it's worse when he shuts his eyes. Memories carry him back to the cave, where sick echoes return to taunt him. But at least the room is reassuring. It smells of medicine and detergent, the electronic bleep of his heartbeat echoing through a monitor. His mother's blue overcoat is hanging from a hook on the wall, yet there's no sign of her wheelchair.

He takes a deeper breath, then there's a sudden crushing pain in his side and an alarm bell shrills in his ear. When a middle-aged nurse rushes through the door, her expression is panicked. He sees her hit a button on the wall before pain sears his ribcage, as if someone is pressing a branding iron to his skin. The boy doesn't notice when two medics strip the blankets away to examine him. His eyes focus on the nurse when she leans over him, her face kind but careworn. It's her gentle expression that makes him recall his captors' desire to see him drown. He whispers the name of the woman that kept him locked up, but the nurse doesn't respond. She just squeezes his hand and tells him not to panic.

57

Mike frowns as we study the list of islanders who own boats sturdy enough to carry Jude out to the *Minerva*. The Kinvers are languishing in holding cells, so they couldn't have left the latest message. Only a small number of islanders own vessels powerful enough to withstand being battered by the Atlantic while Jude made her dive: Elinor Jago, Sophie Browarth, the Polrews, Denny Cardew, Will Dawlish and Jamie Petherton. But it's the sequence of events that I need to understand. Mike spotted the wreck in November last year, and Anna Dawlish died a week later, her body found in Piper's Hole. The next victim was Jude Trellon, then Tom Heligan's abduction, and now Ivar Larsson's disappearance, straight after the boy was found. I rub my hand across my eyes, longing for more clarity, when an idea shifts into place. Jamie Petherton's devotion to Jude means that he would have done anything she asked. His obsession with her may have turned to violence towards the other victims, for reasons that remain unclear.

'Shane or Jude must have told someone,' Mike mutters. 'There's no way Diane would breathe a word.'

Trellon still looks distressed when I say goodbye, as if he can't forgive himself for discovering the *Minerva*. The idea that Petherton could be the killer nags at me. The other names on the list are less convincing. Elinor Jago has spent her life helping people, alongside working at the post office, and Will Dawlish's heartbreak over his wife's death would be hard to simulate. My phone rings while I'm crossing Ruin Beach.

'I've got more details about Jude's bank account,' Eddie says. 'The five grand came from a holding account in the Cayman Islands. I'm trying to trace it back to the Kinvers, but it's been through a money-laundering service.'

'Keep going till you find the source, Eddie. That's the evidence we need.'

'There's bad news about Tom Heligan. He's in intensive care, with pneumonia and a collapsed lung. They say it's touch-and-go.'

I stuff my phone back into my pocket, then stare out at the sea. The ocean knows exactly where Ivar Larsson is being held, but it's guarding its secret, waves battering the shore while my investigation staggers from bad to worse. The wind is growing more intense, whitecaps cresting on the horizon when I drop down onto a breakwater to gather my thoughts. I've believed all along that whoever killed Jude Trellon was motivated by powerful emotions. Now that Larsson is missing, the only other

islander she had been romantically involved with is
Jamie Petherton, who hated her current boyfriend for
ending his relationship with Jude. It's worth confronting the museum manager one more time, for the truth
about what happened.

Morning light is strengthening as I head for Abbey
Gardens, and the island looks incongruously peaceful. There's no sign of Shadow; it's likely that he's
found a quiet spot to sleep in, rather than being confined indoors. The fields are lush green, the landscape
dominated by rounded hills as I pass the Great Pool,
its surface reflecting acres of uninterrupted sky. The
museum's grounds are empty when I arrive, apart
from ranks of figureheads offering me ghostly stares.
When I look through the window, Jamie Petherton
stands in the middle of his empire, peering into a
display cabinet. His expression clouds when he sees
me, his gaunt face marked by a frown, as if he's still
dwelling on our last meeting at the station.

'Put the closed sign on the door, will you, Jamie?'

His movements are jerky as he follows my instruction, as if he's already guessed what I'm going to say.

'Why did you take Jude out to the *Minerva*? You
must have known the dive could kill her.'

He flinches, but his gaze remains steady. 'She begged
me, and I wanted to spend time with her.'

'Jude would never have left Ivar for you. Is that why
you killed her, then attacked him?'

'I never touched either of them.'

'Tell me what happened, or I'll arrest you for her murder.'

'I guessed Jude had found it when I saw all the diving equipment she needed. She had to be looking for something valuable to take that much risk. It was crazy to dive that deep without a decompression chamber on board; I was terrified she'd get the bends.'

'But she resurfaced safely?'

'The wait nearly finished me; she had to stop and use the rebreather three times.' He slumps onto a stool by the counter, as if the memory exhausts him. 'She'd loaded a basket while she was on the seabed. We hauled it to the surface on a pulley, and I couldn't believe my eyes. She'd found coins and masks, jewellery and statuettes, all dating from Roman times. Some of the pieces are worth a fortune.'

'What did you get out of it?'

'To be in her company, like I said.'

'She must have given you souvenirs.'

He shakes his head. 'Only this.'

Petherton takes something from his pocket and drops it into the palm of my hand. It's a thumb-sized version of the mermaid figurine that ended Jude Trellon's life, the bronze polished to a dull sheen, turquoise stones glittering from finely carved eye sockets. He stands at my side while I study it, clearly afraid the amulet will be confiscated. There's relief on his face when I return it to him. The man reminds me of a magpie more than ever at close range, his peculiar gaze drawn by the shiny objects displayed on the museum's walls.

'What happened when you got back to shore?'

'I helped her hide most of it in Piper's Hole, then I didn't see her again until the party on St Agnes. She asked me to take her on another dive, but I refused.'

'Why?'

'I couldn't watch her risk her life again, even though she accused me of being a coward. The only thing she wanted me for was my boat.' There's so much pain on his face, my gut tells me he's speaking the truth.

'Did you tell anyone about finding the *Minerva*?'

'Jude made me promise to keep it secret.' He looks away. 'She never said what she planned to do with the treasure, but she was afraid it might be stolen. When I heard she'd drowned at Piper's Hole, I assumed someone had found her hiding place.'

'Where's your boat, Jamie?'

'St Mary's harbour, being serviced. It's been there all week.'

I leave the museum more frustrated than ever. Petherton has plenty of reasons to carry out the attacks: his passion for history and all that glitters would have made him fascinated by the *Minerva*'s precious cargo and he knew its location, yet I believe his story. He loved Jude even though she was out of reach, and his gentle manner makes him an unlikely murderer. I can't picture him planning a campaign that began with killing Anna Dawlish and included abducting a teenaged boy. I doubt any woman on the island would have helped him carry out such vicious attacks.

When I get back to the incident room, DCI Madron is poking through evidence files, his expression sombre. He informs me that he has despatched Eddie to St Mary's Hospital to check on Tom Heligan's welfare. The news makes me grit my teeth. The DCI seems determined to take over, keeping watch over me while I answer phone calls from concerned locals, when my time would be better spent scouring the island for evidence of Larsson's disappearance. My boss insists on a long review meeting, poring over every detail since Jude's body was found, his grey eyes observing me like a specimen under a microscope. At the end of the inquisition, he offers no feedback on my handling of the case.

'Go and order some food,' he snaps. 'You haven't eaten all day.'

Food is the last thing on my mind, but my position is too fragile to disobey a direct instruction. The bar feels like another world, pop songs whispering in the background while tourists gaze at menus, choosing between Eton mess and banoffee pie. I sit at the bar and order steak and chips, simply because it's quick to prepare. Will Dawlish is missing from his usual place behind the bar, and his assistant takes my order, informing me that his boss has taken the day off. When I look out of the window, the sea is rougher than before, tamarisk trees being lashed by the wind. It's growing dark already, the lights on Bryher starting to shine, and I wish that time would wind back to before Jude's death, when Eddie's duties involved circulating the islands on one of the country's quietest beats, instead of watching a young boy fight for his life. When the food arrives, I swallow mouthfuls too fast to register their flavour, knocking back orange juice to keep my head clear.

The DCI looks calmer when I go back upstairs. He has labelled our evidence files, paperclips stored in a jam jar, reports neatly filed away. It's 8 p.m. and I'm about to suggest he goes home when the landline jangles on the table and he snatches the receiver from my hand. His posture changes as he listens, answering in terse monosyllables before hanging up.

'Someone's reported a man's body, on White Island.'

I'm already pulling on my coat. 'Is it Larsson?'

'They don't know. The woman says it's out in the water, tied to a rock.' He rises to his feet. 'Stay here, Kitto. Call the coastguard while I deal with it.'

I'm about to argue, but the look on his face makes me bite my tongue. It will take an hour to reach White Island and someone must stay here to deal with local concerns. It's clear that my boss has lost faith in me, unwilling to let the investigation take another wrong turn.

I put through a call to the coastguard agency, then stand by the window and watch Madron hurrying down to the quay to take the biggest launch out to White Island. I stay put until it heads south through the sound, then spend a fruitless half-hour going back over the investigation, trying to piece together a new strategy.

I'm still immersed in reports when one of the waiters from downstairs taps on the door. He leaves a small cardboard box on the table, explaining that it was left on the doorstep earlier today. My name is written in block capitals on the packaging, and my heart sinks as I discover that it contains a clear glass wine bottle, stoppered with a cork. I curse under my breath when the slip of paper fails to drop into my hand, then smash the bottle into a waste bin to retrieve the message. This time the killer has abandoned subtlety. I'm expecting a sea shanty or a sailor's prayer but find just two words:

PIPER'S HOLE

For the first time, I realise that the killer must be insane. His writing has changed since the first messages; then it was tight and over-controlled, but now it's like a child's first attempts, the letters scrawled across the slip. I grab my phone and a torch, casting my eyes around for anything suitable as a weapon, but all I can see is a screwdriver lying on the windowsill. I drop it into my pocket, then run downstairs, the wind battering my face as I wrench open the fire escape. I've studied the tide tables so often this week, I know the sea will be racing in by now. If Larsson really is at Piper's Hole there's little time before the cave floods.

I take the most direct route possible, chasing across Castle Down. Tregarthen Hill is in sight when I hear Shadow barking in the distance, but I carry on running; the last thing I need to worry about is a wounded dog demanding my attention. I lose my footing on my way downhill, skidding onto the beach with a few pounds of shale raining down on me. When I stare back at the steep incline, Shadow is picking his way between rocks, still limping heavily, and there's no time to yell at him to get back to safety. The wind is scouring my face, the sea knee-deep as I cross to Piper's Hole. I make a hurried call to Madron, but get his answering service, so I call Eddie to request support, before shoving the phone back into my pocket. Larsson may already be dead, but the killer has played a good hand; the body on White Island was no more than a decoy.

My torch beam is weak as I press through the cave's narrow entrance, its batteries failing. My system is on high alert while the water deepens, the floor of the cave dropping away. I'm already thigh-deep as the passageway widens, then there's a vivid flash of brightness; someone has set up arc lights inside the cave, designed to blind anyone stumbling in from the dark. My torch is fading when the light dies again, leaving me groping along the cave's wall. The sounds change as the passage widens, echoes increasing as water laps against the rock. The stink of rotting seaweed is suddenly so putrid, my breath emerges in ragged gasps, and the sense that I'm being watched makes my skin crawl.

Someone arrived long before me, their eyes accustomed to the darkness. When the light flicks on again, the cave's soaring ceiling is illuminated and I catch sight of something that makes me stumble to a halt. A man's body is hanging above the pool. He's suspended by his ankles, his form so tightly bound it looks like a chrysalis. Ivar Larsson's eyes are closed; there's no knowing whether he's dead or alive before the light cuts out again and I'm alone in the flooding cave, with water lapping at my chest.

'Cowards,' I yell out. 'Show yourselves, for fuck's sake!'

When another flare of white light comes, it's as if I'm caught in a thunderstorm. I can hear the whine of a generator mixed with the waves slapping against stone like riotous applause, but there's no time to question how the killer rigged an electrical system here. All that matters is freeing Larsson, before the sea stops us escaping. The killer must be lurking nearby, but I shove his presence to the back of my mind, until the water lifts me off my feet and I'm swimming through black water. When the searing light flashes on again, I realise it might be on a timer, while the killer and his accomplice stay safe and dry at home. The brief illumination provides enough time to stare up at Larsson's body; I'll have to climb to the cave's highest point to haul him down. There's every chance that he will die in this stinking cave, but I can't abandon him. His daughter's face burns in my mind as I swim through the dark.

When my fist grazes against a boulder, I haul myself onto the wall of rock and climb blindly, my fingers groping for a secure handhold.

'You're safe, Ivar,' I yell out. 'There's a rescue boat outside.'

If he's conscious, I hope the lie will keep him fighting. The next pulse of light is momentary, burning my retinas before dying again. I need to move fast, before the killer cuts the rope and lets him drop into the water below. I'm halfway up the rock face, five metres from the point where Larsson dangles above the pool. As I reach the next boulder, someone shoves me backwards, a rough hand pushing my shoulder. I drop down to get out of his reach, receiving a hard kick to my chest on the way.

There's a gruff peal of laughter as someone tries to push me from the rocks, and he's got the advantage. It's only a matter of time before he pries me from the wet surface, so the next time he shoves me, I grab his arm. There's a muffled cry as he topples forwards, knocking me from the ledge. We hit the water together and I come up spluttering, but when light fills the cave again, I catch sight of Larsson's inert body overhead, swaying like a pendulum. Before I can spin round, someone catches me in a headlock.

'You should have kept out of it, you idiot.' His speech is full of anger, but the island lilt in his voice is familiar.

'Mike,' I choke out his name. 'Why are you doing this?'

He forces my head underwater and instinct takes over. I lash out with my fists; my punches batter his ribs until his grip around my throat loosens by a fraction, and I come up panting for air. There's no sign of him when light penetrates the darkness again. The second attack comes from below; he yanks my ankles until I'm underwater, fighting to free myself. It's only then that I remember the screwdriver in the back pocket of my jeans, but the man is relentless. He's in front of me in the pitch-dark, pushing me under, until I fight free and clamber back onto the rocks. This time I move faster, hands clawing at wet granite.

When I reach the top, I grope along the rock face until my hand touches the rope, and for once my cart-horse build has a purpose. I haul hand over fist, until Larsson's feet are within reach, then drag him onto the ledge. His body is tightly bound, my wet fingers struggling with elaborate knots. When the light flicks on again, his face is ashen, but at least he's breathing. I've just managed to free his hands when someone kicks my legs out from under me, and I topple backwards from the ledge, releasing a yell of anger. My shoulder thumps hard against a boulder on the way down, the pain sharp enough to convert my fear into rage, then I'm flailing through the water again. It could be imaginary, but a woman's soft voice drifts towards me.

'Leave while you can. You don't have to die like this.'

Escape isn't an option while Larsson's lying on the rocks above, too weak to defend himself. I climb the wall of granite from the other side, with adrenalin pumping through me. Light fills the cave as I reach the top and see a man with his back turned, hands bunched around Larsson's throat. It can't be Mike Trellon. The killer's frame is too broad, but his identity makes no difference when I plunge the screwdriver into the wad of muscle between his neck and shoulder. There's a loud cry of pain before he falls from the ledge and blackness surrounds us again. I can hear him splashing in the water below as I kneel beside Larsson. He's regaining consciousness, a stream of Swedish words spilling from his mouth.

'Can you sit up, Ivar?' I ask. 'We have to get out of here.'

'I can't move. My legs are numb.'

'Don't worry, we'll get you home.'

'Is Frida safe?'

'She's fine. You'll see her soon.'

I can hear him weeping while I undo his ties, the man's emotions flooding out at last. When the light flicks on again, there's no sign of the killer, and I hope he's sunk without a trace. The water levels are rising steadily, so I tie a makeshift harness around Larsson's chest and pray that I'm strong enough to fight the tide.

58

Tom can see a light shining up from the depths. It's so vivid, he wants to sink down and bathe in its warmth, but he's rising into the shallows. Dots of colour dance before his eyes, angelfish riding the currents, but the light draws him like a magnet. The wreck is down there, and so is the treasure. He could sleep on the ocean's soft floor, under a blanket of sand, but new sounds are confusing him: high heels clack across lino, and a distant voice is talking about oxygen levels. When he finally surfaces, someone is clutching his hand.

'Thank God, Tom, I've been waiting for you.' His mother is trying to smile.

He tries to speak, but a layer of plastic is covering his face. When he tries to remove it, his mother touches his hand. 'Leave the mask there, love. It's helping you breathe.'

He relaxes back against the pillows, and the pain in his side is milder than before, his thoughts muzzy. Tears trail down his cheeks for everything he's lost. When he shuts his eyes again, he will sleep without dreaming; he will never see the wreck again, his feet stuck on dry land. It's only now that he remembers what he must tell his mother. He tries to say the woman's name, but he's too weak to talk.

'Don't worry about anything, darling.' His mother squeezes his hand again. 'Concentrate on getting well. Try to sleep, then you'll be strong again.'

His mother's cool fingers caress his face, pushing his hair back from his forehead until sleep overtakes him.

59

It worries me that Larsson makes little sound as I lower him from the ledge, telling him to cling to the rocks when he reaches the water. I can't guess how badly injured he is, but it's my only choice; to keep him alive we must leave the cave, and it won't be easy. The bursts of light are less frequent now, each pulse revealing how high the water has risen, relentless waves gushing towards us.

Ivar is barely keeping his head above water when I reach him. I explain that he must cling to my back, but his grip on my shoulders is so weak, the plan may fail. The tide's weight pushes against me as I cross the pool, while Ivar cries out in pain. It would be a challenge to swim out of here alone, but I must do it with a dead weight on my back, and the flashes of light have ended. I'm floundering in total darkness, as well as freezing seawater, with no way to locate the passage out. The oncoming tide keeps shoving me in the wrong direction, swirling currents threatening to pull us under. When a wave breaks over my head, I realise that we're in trouble. Once our exit floods, we'll be forced back into the cave, with no chance of survival. I'm running my hands across the rock face, trying to find the mouth of the passage, when a noise rises above the waves. Shadow's high-pitched howl cuts through every other sound. The dog must be outside the cave, calling for me.

Shadow's guiding call draws me in a new direction, with a wall of water shunting me backwards, but at least Ivar is still clinging to my back. There's only a foot of clear air between our heads and the roof of the passageway as I claw my way along the rocks, hauling us towards the exit, but I've only made a few meter's progress when a rough hand yanks at my shirt, trying to pull me under. This time I lash out without hesitation. I grab my attacker and pound his skull against the granite. There's a dull moan as I hurl him back into the water, certain the tide will finish him once and for all. When I turn round, Ivar is shivering as I lift him onto my back again.

'Stop this,' he mutters. 'Go on without me.'

'You'll die if you stay here.'

'We both will if you try and save me.'

'Don't be a fucking hero. Just hang on, we're almost there.'

It's a lie, of course. We must fight through metres of pitch-black water, but at least his grip is stronger than before as I haul him through the torrent. A slight bend in the passage gives us a moment's shelter and the

380

dog's howling is closer than before. There's a crack in the darkness ahead, but the tide is almost touching the ceiling. If I slow down, we'll have to finish the last part of our swim underwater.

When I finally drag Larsson from the mouth of the cave, Shadow is poised on a lip of rock directly above us, barking at full volume. I reach up and touch his flank before helping Larsson onto a dry rock, then let myself collapse. Ragged breaths shudder from my lungs, cold and exhaustion weakening me. When my eyes open again, the moon is breaking from a bank of cloud and Denny Cardew's ancient fishing boat is bobbing on the waves. A weak laugh slips from my mouth. The man has helped me from the start, so it seems fitting that he will rescue us, and this time he deserves more than a bottle of wine. When I rub the brine from my eyes, there's no sign of him on board. If Cardew tried to swim ashore, his chances of survival are thin, but I'm too busy checking that Larsson is safe to fret about the fisherman. The sea is lapping closer, forcing me to carry him to a higher ledge. Before long there will be only the sheer wall of the cliff to cling to, while the tide tries to rip us from its surface. I dig my phone from my pocket, but saltwater has ruined the mechanism. I can only hope that Eddie put through an emergency call straight after I phoned him.

It's a huge relief when the lifeboat finally arrives, its powerful lights almost blinding me. My respect for the volunteers rises as one of the men leaps into the sea, while the female skipper keeps the vessel steady. I wish I could get Larsson to safety immediately; the big, orange boat looks so inviting, with light beaming from its portholes, promising warmth and shelter. Somehow they manage to rig a rope and pulley to winch Larsson aboard. When they come back for me, I lift Shadow into my arms and abseil from the rock face, while the lifeboat rocks from side to side on the cresting waves.

'The killer's still in the cave,' I tell the skipper. 'We have to check the fishing boat too, another man may have drowned.'

She looks bemused but sends two of her crew back to check Piper's Hole. My guess is that the killer's body won't be found until morning; currents will pin it there until the tide recedes. Denny's boat, the *Tresco Lass*, is bobbing helplessly on the waves, anchored too near the rocks to be left unattended. When the rescue boat swings alongside it, I manage to scramble onto the deck with another lifeboatman behind me. There's no sign of anyone on board, but a woman's thin scream reaches me from the galley. I can't make out who's crouching there until she turns round. Sylvia Cardew's yellowy hair is plastered to her skull, her clothes soaking. She's holding a large fish hook raised above her head like a weapon.

'I'll hurt you if you come any closer.' The hook has a vicious point, sharp enough to gouge out someone's eye.

'Put it down, Sylvia. Tell me what's happened.'

'This is your fault. Why couldn't you leave us

alone?' She's weeping now, tears sliding down her face unnoticed.

'Where's Denny?'

She stares out of the porthole. 'I knew he'd die at sea, but he never listened.'

'You're not making sense, Sylvia.'

I'm still struggling to understand as the lifeboatman coaxes the hook from her hand, then leads her up the metal steps. By the time we get her onto the rescue boat she's slipped into her own world, whispering quietly to herself, her gaze unfocused, while one of the crew wraps a thermal blanket around her shoulders. The picture only becomes clear when another victim is winched to safety. Denny Cardew's face is badly injured; dark bruises are erupting across his forehead, blood pouring down his cheek. I feel a rush of relief that at least he's alive, until one of the lifeboat officers explains that he was hiding inside the cave's entrance. Cardew fought off their attempts to rescue him until they managed to restrain him. When I look more closely, I see the deep wound where my screwdriver gashed the side of his neck. A sense of disbelief hits me as the boat speeds towards St Mary's. Denny Cardew didn't sail his boat to the mouth of the cave on a rescue mission: he was waiting inside, to watch us die.

60

It's the middle of the night when the boat docks in Hugh Town Harbour, and I focus my mind on practicalities. The ambulance on St Mary's is waiting to take first Ivar Larsson then the Cardews to the island's hospital. The lifeboat crew have to help Larsson into the van because he's almost too weak to stand, but at least he can move his legs. Shadow is sitting patiently at my feet; his shivering is so severe that I ask Lawrie Deane to take him back to the station to warm up. Then I have to keep watch over Denny and Sylvia until the ambulance returns, while three lifeboatmen stand guard, as if the couple might run for cover. We sit in a wooden shelter on the quayside in silence. The fisherman is nursing his wounded cheek with his hands, while blood drips from his nose, and by now my own muscles are aching. My left shoulder burns whenever I move, but the pain is dulled by the adrenalin still coursing around my body. When I look up again, Sylvia Cardew's face is moonlit; her bleached hair appears as glossy and unnatural as the figureheads in the Valhalla Museum. She's muttering to herself, but her words are too quiet to hear, as if she's spitting out a mermaid's curse. When the ambulance returns, it's a relief to see the pair locked inside.

My legs feel unsteady as I walk east along the quay. My clothes are still saturated, and for a second time during the investigation the sea has baptised me against my wishes. When I pause to catch my breath, my shoulder is still burning, but my mind is causing more pain than my body. I should feel elated that Larsson will soon be reunited with his daughter, but the reasons for Jude Trellon's death remain unclear.

When I gaze back at Hugh Town, the sight is reassuring. It looks as peaceful as it did during my childhood, fishermen's cottages huddled against the breeze, lobster boats marooned on the harbour's mud until morning arrives. The sea has retreated for once, the tide calmer than before. On an objective level, the Atlantic looks majestic, but I'm tired of its split personality. Its tranquillity is just a pretence; an hour ago it was battling to take my life.

The hospital is buzzing with activity when I arrive. A relief doctor has been roused from his bed to tend the casualties, and I catch sight of Dr Barrett emerging from one of the treatment rooms. She fiddles with her stethoscope when I ask about Larsson's condition, as if she's longing to take my pulse.

'He's in shock, but he'll recover. I'd like a CAT scan on his back in the morning, to check there are no serious injuries, but the numbness in his legs is probably just bruising to his spine.' A sudden loud noise from along the corridor interrupts the doctor's explanation; a man bellowing at the top of his voice. 'Mr Cardew will need facial surgery once we fly him to Penzance. The poor man's taken a battering, but he's getting morphine for the pain.'

Dr Barrett listens in silence when I explain that Cardew and his wife are murder suspects; their rooms will have to be guarded overnight. She nods her assent, but the medic's expression is disbelieving when she walks away. Exhaustion sets in once I'm alone in the corridor, resting on a hard plastic chair. The place is the polar opposite of Piper's Hole, its tiled floor scrubbed to a high shine, overhead light bouncing from the white walls, the air smelling of room freshener and menthol. Normally I hate hospitals, but tonight its cleanliness and lack of shadows are a welcome relief.

When I get to my feet again, I take a tour down the corridor. Both doctors are busy dealing with Denny Cardew, but when I peer through the window of his wife's room, Sylvia is bolt upright on the bed, staring at the wall. She doesn't register my presence when I enter her room, but curiosity is nagging at me, and I'm legally entitled to question her. I read both of them their rights when we were in the lifeboat.

'What made you do it, Sylvia?'

She doesn't reply. Her hands are fiddling with the buttons of her cardigan, her gaze unfocused.

'I bet you visited loads of websites to copy the symptoms of agoraphobia so accurately. You had all of us convinced, and pretending to be ill gave you the perfect cover, but you care more about dogs than humans. It was you that broke into Ivar's house when Denny was at the wake. Your husband killed Anna for you, didn't he? Or did you finish her yourself? You blamed her, not Will, for losing your job.'

When her gaze lands on my face, her watery blue stare is furious, but it soon flits away. She carries on staring at the wall, while a low slur of words issues from her mouth. She must be expecting leniency from the courts by pretending to be unstable. I leave her room without bothering to say goodbye; there will be plenty more opportunities to talk in the days to come.

Ivar Larsson is sound asleep when I peer through his door, more colour in his face than when I hauled him from the cave, but it's Denny Cardew that I really want to see. He's lying on a mound of pillows in the room next door, and his face has been scrubbed clean of blood, revealing the full extent of his injuries. His cheek is puffy and distorted, a splint taped to his nose and another bandage covering his neck wound. Two bloodshot eyes observe me intently, but the fury in them has burned away. The feelings churning inside my gut include pity, anger and disappointment: the man's wife is just pretending to be mad, but he must be genuinely ill to commit such crimes.

'Do you want to talk, Denny? You'll be interviewed formally in the morning, but I'll listen now, if you want to get it off your chest.'

'You're just like your father, nothing ever riled him.' His voice is groggy when he replies. 'I wish I was the same; everything gets under my skin.'

'Shall we leave the talk till tomorrow?'

He shakes his head, then winces in pain. 'It started when Sylvia lost her job. Anna accused her of stealing from the till, but it must have been someone else. My wife's got too much pride. She was a sly one, that Anna. I started following her around, to find out why she lied. I heard her and Jude having a conversation at the diving school in November, last year. Jude was telling Anna about her dad finding the *Minerva*. That's what decided it in the end.'

'How do you mean?'

'I've dreamed about that ship all my life. After forty years risking my life at sea, no one deserves the reward more than me. Jude talked about the wreck like it was a bank she could steal from whenever she liked. Everything she took was mine by right.' There's a mad fervour in his tone as he finishes his speech.

'What did you do then?'

'That evening I followed Anna round the coast. I thought Jude would have told her the wreck's location, but she pretended not to know. I didn't mean to kill her; I just gave her a push and she fell on the rocks, so I dragged her into Piper's Hole and left her there.'

'Knowing that she'd drown?'

Tears leak from under his bandages. 'She destroyed my wife's life. Sylvia loved working in that pub, long before they took over. She gave that place the best years of her life.'

'Is that when you started leaving messages for Jude?'

'My wife and I needed that money, but we wouldn't have damaged the wreck. We'd have reported the location and claimed the finder's fee. The messages in bottles were Sylvia's idea: she loved the sea shanties her dad sang when she was a girl. I saw Jude and Jamie Petherton coming back from their dive when I was in my fishing hut. They thought they had the quay to themselves, but I heard every word.'

'What did they say?'

'Jude went on about needing a safe hiding place. When they talked about Piper's Hole, I knew she'd leave things, or collect them, if I waited there each night. That couple from London took the pieces and sold them for her.'

'The Kinvers?'

'Ivar sold things too, I'm sure of it. That's why he goes back to Sweden every few months.'

'You can't prove that, Denny. He could just be visiting his family.'

He ignores my reply. 'Jude had the chance to hand everything over to me, but she refused. When she came to Piper's Hole, I found that mermaid figurine in her kitbag, and I was sick of her arrogance.'

'Why did you take Tom Heligan?'

'That boy must know where the *Minerva* is, but he wouldn't say. He's a tough little bastard.' His eyes close as he leans back on his pillows, his voice tailing into silence.

'All right, Denny, you can sleep now. We'll get everything you told me down on record tomorrow.'

'What do you mean?' His blank eyes stare at me. 'I never said a word.'

There's every chance that the fisherman will change his story tomorrow, but his statements have an insane logic. He hated Anna Dawlish for denying Sylvia her job, and killing her must have felt like retribution. Then his obsession with the *Minerva* started to blossom. He was struggling to make ends meet, and believed that a lifetime spent battling the ocean meant that its bounty was his by right. It incensed him that Jude's family planned to cash in on the *Minerva*'s treasures, while he struggled to get by.

When I return to the corridor, Dr Barrett is waiting for me, with a determined look on her face.

'Come to the treatment room now, Inspector. It's your turn to be examined.'

'There's no need.'

'I don't agree.' She points at my hand. 'That cut needs stitches.'

When I look down, there are splashes of blood at

my feet, the cuff of my jacket torn away. My hands are covered in grazes from my efforts to escape the cave, but I've been too busy to notice them until now.

There's something oddly soothing when the medic dresses my wounds, the smell of iodine filling my airways. The doctor recommends an X-ray tomorrow, to check that my shoulder blade is intact, but I draw the line when she suggests spending the night on a gurney. There's no way I could sleep soundly so close to the Cardews, even though they're locked in their rooms and Lawrie Deane has arrived to guard them until morning.

I thank the sergeant on my way out and he manages a grudging smile. Shadow is whimpering for food when I get back to the police station, but all I can provide is a bowl of water and an apology.

'You'll get a feast tomorrow.'

The dog favours me with an old-fashioned look, tired of my promises, but this time I mean it. Without his call to guide me to the mouth of the cave, I could never have escaped alive. No hotel in Hugh Town will rent me a room with a dog in tow, so we hunker down on the floor of Madron's office, with only a thin layer of carpet to soften the concrete, but I'm too exhausted to care. Shadow curls up beside me as I shut my eyes and let sleep wipe my memory clean.

61

Wednesday 20 May

Madron arrives at 8.30 a.m. Luckily, Shadow is in the yard behind the station, tucking into the fillet steak the butcher sold me long before his shop opened for business. I hope he has the good sense to stay out of sight while the DCI vents his spleen; the man's expression is so tense it looks like he's about to fire me instantly for breach of protocol.

'Start at the beginning, Kitto, I want every detail.'

He listens in silence to the whole story, from Cardew guiding me to Jude Trellon's body on the first day so he could watch my reactions. The fisherman was a constant presence during the case, pretending to help at every stage, including searching for Tom Heligan. I explain that his wife's agoraphobia was a ruse to make her seem too vulnerable to step outdoors, let alone harm anyone. Madron's shrewd eyes observe me while I speak, listening so intently that he doesn't move a muscle.

'Denny Cardew admitted all this last night, did he?'

'Morphine must have loosened his tongue. I'll interview him again today, but there's enough proof to convict them both, if he tries to wriggle.'

'No, you won't. You're taking the day off,' Madron says firmly. 'What do you plan to do with Stephen and Lorraine Kinver?'

'There's enough evidence to try them for smuggling; it looks like they've been laundering money along the way. I should sort out court application papers for the CPS.'

'I'll get that done; we can manage without you for twenty-four hours. The Cardews are being flown to the mainland later this morning. Denny's booked for surgery and Sylvia will have a psychiatric assessment, so you can recover at home.'

The DCI remains silent when I get up to leave. I'm halfway out of the door before he speaks again. 'Congratulations on getting Larsson out of that cave. I've never doubted your commitment, Kitto, but your methods leave a lot to be desired.'

The man is so hard to read. It's impossible to know whether he plans to terminate my contract at my review meeting or provide a ringing endorsement. When I collect Shadow from the yard, my head is too full of the case to let me relax, so I double back into town to buy items I'll need during the day. The dog is in good spirits after yesterday's adventure, his tail wagging as we wait for the ferry back to Tresco.

The boat ride eases some of the tension from my

system: the water is mirror-smooth today, reflecting miles of summer-holiday blue sky. The tourists that pile into the boat are all middle-aged gardeners, equipped with guidebooks on the exotic plants and trees in the Abbey Gardens. The group set off at a brisk march when we reach the island, while my pace is slow. The hammering I took against the rocks is catching up with me, but I've always hated unfinished business.

My first task is to return to our makeshift incident room, where Eddie is packing files into lockable boxes for transportation back to St Mary's, to be used during the Cardews' prosecution. His face glows with excitement when he hears details from last night's adventure in Piper's Hole.

'I can't believe it was Denny,' he says, quietly. 'He always seemed like a decent bloke.'

'Anyone can flip, Eddie. All it takes is a run of bad luck.'

I stay for another couple of hours, helping him tidy the place, while he begs for more information. There's something cathartic about getting the events out into the open, so they don't curdle at the base of my stomach, and Eddie has passed a new milestone. He completes a whole conversation without calling me 'sir', which is a welcome relief. I'm glad there's no sign of Will Dawlish when I return downstairs. I need to regroup before breaking the news that his wife didn't die from a fall on the beach; she was murdered by a man who blamed her for his wife's misery.

My next port of call is the Trellons' large house by Ruin Beach. When I peer through the front window, Frida is curled up on the sofa beside her grandmother, looking at a picture book. Diane's face lights up when she sees me. Even though there's been no formal announcement, it's impossible to keep secrets in a place this small. The whole island must know that the Cardews have been arrested in connection with Jude's death. Diane doesn't say a word when she welcomes me inside, her eyes cloudy with tears. I can't imagine what she's feeling, but I can take a guess. Knowing who killed her daughter will offer some peace of mind, but it will never replace everything she's lost.

Frida's face breaks into a smile when she looks up at me.

'These are for you,' I say, as I hand over a box of marker pens. 'Your dad will want a picture when he comes home.'

'I did one of you.'

The girl pulls a piece of paper from a pile on the floor. A black-haired man stands at the centre of the page, taller than the trees and houses that surround him: a broad-shouldered giant, with a lopsided smile. She beams at me again when I thank her for my portrait, but it's obvious she wants to return to her story, and my concerns are fading. The kid's grandparents adore her and she already knows how to protect herself; she'll get by with one parent instead of two.

My strength is waning when I walk back across the

fields, with Shadow limping between rows of ripening wheat. I could use three Nurofen and a comfortable bed for the rest of the afternoon, but David Polrew is striding towards me, his craggy features set in a cast-iron frown. Whether the historian is out for an afternoon stroll or looking for a fight, I'd rather avoid him until my strength returns.

'I'll be filing a complaint, Inspector,' he says. 'The way you hounded me during your investigation was unforgivable, and you've been contacting my daughter against my wishes.'

'Gemma phoned me yesterday because she's too afraid to confront you.' My dislike for him turns my voice bitter. 'I'm taking her to the mainland tomorrow, to see Tom Heligan in hospital. He's been asking for her.'

'I won't allow it. Her exams start next week.'

'Didn't she tell you, she's decided to study horticulture instead? Gemma's going to train as a gardener in the Abbey Gardens. I'll call for her first thing tomorrow morning, and if I hear you've laid one finger on her, or your wife, you'll be prosecuted for assault.'

There's a hissing sound as air emerges from Polrew's mouth, like gas releasing from a hot-air balloon. It's a pleasure to render the man speechless for once as I wish him good day and head for the harbour.

When I finally get home to Hell Bay, Shadow stretches out on the settee and shuts his eyes, as if he's witnessed enough trouble to last him a lifetime. Maggie has left a shepherd's pie, a loaf of bread and a bottle of wine on the table, in line with island tradition. I grew up certain that every problem could be fixed by a square meal, but last night's poor sleep has finally caught up with me. I serve the dog half of the pie, then go into my room and lie down without bothering to remove my shoes.

It's late afternoon by the time I wake up. My head's groggy with bad dreams about evil mermaids with vivid yellow hair, but the pain in my shoulder is fading, my body slowly recovering. I put on swimming shorts and a T-shirt and sit on the bench outside my house, letting late afternoon sunlight soak into my bones while I drink a cold beer. The dog is amusing himself by batting an empty sea urchin shell across the beach, and my eyes are fixed on the surf when Zoe appears on the gravel path. She looks gorgeous as usual, in the smallest pair of shorts imaginable and a white vest that accentuates her tan. She sits beside me and steals a swig of my beer; when she turns to me again, her eyes are round with interest.

'What happened in that cave, Ben? Everyone's calling you a hero.'

'I was just doing my job. Why don't you entertain me, for once?'

'You can have a song, if you want. But I need more beer first.'

I hand her my bottle. 'It's a deal.'

Zoe tips her head back and sings 'Cry Me a River'.

Her voice is so achingly sexy, it sounds like Ella Fitzgerald is serenading me, and I have to cross my arms to stop myself from reaching for her. I give a slow round of applause when she finishes.

'Stay there, I've got something for you.' I go inside to collect the box, but her smile fades when she looks inside.

'You got me some bulbs?'

'I spoke to the guy in the garden centre on St Mary's. They're alliums; if you plant them now they'll be flowering when you get back from India, to welcome you home.'

Her jaw drops open. 'How did you guess that I'd signed the contract?'

'Because you never refuse a challenge.'

'We've got that in common.' She plants a kiss on my cheek. 'Maybe I was wrong to make you swear never to ask me out.'

'Your loss is the rest of womankind's gain. Let's go for a swim.'

'I didn't bring a costume.'

'Never mind. I won't arrest you for indecent exposure.'

'All the hotel guests would see me; I'll have to change.'

She heads for home, but I'm too impatient to wait. The tide is rolling towards Hell Bay in a series of low waves when I reach the water, to find it soft as a caress. Shadow is sniffing along the tideline, hunting for something disgusting to roll in, and soon Zoe is running across the beach in a scarlet bikini that makes me feel glad to be alive. I won't let myself imagine her leaving until it happens, and there's no point in worrying about my professional future until after my review meeting.

Out of nowhere, the human waste I've witnessed in the past ten days catches up with me. Denny and Sylvia Cardew's bitterness has left two men without wives, and a young girl motherless. The only beneficiary will be the Valhalla Museum, when the *Minerva*'s bounty is finally salvaged. I drift on the water's surface, aware that hundreds of undiscovered wrecks lie fathoms below me on the ocean floor. All I can hope is that the underwater graves will be left in peace for a long time to come.

Author's Note

I have blended truth with fiction in *Ruin Beach*, and hope my book will not offend inhabitants of the Scillies. The islands are one of my favourite places, so I would hate to lose my usual warm welcome! I have twisted and turned the landscape slightly for the sake of a good story. All of the locations mentioned in my novel are real, including the famous Abbey Gardens on Tresco, which contain the Valhalla Museum, with its atmospheric display of mastheads and items reclaimed from shipwrecks. Piper's Hole exists too, on Tresco's northern coast, but I have exaggerated its dangers. Plenty of myths exist about the cave's deathly atmosphere, but its pool is far shallower than I describe. None of the people mentioned in this book are real, but both the New Inn and Hell Bay Hotel do exist, and are great places to stay while you get to know the Scillies' haunting landscape.

The islands' archaeology and shipwrecks have always fascinated me. For anyone with an interest in early civilisation, the Neolithic dwellings scattered across the Scillies are well worth visiting, as are the remains of a Roman temple on Northwethel. But the thing that fascinated me most when researching this book is the multitude of wrecks that litter the islands' shorelines, making the area a magnet for divers. Geologists believe that the archipelago was one united land mass before sea levels rose, and now only the highest peaks of mountains remain, with hill graves exposed, making the islands the largest ancient graveyard in the world. Marine archaeologists estimate that only a tenth of shipwrecks on the seabed around the islands have been explored, the rest buried so deep beneath the waves they have not yet been found.

Acknowledgements

My thanks are due to my excellent editor, Jo Dickinson, for her kind encouragement and great editing skills. Thanks too to all of the lovely, supportive team at Simon and Schuster, including Jess Barratt, Carla Josephson, Maisie Lawrence and Helen Upton, and to my copyeditor, Fraser Crichton.

I owe a great deal of thanks to the kind staff of the New Inn on Tresco, for answering all of my questions about Piper's Hole and local tide patterns. Thanks also to Martin Owens for taking me out on his boat on a blustery day. Touring the coast of Tresco on a rough sea gave me plenty to write about, Martin, thank you! It was well worth getting soaked to the skin.

Thanks as ever to all of my writing pals: the Killer Women, the 134 Club, Penny Hancock and Miranda Doyle. Twitter friends are too numerous to mention, but I owe Peggy Breckin and Julie Boon a debt of gratitude for supporting me right from the start.

My excellent husband, Dave Pescod, deserves the largest amount of gratitude, for being my first reader, best critic and provider of endless cups of tea.

Love DI Ben Kitto?
Read on for an exclusive extract
from the new thriller by Kate Rhodes,
coming 2019 ...

BURNT
ISLAND

Friday, Nov 5th

The sun is rising when Jimmy Haycock sets out on a cold November morning. He passes the lighthouse first, its tall form looming over St Agnes like a winter ghost. The building is one of his favourites, even though its light was removed years ago, but there's no time to stop and admire it. Jimmy's friends are waiting and he can't disappoint them. He takes his usual route to the lake, with his binoculars hidden in his pocket.

Jimmy walks north through Middle Town, where the stone faces of a dozen houses observe his progress. The man keeps his head down, to avoid the blank stares of shuttered windows, only relaxing once he reaches open country, where no one will disturb him. The meadow is crisp with frost, grass crunching under foot, his heart lifting when he spies the Big Pool. The expanse of water is as flat and shiny as polished glass today, tinted pink by early sunlight. None of his friends have come to see him: the sky is empty, not a single cry of welcome. Jimmy is about to return home when seagulls descend suddenly in a swirling cloud. The flock circles overhead, close enough to touch, bawling out raucous greetings. When he throws scraps of bread into the air, they battle for each crumb. He can smell brine on their wings, wet feathers stroking his cheeks. The creatures stay long after his food supply is exhausted, then disappear back into the sky, leaving only a handful of his favourite creatures behind. Oystercatchers wade towards him through the shallows, absorbing his attention.

His fingers are numb with cold by the time he slips his binoculars back into his pocket. There's an odd smell on the air – a stench of fuel burning, mixed with a sweetness he can't identify. Now that the birds have gone he notices smoke billowing from Burnt Hill, as if someone is sending him a signal. He leaves the pool behind then picks his way across the sandbar that stretches from Blanket Bay.

Jimmy's pace slows as he approaches the source of the fire. The smell is stronger now; its sickly taste irritating the back of his throat. He's panting for breath by the time he reaches the peak of the hill. The sight that greets him there makes little sense at first. A mound of charred sticks is glowing a dull red, paraffin cans abandoned on the grass nearby. When he looks again, small flames surround a blackened mass at the heart of the bonfire. His stomach rolls with nausea, because there's no mistaking the shape that lies among the ashes. A face leers up at him, melted flesh hanging from exposed cheekbones, empty eye sockets giving him a direct stare. The dead man appears to be asking for his help, and Jimmy's unable to refuse. He witnessed another life slipping away when he was a boy; this is his chance to make amends.

'I'll find out who hurt you,' Jimmy mutters.

He can't even tell whether the body is male or female as he makes his promise. The sight sends him reeling backwards, desperate to escape, but his conscience won't let him run away. He recalls something his mother used to say: *always leave something for the dead, to show your respects.* His eyes smart with smoke and tears as he throws his sheepskin coat over the fire, extinguishing the last flames. Jimmy recites the start of his mother's favourite prayer: *Our Father who art in heaven, hallowed be thy name,* but his words vanish in the smoky air. His grey hair flies on the breeze as he stumbles towards safety.